Butterfly Mother

Miao (Hmong) Creation Epics from Guizhou, China

BUTTERFLY MOTHER

MIAO (HMONG) CREATION EPICS FROM GUIZHOU, CHINA

Translated by Mark Bender

Based on a version compiled by Jin Dan and Ma Xueliang

Hackett Publishing Company, Inc.
Indianapolis/Cambridge

Copyright © 2006 by Hackett Publishing Company, Inc.

All rights reserved
Printed in the United States of America

09 08 07 06   1 2 3 4 5 6 7

For further information, please address
Hackett Publishing Company, Inc.
P.O. Box 44937
Indianapolis, IN 46244-0937
www.hackettpublishing.com

Cover design by Abigail Coyle
Interior design by Elizabeth Wilson
Composition by William Hartman
Printed at Edwards Brothers, Inc.

Library of Congress Cataloging-in-Publication Data

Butterfly mother : Miao (Hmong) creation epics from Guizhou, China / translated by Mark Bender ; based on a version compiled by Jin Dan and Ma Xueliang.
    p. cm.
    Includes bibliographical references.
    ISBN-13: 978-0-87220-849-0 (pbk.)
    ISBN-10: 0-87220-849-4 (pbk.)
    ISBN-13: 978-0-87220-850-6 (cloth)
    ISBN-10: 0-87220-850-8 (cloth)
    1. Epic poetry, Hmong—Translations into English. I. Jin, Dan. II. Ma, Xueliang. III. Bender, Mark.
    PL4072.7.B88 2006
    895.9'72103208—dc22

                                              2006007230

The paper used in this publication meets the minimum requirements of American National Standard for Information Sciences—Permanence of Paper for Printed Library Materials, ANSI Z39.48–1984.

for Fu Wei and Marston

Contents

Acknowledgments	viii
Key to Pronunciation for Eastern Miao Dialect Romanization	x
Map of Miao (Hmong) Areas in Southern Guizhou Province	xii
Preface by Jin Dan (Jenb Dangk)	xiii
Introduction	xv
Traditional Culture and the Epics	xvi
The Epics and Their Performance	xxvi
Part I, *Prelude*	**1**
Introduction	1
Prelude	4
Part II, *Song of Gold and Silver*	**8**
Introduction	8
Creating the Sky and Earth	11
Transporting Gold and Silver	19
Creating the Suns and Moons	49
Shooting Down the Suns and Moons	66
Part III, *Song of the Ancient Sweet Gum*	**71**
Introduction	71
The Seeds' House	73
Seeking the Tree Seeds	82
Plowing and Harrowing the Earth	92
Sowing the Seeds	103
Cutting Down the Ancient Sweet Gum	108

Part IV, *Song of Butterfly Mother* — **111**

    Introduction — 111
    The Birth of Butterfly Mother — 113
    The Twelve Eggs — 115
    The Brothers Divide — 122
    Killing the Centipede — 128
    Searching for the Sacrificial Drums — 136
    Searching for the Sacrificial Ox — 140
    Searching for the Sacrificial Vestments — 146
    The Ancestor Sacrifice Hunt — 152

Part V, *The Great Flood* — **157**

    Introduction — 157
    The Great Flood — 159

Part VI, *Westwards, Upriver* — **169**

    Introduction — 169
    Westwards, Upriver — 170

Notes — 189
Selected Bibliography — 212

Acknowledgments

Over the years a number of people have helped out in various ways to realize the goal of introducing the Miao (Hmong) epics to readers of English. First, I would like to thank the original compilers of the epics. The late Professor Ma Xueliang of the Central Nationalities University (*Zhongyang minzu daxue*) in Beijing was a pioneering ethnolinguist who as a young man took a deep interest in the languages and oral traditions of several of the southwestern minority cultures in China, a passion that remained with him for the rest of his life. He engaged in extensive fieldwork on every language and culture he studied, always an advocate for accuracy in the collecting and presentation of materials. Jin Dan (Jenb Dangk in Miao) was the essential figure in collecting the present epics from a number of singers in the 1950s and re-collecting portions in the late 1970s and early 1980s. He initially translated them into Chinese, providing a wealth of personal background information—this due to his unique position as both a researcher and a singer. Long an editor in the Nationalities Publishing House (*Minzu chubanshe*) in the city of Guiyang, Jin has produced a number of other publications on the local Miao cultures, work now engaged in by his son Wu Yiwen, daughter Wu Yifang, and son-in-law, Qian Dongping (a member of the Zhuang ethnic group). In 1985 Jin Dan accompanied me on my first visit to the "hometown" of the epics in the Taijiang region of Southeast Guizhou and answered innumerable questions on the text and aspects of local culture and performance. His wife, Yang Meitao, offered immense hospitality during that and subsequent visits. This cooperation has lasted over two decades and continues today. Without his enduring help, and initial encouragement from Professor Ma, this English translation would never have been realized.

My wife, Fu Wei (Wei Fu Bender), has helped me greatly throughout this project—first by accompanying me during the initial fieldwork trip in Guizhou and later in reading the manuscript, organizing the endnotes, troubleshooting computer glitches, and innumerable other tasks. I thank her deeply for putting up with me over the years.

Annette Murphy and my brother, Nathan Bender, provided comments on an early draft of the translation. In later stages, my sister Karen

Bender and Brian Bare meticulously proofread the entire manuscript. Ok Joo Lee deserves special mention for her help on the pronunciation key. My students Max Bohnenkamp, Peace Lee, Wu Shan, and Kou Yujia helped in a variety of ways during the project.

I have benefited from the advice and encouragement of many other people. I will mention a few of them here: Zhong Jingwen, Li Zixian, Anthony Walker, Sun Jingyao, Frank Hsueh, Chen Ju, Shi Kun, John Deeney, Lawrence Tyler, Mary Tyler, Royall Tyler, Gary Snyder, Timothy Wong, Victor Mair, John Miles Foley, Frank Stewart, John Balaban, Peter Knecht, Kevin Stuart, Chan Park, Shelley Quinn, Huang Jianming, Wang Jichao, Chao Gejin, Bamo Qubumo, Luo Qingchun, Wu Xiaodong, Luo Danyang, Kong Yanjun, Deng Erlong, and Weng Wenzhong.

The late Zha Ruqiang of the Social Sciences Institute, Beijing, helped in many lasting ways during my early years in China. I would also like to remember the help from various officials at Guangxi University, including President Hou Depeng and Zhang Congde. Thanks are due to the staff of the cultural bureau and other agencies in Taijiang for help in arranging recent local visits and in particular to Li Meiren, Fang Kang, and the epic singer Tian Jinfeng. Deep thanks go to Deborah Wilkes at Hackett Publishing Company for her care and encouragement. Many thanks are due the anonymous outside reader for a host of thoughtful comments. Hearty thanks are offered to Liz Wilson and others at Hackett Publishing for their much-appreciated efforts. Thanks of another order go to my parents, Rev. George E. Bender and Pauline Ella (Pike) Bender, my sister Pam Bender, and other family members, friends, and colleagues not mentioned by name. And finally, a special "thank you" to my intrepid son Marston, whom I hope will somehow engage the epics.

Key to Pronunciation for Eastern Miao Dialect Romanization

With few exceptions, most of the non-English words represented in this book are Romanizations in the language of the Miao ethnic group as spoken in Southeast Guizhou province and known as the "Eastern dialect." Like Standard Chinese, the Miao language utilizes tones to aid in differentiating words. In the Romanization system used to represent the sounds in the Eastern dialect, consonants are placed at the end of words to represent the language tones. *These final consonants are not pronounced—rather they guide the reader in the use of the proper tone when saying a word.* For instance, the most common ethnic name (ethnonym) used by members of the Miao ethnic group in Southeast Guizhou is "Hmub," though the term "Hmongb" also occurs. Written without the tone markers, the terms are "Hmu" and "Hmong," respectively. This notation of tones is very different from the set of iconic diacritics used to represent tones in the Pinyin Romanization system (the official Romanization system for Standard Chinese) and can be quite confusing for readers not familiar with this convention. For this reason, the tone markers have been dropped for all of the Miao words in the epics, with the exception of words that appear in the Introduction and Notes, where they are included in parentheses for those with especial interests in the language.

The eight tones represented in the five-level numeric scale (adopting Chao, "1" is the lowest pitch value and "5" is the highest pitch value within a speaker's normal pitch range) are listed in the chart based on a similar one in Wu and Qian (380). In the example, the consonant used as a tone marker is in italics.

Number	Tone marker	Tonal contour	Example
1	b	33	da*b* (answer)
2	x	55	da*x* (come)
3	d	24	da*d* (long)
4	l	22	da*l* (lose)
5	t	44	da*t* (morning)
6	s	23	da*s* (die)
7	k	53	da*k* (wing)
8	f	21	da*f* (erect)

A few other conventions in the Romanization system may seem difficult for some readers. Most of these have to do with initial consonant clusters (in some cases, unvoiced nasal sounds) at the beginnings of words (hm, hf, hn, etc.) that represent sounds found neither in modern English nor Standard Chinese. In other instances certain sounds are represented by the letters found in the English alphabet (such as "x") but pronounced differently (though in some instances they are similar to the sounds represented by the same letters in the Pinyin Romanization for Standard Chinese). As a detailed treatment of the intricacies of the pronunciation of Eastern Miao is beyond the scope of this book, a table listing some of the more difficult sounds for non-native speakers and their English approximations is given here. Linguists will need to seek other sources for a more thorough and accurate explanation. (See Wu and Qian, 379–80, for a complete chart of the sounds with equivalents in the International Phonetic Alphabet.)

Initial consonants:
x (as "sh" in "sheet")
q (as "ch" sound in "cheek")

Consonant clusters: hm, hf, hn, dl, hl, ng, hv, gh, kh
In approaching such sounds, imagine the principle of trying to say the consonant in the English word "knight" by pronouncing a nasalized "k" followed by a clearly articulated "n" sound.

Final vowel sounds:
i (as "ea" in "leave")
e (as "a" in "about")
a (as "a" in "father")
o (as "o" in "sorry")
u (as "oo" in "moon")
ai (similar to "eye")
ee (as "ee" in "beet" but longer)
ao (as "ow" in "how")
ei (as "a" in "father" but longer)
ang (as "ong" in "gong")
ong (as "oo" in "moon" plus "ng" of "wrong")

Finally, in some cases the names of geographical features (particularly towns and rivers represented on modern-day maps) and a few widely used local names for plants and material objects (like the sticky-rice *baba* cakes—printed in italics) are represented in the Pinyin system used for Romanizing Standard Chinese.

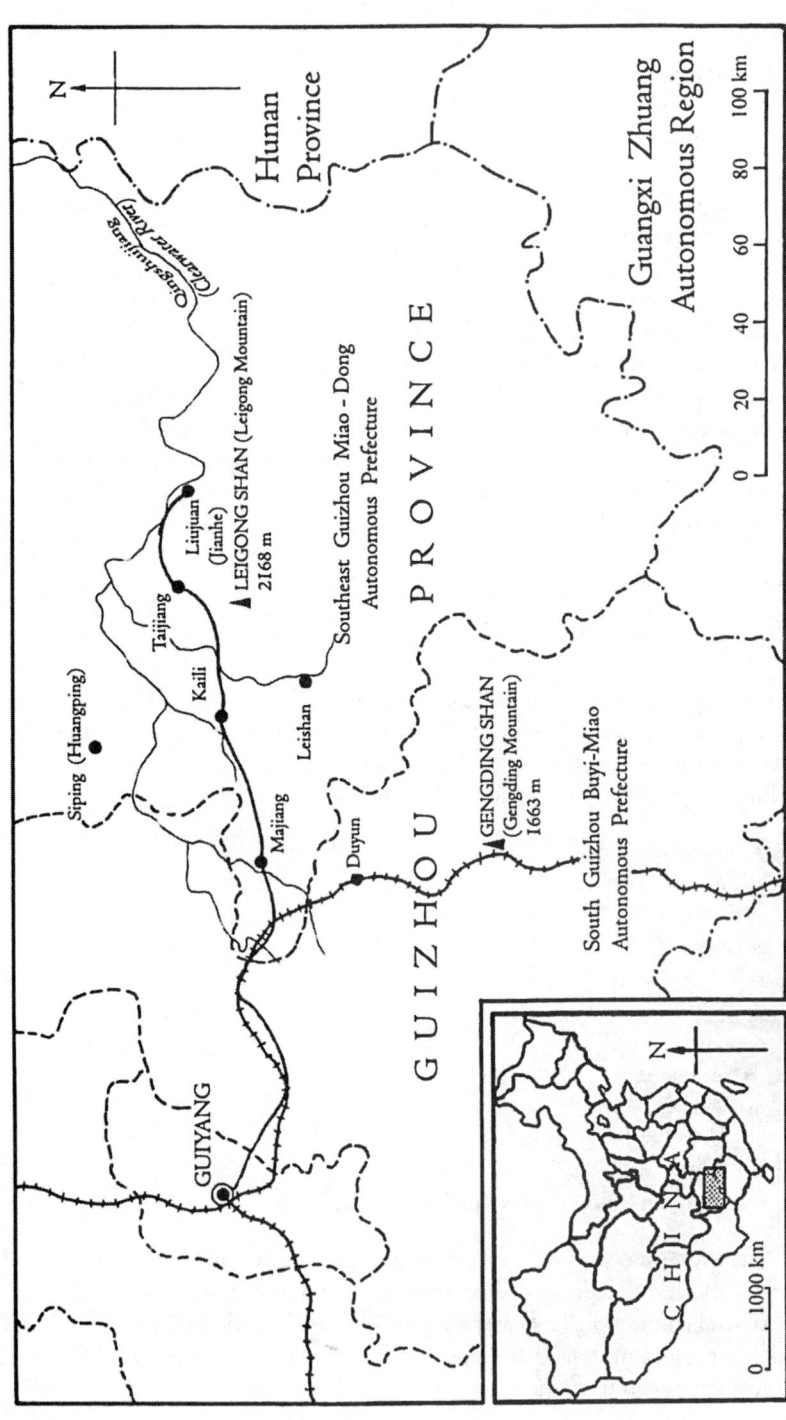

Miao (Hmong) Areas in Southern Guizhou Province, China (reprinted from Bender, *Hxak Hmub*, 96).

Preface

By Jin Dan (Jenb Dangk)

I grew up in the Miao (Hmong) ethnic areas in Southeast Guizhou, a region of China long known as a "sea of song and dance." My father was a well-known singer in our area and knew many of the ancient epics. He was also fond of improvising songs, and still sang when he was in his eighties. Encouraged by my family and the society at large, I often went to listen to epic recitals as a child and gradually learned to sing them myself. I felt the urge to preserve them in writing, but before 1949 the Miao in my part of Southeast Guizhou did not have their own writing system. Everything was remembered and passed down orally. I tried writing down the songs phonetically using similar sounding Chinese characters but was disappointed by the results. In the years that have passed, those songs I wrote down in such a way are long forgotten, but those I remembered by listening come easily to mind.

When I first fell in love with the Miao songs, I regarded them as beautiful expressions of language that revealed things difficult to express in regular speech. As I grew older and received more education, I began to realize that the songs reflected much about history and culture and that they were part of a valuable heritage. I now better understand the proverb, "A word that is sung can equal a hundred that are spoken." Translating the songs into the Mandarin Chinese language then became my goal. How clearly I remember my anticipation when I sent my first translations of a few love songs to the journal *Telling and Singing (Shuoshuo changchang)* in the early 1950s. Quite unexpectedly, they were published, and the editor, the famous writer Lao She, invited me to see him in Beijing, where he gave me great encouragement. Later, I became a teacher in the minority languages department in the Central Nationalities University in Beijing. It was there, under the influence of Professor Ma Xueliang, that I became absorbed in the collection, study, and translation of Miao folk literature. For a time I stepped into the shoes of a part-time folklorist, but for reasons everyone knows all too well, my work was stopped for many years, though I never forgot it. Through all those years, I did my best to hang on to as much of the material I had collected as possible—through a time when all such things came under the heading of the "Four Olds."[1]

My major translations are the Miao epics, best represented by *Hxak Hmub: Miao Epic Poems*, produced in collaboration with Professor Ma. In completing *Hxak Hmub*, we relied on versions of the songs sung by Ghe Hfu Dlen of La Ci village in Taijiang county. Other singers included Ghe Dang Sang Ma, Ghe Dla Dang, and Ghe Ba Hlo, all of La Ci. Their songs were transcribed either in the then new Miao Romanization system or in the International Phonetic Alphabet, before being translated into Chinese. In the process of editing, we stressed the scientific value of the texts and refrained from deleting things that were contrary to prevailing ideas. On a few occasions, we felt that certain lines were best put in the endnotes for reasons explained therein. Above all, we stressed accurate translation.

Certain of the epics, such as *Song of Gold and Silver*, and *Song of Butterfly Mother*, were published in *Folklore (Minjian wenxue)* in 1955 and 1956, respectively. Those original translations have been revised.

I am so grateful to my ancestors for producing such fine songs. What a shame it is that there is a limit to what can "come across" in translation! But we must make do.

(1986)[2]

Introduction

Butterfly Mother is a collection of epic songs from the rich oral tradition of the Miao ethnic group (or "Miao nationality") located in the southeast corner of Guizhou province in China.[1] The songs detail the origins of the sky and earth, heavenly bodies, landforms and water, plants and animals, farming practices, ritual activity, and the various local peoples. A world is created in which everything is alive: listeners find that besides mountains, rivers, trees, and creatures, even such inanimate objects as metals, plows, and drums were "born" and have spirits. Major actors in these stories of creation are the mythical Ancestors—giant supernatural beings in human and sometimes animal form. Central among these beings is Butterfly Mother, a mythical butterfly who is impregnated one day by sloshing wave foam.[2] Then, in a sweet gum tree, she lays twelve eggs—one of which contains a clever, capable culture hero who eventually plays a direct role in the creation of humankind. Normally sung in the form of a dialogue between two pairs of singers who are steeped in tradition (represented by "A" and "B" in the text), the epics are a virtual encyclopedia of myth, legend, and folk custom of the local Miao people.

The Miao in Southeast Guizhou are part of one of the largest of China's fifty-six official ethnic groups. The majority ethnic group (comprising about 91 percent) is known as the "Han" Chinese, and the other fifty-five are classified as minorities (*shaoshu minzu*). These ethnic minority groups (or "minority nationalities") vary widely by custom, language, area of habitation, livelihood, history, and population. The Miao ethnic group (*Miaozu*), as officially recognized by the government, presently numbers between seven and eight million people. Like other large ethnic groups in China, the formation of the Miao group is complex. It is comprised of dozens of diverse subgroups of related peoples that go by many different names, creating many issues of identification and inclusion (Schein, 37–41; Wu and Qian, 64–8; Tapp, *The Hmong of China*, 7–11).

Most Miao reside in mountainous areas in the provinces of Guizhou, Hunan, Yunnan, Sichuan, a few areas of Hubei, and in the Guangxi Zhuang Autonomous Region. Related peoples, often calling themselves "Hmong," live in Southeast Asia and in recent decades have immigrated to countries around the globe. Traditions of clothing, customs, dialects, and performance may differ widely in the various Miao or Hmong areas. Thus, while certain aspects of the Butterfly Mother epics can be found in the oral traditions of many of the Miao/Hmong subgroups, they are best understood as being a part of a specific local Miao culture in Guizhou province in an area officially known as the Southeast Guizhou Miao-Dong Nationalities Autonomous Prefecture (*Chendongnan Miaozu Dongzu zizhizhou*). In Southeast Guizhou, many Miao were once known in Chinese as the "Black Miao" ("Hei Miao") (de Beauclair). While that term is seldom heard today, traditional native names are still used when speaking Miao. The most common native designation in Southeast Guizhou today is "Hmu" (Hmub), though some groups in the area use other designations, including "Hmong" (Hmongb). (Please see Key to Pronunciation for Eastern Miao Dialect Romanization.)

This Introduction provides background information on the epics and the culture that created them. The first part gives useful background information on the Miao in Southeast Guizhou, and the second part positions the epics in relation to other poetic narratives in China and presents detailed information about form, content, performance, and the translation process. Each section is prefaced with a short summary of events and additional background information.

Traditional Culture and the Epics

Low mountains of earth and limestone rise in endless succession along free-running rivers like the Clearwater (Qingshuijiang) and Sword (Jianhe) in Southeast Guizhou. With an average elevation of 2,000 meters, the region was once heavily forested with lower temperate zone flora, though today terraced rice fields are the most outstanding feature of many green valleys. Although opinions on the "origin" of the Miao ethnic group are numerous, exactly when the historic Miao lifestyle began in the hills of southeastern Guizhou, and what types of cultural adaptations (such as hunting and gathering economies) may predate it, are still mysteries (Schein, 44–9; Wu and Qian, 44–55).

Chinese records of Miao presence in Guizhou date to the Song dynasty (960–1279), although the much talked about but probably unrelated tribes of the "Three Miao" are recorded as having lived in central China over 3,000 years ago. According to legend, at some time in the distant past ancestors of the present Miao ethnic group migrated south from a hearth on the Yellow River to the banks of the Yangzi River (Wu and Qian, 69–78). Some scholars claim that ancestors of the Miao were living in Hunan province by the Qin dynasty (221–207 B.C.). Whatever the case may be, over the ensuing centuries Miao groups appeared in what are now Guizhou and other areas of the southwest. Some of these movements, particularly those after the Song dynasty, are mentioned in historical records. To complicate things, Miao in Southeast Guizhou often claim that their ancestors came from Jiangxi province to the east, and some claim that they were once part of the Han ethnic group (China's majority ethnic grouping). Culturally and linguistically, the Miao in Southeast Guizhou are closest to certain subgroups of the Yao ethnic group, another mountain-dwelling people of south China. They also have considerable cultural affinities with the Dong (or "Gaem") ethnic group in Southeast Guizhou and nearby areas in Guangxi and Hunan.

Though various ancient kingdoms exerted influence over the area as early as the Qin dynasty, the Han controlled what is now Guizhou long before it became a province in the Ming dynasty (1368–1644). Under the Manchu government of the Qing dynasty (1644–1911) military posts were spread throughout minority areas in the mountains of southwest China in a system designed to undermine local control. Village headmen were replaced by native collaborators or government officials in the local *yamen* (district office) and large numbers of Han immigrants from other areas (including Jiangxi province) were relocated in Guizhou. Most Han living in the Taijiang region before the mid-nineteenth century, however, were soldiers, some of whom married Miao wives and then raised their children as natives.

Beginning in the early eighteenth century a long series of rebellions shook minority areas in Hunan, Guizhou, and Guangxi. In 1854, a man named Zhang Xiumei (Miao were forced to take Han surnames in the Qing dynasty) led an uprising that was influenced by the Taiping Rebellion (1851–1864) that had begun in the Yao and Hakka regions of neighboring Guangxi. The Miao rebellion lasted eighteen years and was at times supported by Taiping troops, whose leaders ultimately failed in their bid to control China. Tens of thousands of Miao were beheaded after the demise of their rebellion in 1871. Uprisings, however, continued until 1949. In the long history of insurrection hundreds of thousands of Miao died of starvation, in battle, or by the executioner's sword. The survivors were often reduced to the status of feudal peasants under Han or favored Miao landlords.

Today, Southeast Guizhou is rapidly joining the rest of China in the swift-paced march to modernization and is also being heralded as a center of Miao culture. In Taijiang County, a major district in the Miao-Dong prefecture and one of the most concentrated Miao areas in China, the Miao ethnic group comprises 96 percent of the total population. A number of projects there and elsewhere in the area are currently underway to highlight and preserve aspects of the local traditions. These projects include government-sponsored traditional arts festivals, tourist venues featuring song and dance routines, museums exhibiting aspects of arts and crafts, and the production of digital videos on folk customs, dance, and music.

Traditional Society and Life Cycle

Although many aspects of Miao culture in Southeast Guizhou have changed since the initial collection of the epics in the early 1950s, and the more developed towns are increasingly being integrated into national social and economic patterns along with the rest of southwest China (Schein), the more traditional villages in upland rural areas still offer parallels to aspects of the life ways described or alluded to in the epics. The following overview of local Miao society depicts a lifestyle from earlier in the twentieth century that was still current at the time of the initial collection of the epics. In the years since 1949, outside influences have increased markedly, sometimes in conjunction with political experimentation and extremism from 1949 until the late 1970s. Events went in a different direction with the introduction of economic reforms that rapidly gained pace throughout the 1990s and into the twenty-first century, increasing individual mobility (with many young people heading for the cities in search of work) and introducing a modern, money-based economy and ethical system powered in part by television and other media.

Family and Village

Miao settlements in Southeast Guizhou are permanent and range in size from a few homes to tens of thousands of households. The size of these communities (compared to the historically less sedentary Hmong communities in Southeast Asia) may be due to the relative abundance of cultivatable land. In parts of Southeast Asia, some Hmong rely on slash-and-burn agriculture and grow little wet-field rice (though governments may pressure them to settle down) (Geddes; Tapp et al.). Such practices entail constant cycles of village building, abandonment, and migration because of resource depletion. It may be that similar cycles involving short- and long-range migrations were once the norm among the Miao in Southeast Guizhou. This might explain, in part, the numerous origin legends and the persistence of the theme of migration in the epics.

In terms of family structure, Miao families in Southeast Guizhou are patrilineal and patrilocal. Before the *yamen* system of local government was introduced, Miao headmen were chosen for clan affiliation and personal qualities such as ability, honesty, and fairness. Wisemen, known as *lu* (*lul*), were the equivalents of judges. Various ritual specialists were important until recently for doctoring the sick, dealing with ghosts and other supernatural beings, and overseeing certain ceremonial activities. Rural women have important roles in certain ceremonies, courting activities, agriculture, marketing, childcare, handicrafts, and more recently, in the tourist industry. Positive images of women are common in Miao folklore, including many of the epics in this volume.

Families are basically organized around small households of parents with children. Relatives and friends mutually benefit each other by interacting at house-raisings, weddings, funerals, and religious ceremonials. Special relationships are recognized as existing between uncles and nephews and aunts and nieces. Cross-cousin marriage was once common, and today a bride must still formally ask her mother's brother for permission to marry (outside the family), as traditionally she was obligated to marry one of his sons. Brothers-in-law are often considered the equals of blood relatives. Knowledge of kinship ties is of extreme importance, as participation in the ceremonial drum societies depends on clan affiliation. Kin are invited to social and ceremonial events in a strict order of blood affinity. Forgetting to invite a close blood relative may result in a quarrel. Though elder sons set up separate households when they marry, the youngest son will stay in the parents' home. Sons inherit all parental property, but daughters are given silver heirlooms when they marry. Men do the strenuous fieldwork such as plowing and harrowing and care for the larger animals. Women cut firewood, tend small garden plots on the hillsides, and manage household chores. The summer months are times of the greatest activity. During the winter, traditionally, the men spent much time around charcoal burners smoking and chatting while the women wove cloth on their looms.

Economy and Material Culture

Miao in Southeast Guizhou are wet-field rice farmers. In the Taijiang area one crop of rice is raised each year in fields built in narrow river valleys, along stream banks, or in hillside terraces. Bottomland is at a premium. In recent years modern techniques of crop rotation and the use of chemical fertilizer have been adopted. Maize, yams, green vegetables, vine crops, and tobacco are grown in plots dug high on the hillsides. Water buffaloes and smallish, yellow cattle are kept as draft animals in wooden pens, while pigs, chickens, ducks, and geese are raised for meat. Fish are sometimes raised in the rice fields.

Favorite foods include salted and pickled fish (which can keep for over a year), crushed and pickled red peppers mixed with glutinous rice flour, a special sour drink made of pickled greens, and homemade distilled alcohol. Glutinous rice cakes (known as *baba* throughout Guizhou) are made by using a giant wooden mallet to pound a special variety of rice into a sticky paste in a carved out log. Though Miao banquets do not include a great number of dishes, guests can expect some combination of fish, fowl, meat, soup, and alcohol. Hogs may be butchered and preserved at New Year's Festival and eaten for several months afterward.

The main farm tools, which are mentioned repeatedly in the epics, are the plow and harrow. Plows, made of wood with an iron or steel share, are light and compact—just right for maneuvering in mountain fields that can sometimes be jumped across. The wooden harrows, used to break up the plowed soil, have eleven iron teeth and are reinforced with iron bands (just as reported in the epics). Other tools include axes, hammers, chisels, rakes, hoes, sickles, ink-lines, and specialized tools for carpentry, silversmithing, and iron work. In the past, many of their worked metal goods were obtained in trade from the Han in exchange for raw gold and silver mined on a limited scale.

The traditional wooden houses are large and roomy, with frames made of fir posts and sided with fir boards. Though most houses in the larger valley settlements have solid foundations, houses on hillsides are often built on posts, leaving a space beneath for tools or animals. Baked tile roofs cover most homes; otherwise, bark or split planks are used. Since the houses are never painted, they develop a rich dark brown hue that is pleasing to behold against the green hillsides. In villages, houses are built so close together that they sometimes touch, and in smaller settlements they are built right up the steep hillsides. The references in the epics to the "foot" of a village refer to the lowest tier of houses on a hillside. A few large sweet gum trees are usually found in the villages and small shrines to the Earth God (called the "Earth Buddha" in the Taijiang region) are located at various spots in the village or on nearby ridges. Animals are kept in small pens or barns. In some river towns giant three-hulled dragon boats over twenty meters long (used for racing at festival times) are stored in long sheds.

Miao embroidery has been famous in China for centuries. Tunics women wear on special occasions are made of cotton dyed with indigo then coated with egg whites and pounded, when dry, with a wooden mallet until shiny. The tunics are then decorated on the cuffs, sleeves, breast, and collar with colorful embroidery or brocade. Motifs include cross-stitched geometrical patterns, such as swastikas (an ancient pattern possibly derived from the hair whorls on the shoulders of water buffaloes), triangles, diamonds, stylized flowers, butterflies, pond algae, and birds. Fantastic lions, insects, birds, and flowers sewn with bright synthetic colors have become popular in recent years. Traditionally, a young woman would leave a small portion of one design unfinished to signify continued diligence. There are many styles of looms, both large and small. The biggest have wooden frames, though the tension on the warp threads is supplied by a back strap fastened around the worker's waist, as in smaller looms. A long bamboo needle used in brocade work is mentioned in the epics. Cotton cloth shoes are embroidered. Rather stiff, knee-length skirts with hundreds of tiny pleats (compared to mountain ridges in the epics) are dyed seven or eight times in indigo until they turn nearly black. Some women wear protective indigo puttees wrapped around their calves.

In recent years, younger Miao have tended to adopt more Western-influenced dress styles for all but festival occasions, though many women and girls still wear their hair pulled up in topknots. In the Taijiang area, many hairdos are decorated with a nine-inch silver pin, a wooden half-moon comb, and sometimes a calico turban. Some women also twist several locks of human hair (available in local markets) into their own in order to fill out their topknots. The heads of many little girls are shaved, except for a tiny topknot, in the belief that their hair will grow thickly when they mature. At festivals, teenage girls from richer families bedeck themselves in heavy silver earrings, bracelets, neck rings, giant hollow pendants, and elaborate headdresses with crescents, antlers, birds, and danglers—a silver costume worth many thousands of Chinese *yuan*. The most elaborate costumes are worn only at spring or winter festivals; dress for summer festivals is very colorful but much simpler (and cooler), consisting of simple topknot decorations such as plastic or metal flowers, combs, and silver pins. Simple bibs of velvet or pink or bright green or sky blue blouses are typical. Some older men wear the traditional dark cotton clothing with turbans or huge bamboo hats, though young men prefer newer styles.

Marriage

Young people have traditionally had plenty of opportunity to meet members of the opposite sex before marriage. Traditional courting activities called *ye fang* (*yet fangb*) consist of antiphonal singing of love songs, playing the *lusheng* (a type of bamboo reed-pipe, common among several southwestern minorities, called *gi* [*gix*] in the local Miao dialect), blowing tunes on tree leaves, dancing, and other more intimate activities. Boys and girls may gather in small groups in the evenings at a customary spot such as a tree or at the village center to *ye fang*. Often, boys from other towns will come to seek girls with different clan names, since many towns consist of persons having the same, or at most, a few clan names. Those who violate local courting customs, however, may be beaten and driven away. Large song festivals are held several times throughout the year, providing a wide choice of prospective marriage partners for the young people. Larger festivals attract thousands of people, young and old, and last several days. It is common for mothers to act as chaperones for their daughters, and older women sometimes prompt girls who are singing antiphonal love songs. Though in the past these song festivals may have had religious significance in the agricultural cycle, they are now primarily secular activities. Festivals are usually held along stream banks or at an unusual natural formation, such as Censer Mountain near the city of Kaili, which according to the epics is a site where one of the pillars supporting the sky was set during an early phase of the creation.

In former times, there were two ways to marry. The simplest method was for the groom and several friends to go to a neighboring village to escort the intended bride back home, where she was feasted by the groom's family. After thirteen days the bride returned to visit her mother. There was no official ceremony and the groom wore everyday clothes; at most the bride might wear a suit of new clothes. This sort of wedding was common among poorer families. The second type of wedding was more elaborate and was usually arranged by the respective families. The boy's family presented a money gift to the bride's maternal uncle's family. Until the money was given, the bride could not leave. The escort party from the boy's family arrived at the bride's home on the day of the wedding laden with pork, fish, chicken, and *baba* cakes the size of wash pans. The bride's family returned similar gifts, and the bride was escorted to the groom's home dressed in her finest garments and silver ornaments.

Most weddings still take place after harvest or in early spring. In the past, the majority of people married in their late teens. In some places many of these customs are still popular, though Han and Western influences have increased in recent years (Schein, 262–67).

Funerals

Funerals were presided over by ritual specialists. Ideally, persons were not allowed to die on a regular bed, and the coffin of the dead was kept outside the home. If a person died in bed, the clothes, shoes, and straw mattress belonging to the deceased were burned. A special couch was often made for those near death to rest on. Deceased old men were dressed in special long gowns, and old women were dressed in clothes laid aside for the occasion. Burials were made in the mountains. The soul of the deceased was instructed by a ritual specialist to follow the path back to the east—the legendary ancestral home (souls of the Han Chinese are said to travel west). Silver and gold were often buried with the body, but copper was forbidden in graves, as luck-bringing dragons fear the metal. Children of the deceased would bring pork and rice, while friends would bring rice or wine to feed the guests. During the days of the funeral, the family members did not wear special clothing, though in some places, when the coffin was escorted up the mountains, family members wrapped their heads in rough hemp. Some of these customs continue today, though Han ways (which are somewhat similar) have been adopted in many places.

Beliefs

In Southeast Guizhou, the local Miao have been influenced in varying degrees by Buddhism, Taoism, Christianity, and prevailing ideologies of both historic and modern Chinese governments. Along with these elements of worldview, a strong current of animism ran through traditional thinking, and everything from mountains to metals was believed to be alive (though only certain things, such as unusual rock formations or weirdly gnarled trees, were thought to have souls). There is also a strong belief in ghosts and ghost families. The most important ceremonial activities continue to be sacrifices (*bu mai* or *but mais*) to the mythic Ancestors, especially Butterfly Mother, and the Ur-parents Jang Vang (Jangx Vangb) and his sister (who married him after a disastrous flood that killed everyone else on earth).

Aside from the sacrifices, there are the Miao New Year, the Chinese New Year, and various festivals for cleaning villages, propitiating dragons and ghosts, racing dragon boats, and courting. Some local governments have recently promoted annual festivals in order to attract tourists. One of the most lavish is the "Sister Festival," in which young, unmarried women gather to eat a special kind of glutinous rice and display themselves clad in elaborate traditional costume replete with silver ornaments. Folksong singing, dancing, traditional games, and other activities are held for several days and nights.

Since the Ancestor Sacrifices are central to the epics, a more thorough description is essential. In Southeast Guizhou, the areas of Taijiang, Jianhe, Leishan, and Kaili are all regions where water buffalo bull sacrifices, sponsored by clan drum societies, were held in twelve-year cycles.³ Other areas held sacrifices every three, five, seven, or nine years. Epidemics or other natural disasters sometimes prompted ritual specialists to set up special dates for sacrifices. All blood relatives were members of a drum society, though in some areas, because of population changes, persons of different clan names were admitted. The drum society was at once a religious, political, and military institution, and its major function was to ensure that the cycle of sacrifices continued. Drums, central to drum society activities, were regarded as being alive and the living places of the mythical Ancestors. The sacrifices were held to remember the Ancestors (who are very different from the deceased relatives of Han ancestor reverence), to ask them for prosperity, and to strengthen clan unity.

The sacrificial cycle was complex and entailed many restrictions, particularly on leaders (Yang, 374–7).⁴ A capable, affable master of ceremonies at least thirty years of age was chosen by the clan to lead a particular sacrifice. Though the position prevented him from regular farming and put a great strain on his family's food reserves, the chosen could not refuse. Those making that mistake were ostracized, finding themselves without help at marriages, funerals, and house-raisings. The community punished persons associating with such shirkers. Besides the master of ceremonies, about ten other lesser leaders were chosen to carry out various activities. Four epic singers were included in this group.

Three drums were used in the twelve-year ceremonies. The largest pair was chiseled out of *nanmu* (*Phoebe nanmu*) logs and the ends were covered with the skin of a yellow cow. These drums were about five-and-a-half feet long and a foot in diameter. Handed down from sacrifice to sacrifice, they were kept on racks, between ceremonials, in the house of a family willing to care for them, often in a home without sons. A smaller single drum was made especially for each sacrifice. Each sacrifice took several years to complete. On the fifth day of the second lunar month at the beginning of the new sacrificial cycle, the pair of large drums was escorted from the keeper's home to that of the new master of ceremonies. On the first day of the tenth lunar month a group went to the mountain hiding place of the small single drum to perform a ceremony known as "Turning the Drum," in which the old drum was rolled over and the Ancestors told that a new sacrifice was beginning. The old drum was then symbolically escorted down the mountain, though in fact, it was left to molder. The next day was the Miao New Year, so everyone young and old in the drum society danced the "Wooden Drum Dance."

The next year the mountain drum was also turned once on the same date as the first ceremony. In the third year, the time of the most complex and serious ceremonials, the water buffalo bulls were sacrificed. On the third day of the fifth lunar month, a *nanmu* tree was cut to make the new drum, and on the third day the bulls fought each other. Great crowds gathered to watch the strong bulls with distinct hair whorls on their shoulders rack horns. It was unusual for bulls to fight to the death. Instead, the winner overpowered the loser, or pushed it out of bounds. Visitors who were not members of the sponsoring drum society ate and stayed with relatives, or were fed and housed by the master of ceremonies. (There were certain times during the sacrifices, however, that non-blood kin would present gifts to the hosts.)

On the third day of the seventh month a yellow cow was killed for its skin. The next day was a rice harvest festival called "Eating the New" when a ceremony was held to turn the new drum. The following day the skin was fastened on the new drum before the instrument was sent to the master of ceremonies' home for the society members to dance around during the sacrificial ceremonies.

On the sixth and twelfth day of the seventh month the water buffalo bulls, having been fattened for three years, were killed after the bullfighting had ended. In some villages hundreds of bulls were sacrificed, as ideally each household would offer one beast. In reality, not every family could afford to do so. Some poorer families might afford only a piece of beef. Some well-to-do families might offer several animals. The bulls were slaughtered by having their throats cut with a huge knife. In some areas the bulls were painted black with tung oil and their necks were draped with live chickens and ducks.

During the fourteen days after the butchering of the bulls, various ceremonies were held. On the eleventh day, eight or nine ceremonies were held and the reed-pipes were played day and night. On the fourteenth day people danced around the beating drums, thus ending the third ceremonial year. Both the paired drums and the single drum were kept in the house of the master of ceremonies, where at later ceremonies members of the drum society would come to dance.

The fourth year was the final year. On the first day of the tenth lunar month the "drum pig" was killed. The responsibility for this ceremony was delegated to the second drum master. The day before the pig was killed the paired drums were moved to the second master's house for dancing. The next fourteen days were similar to those of the third year, except that the bamboo reed-pipes were played day and night on the thirteenth and fourteenth days. At midnight of the final day, the paired drums were moved to the home of the new host family. The single drum was then escorted to the mountains where it was left to rot, ending the ritual activity. In some communities today, simplified versions of the sacrifices are still conducted.

The Epics and Their Performance

In recent years, many scholars worldwide have engaged in debates over some basic questions about the nature of epic narrative. According to Lauri Honko, a Finnish epic scholar, the traditional Western notions of epic—predicated on notions of Greek heroic epics like Homer's *Odyssey*—as being stories of history and heroes has gradually expanded to include many poetic narratives from around the world that by criteria of length, form, and content have been classified under the now international term "epic." Not just limited to the exploits of male heroes, epics may feature heroes of either gender, who are physical, moral, or intellectual "exemplars" (Honko, 22–3; 28). The poems may vary in length from a few hundred lines to many thousands, concern events and the doings of individuals in circumstances that are not limited to combat, and are not necessarily performed by a single bard or singer, but possibly by multiple singers and other participants, who may include audience members. Another recent realization is that epics tend not to be told in strict linear series of episodes. Moreover, one or a group of singers may know only a portion of a potentially "complete" story. Thus, at a given performance of an epic, one is more likely to hear at most a few episodes (and those not necessarily in sequential order), rather than the "whole" story. The "whole" story, however, may be more or less known to the community of audience members, but its telling may seldom if ever take place as a complete cycle. Also, it is now being understood that the ways in which singers conceptualize the stories may often differ from those of scholars who have examined various written transcripts of performances. What the scholars may see as relevant to the telling may be recognized as optional or incidental to singers who may add or delete portions of the story from the "mental texts" residing in their minds. Honko (92–9) has described these unwritten story texts as the sum of mental resources that to some extent become actualized (or made "immanent" [Foley, 113–14]) in specific acts of performance. At each performance singers draw on their core bundle of content and associated epic lore to recreate the segment of the story they are telling, which seems to come out differently each time, though thematically is the "same" story. Such is certainly the case for the *Butterfly Mother* epics, in which two pairs of singers help each other unfold the main storyline, which they call the "bone," while interspersing the story with many colorful asides in the form of lyric poems called "song flowers." Thus, as a unique form of oral narrative, the *Butterfly Mother* epics help us to extend our understanding of oral epic traditions worldwide.

Epics in China

The Miao epics from Southeast Guizhou (which are also sung in parts of northern Guangxi) are only a small part of a vast web of epic traditions historically circulating within the boundaries of China. Although until fairly recently Western scholars believed that China was bereft of an epic tradition, within the country's borders exist a number of traditions of long narratives delivered or written as poetry or as mixtures of prose and poetry. Some of these traditions fall easily into earlier categories of epic, while others might be considered for membership under the now emerging sense of the term. In the north and west are ancient traditions found mostly among herding or hunting peoples that meet many of the criteria for heroic epics in the West. The most famous of these epics is the Tibetan narrative of King Gesar of Ling, a story also told among the Mongols and related groups. The Mongol epic cycle of the super-hero Janggar features a powerful khan and his band of heroes who spend their time banqueting and fighting off multiheaded giants called *manggus*. Heroic epics such as these feature the deeds of mounted, sword-wielding, monster-slaying heroes of divine birth, and are found as far east as Heilongjiang province, where forest-dwellers like the Daur people live, and spread west across Central Asia to the gates of Europe (Bender, In the Oral). Epics of culture heroes are also found in the southwest of China, for instance, the tales of Zhyge Alu of the Yi people living in the mountains of Sichuan and bordering areas of Yunnan. Sharing parallels with myths of the Han and several other southwestern minorities (including the Miao), the story of Zhyge Alu tells how he was conceived out of wedlock by an eagle dripping blood on his mother's skirt. The fatherless child was abandoned in the mountains where he was raised by dragons. Becoming a skilled archer, Zhyge Alu later shot down the extra suns and moons, saving the earth's people from an early version of global warming.

In the south and southwest of China, however, most of the long narrative poems of these primarily agricultural peoples deal with creation, and the heroes are often as not mythical heroines or non-martial exemplary figures. Usually shorter in length than the heroic epics of the steppes, and often sung antiphonally by two to four singers, these epics speak of origins, some also including accounts of the harsh migrations through the rugged mountains of Yunnan, Sichuan, Guizhou, Hunan, and Guangxi. Among the ethnic groups that count such narratives in their oral traditions are the Yi, Hani, Lahu, Jingpo, Drung, Naxi, Wa, Dai, Zhuang, Dong, Bouyei, and Yao (Zhu and Li, 146–47).

Common themes in the epics collected in southwest China include the creation of the sky and earth from amorphous matter, the propping up of the sky, the shooting down of excess suns and moons, the creation of forests and agriculture, a great flood, a calabash that acts as a sort of Ark, incest between a brother and sister who are the sole survivors of the flood, the consequent birth of a flesh ball (or other abnormal "child" such as a piece of wood), followed by the division and dispersion of various ethnic groups when the offspring is chopped up (Zhu and Li, 153; 157–58). Creation is often a joint activity and may include both male and female creators. Though the mythology of the Han, China's majority ethnic group, finds less expression in contemporary oral cultures, many of the recorded myths that have weathered the censor's brush during the long imperial period share motifs found in epics of the southwestern minorities (Birrell).

In recent decades, many minority epic narratives, such as the texts in *Butterfly Mother*, have been collected and edited by folklore researchers, sometimes in large folklore collection projects that were carried out in the mid-1950s and again, after years of political turmoil, in the 1980s and 1990s. In China, as elsewhere, once oral epics are collected they usually become involved in formal aspects of what Honko has called the "process of textualization" (3–4; 17). In this process, epics are collected from oral performers by scholars who transcribe them in printed or electronic formats and render them into print or other media. In the process, various modifications are made. Aside from simply playing video recordings of actual performances, any attempt at transcription (the writing down of the sounds of the original language) and translation—the attempt to move meaning from one language to another—involves compromises on the parts of translators, editors, and publishers in order to create readable texts for literate audiences. In some instances, editors may take out certain parts, or enhance others in order to create a more aesthetically desirable or politically correct product. In other instances, they may take parts of several versions to make a more complete "master" text, or may even simply use portions of oral transcripts as inspirations for more literary compositions. Honko has explored many of these questions in great detail and has coined the term "tradition-oriented" epics to describe those epics that have undergone more extensive editing or been creatively modified to make them more artistically interesting. Since 1949, probably a majority of the epics published in China could be placed under the "tradition-oriented" label, with outright fabrications on one end of the scale, and lightly edited versions made with the goal of being more easily readable in print on the other end. The best versions are probably those lightly edited versions in Chinese translation that are supported by accurate footnotes and include all or part of the original language transcripts.

Most versions of the Miao epics, including the Ma and Jin version used as a base for the present English translation, fall into this latter classification, though only a few contain original language samples or transcripts. In general, published epics have become more accurate since the early 1980s, after a period of intensive censorship in the 1960s and 1970s during the Cultural Revolution.

Outline of the Epic Narratives

In the local Miao language the epic songs are referred to as "old songs" (*hxa lu hxa gho* or *hxak lul hxak ghot*). This is similar to the Chinese term "ancient songs" (*guge*), an appellation sometimes applied to creation epics from the ethnic groups in southwest China. In actual performance, the Miao epics are not necessarily sung in the order presented in this volume and the whole cycle would not normally be sung at one event. The songs may also go by other names and be grouped differently. In some cases, the performance situation may also vary, especially for certain songs in the section entitled *Song of Butterfly Mother* that are performed by ritual specialists at specific points in the ceremonial sacrifices to the mythical Ancestors (described above). The epics, however, can be arranged as a narrative cycle for the convenience of reading audiences, and major figures such as the trickster-hero Jang Vang (Jangx Vangb), Butterfly Mother, the flesh ball, Gho Do (Ghot Dol), and the creator Bang Xang Ye (Bangx Xangx Yel) appear or are mentioned in many of the episodes.

When the songs are placed in chronological order, the cycle begins with a prologue similar to what might appear before any of the individual songs. We witness a cosmic panorama in which the earliest mythic figures are born. All does not proceed smoothly, and some of the early gods die. Later, a mythic egg is hatched and the pieces of the eggshell change into five gods who all have important tasks in the creation.

In *Song of Gold and Silver,* we see the sky and earth created and the pillars that hold up the sky set at various places within the Miao universe. A tiny crab and Hxu Niu (Hxub Niux), a mythical unicorn (possibly a rhinoceros), open the waterways to allow the personified metals, Gold and Silver, to be transported to make the suns and moons. In the portion of the song called *Transporting Gold and Silver,* the fascination with metals, particularly gold and silver, which take precedence over the lesser metals such as tin, copper, lead, and iron, is obvious. As everything else in the epics, the metals are "born."[5] They suckle their mother, have their hair cut, their faces washed, and marry. Though such personification is sometimes bewildering, the view is animistic: in this mythic age everything is alive.

Certain similes, such as a leech forming the bolt of the fire tongs in the cosmic forge, are also arresting in their aptness, reflecting the close study of local natural conditions. The events described are serious, but the tone is often light-hearted and even mischievous, as when it is asked what sort of horseshoes the transport boats wore.

When Gold and Silver's ox (water buffalo) leaves for the east to have its hair whorls painted on its shoulders and its horns attached for the Ancestor Sacrifice (a theme expanded upon in *Song of Butterfly Mother*) the metals all follow, later to be pursued and captured in the east. They are finally transported home in a journey paralleling *Westwards, Upriver*, the legendary account of a migration from east to west. After the suns and moons are made, the tools are all escorted to various places and then change into other things, a motif occurring several times in the epic cycle. When it is found that too many suns and moons have been made, the archer Hsang Sa (Hsangb Sax) shoots down all except those that remain today. Afterwards he unknowingly kills his own son after testing the boy's skill in arrows, fearing that the young archer might someday displace him.

In the *Song of the Ancient Sweet Gum*, the various tree seeds are born, then raised in a house built by the mythic being Fu Fang (Fux Fangb). His mythological house building methods are contrasted with those of Jang Vang who, though a mythic being like Fu Fang, often represents humanity in the epics. Human actions (the actions of "our parents" or "Mother," etc.) are often compared directly with the feats of the gods.

Later, the seeds' house is burned down by Grandma Niu Xang (Niux Xangb), one of many of the mythical grandmothers who appear in the epics. The seeds escape east and are pursued by the mythic being Xang Liang (Xangb Liangx), captured, and returned to the west. He then plows the fields and we are introduced (in great detail) to the plow and the harrow, tools basic to wet rice agriculture. The tree seeds are planted and a sweet gum grows beside a pond where Xang Liang raises fish. When cranes steal some of his fish, Xang Liang accuses the sweet gum, for its leaves are covered with fish scales dropped by the feasting birds. Yet the tree is unable to speak in his own defense. Several wisemen are invited to defend the tree in court, but all fail and the tree is felled as punishment. As with the body of the early creator Bang Xang Ye, the shattered tree's parts change into a myriad of beings, including Butterfly Mother and the Ji Wi (Jib Wix) Bird that comes to hatch Butterfly Mother's eggs in *Song of Butterfly Mother*. The trial of the sweet gum parallels the trial of the eagle in *Westwards, Upriver*. In the past, such creatures as tigers or eagles captured by hunters were tried for their "crimes" and rapped on the head with a special stick when "sentenced" to death.

The *Song of Butterfly Mother* was only performed by ritual specialists every twelve or seven years during sacrifices made to the Ancestors. The cycle describes the birth of Butterfly Mother from the heart of the sweet gum tree, her lovemaking with Wave Foam, the birth of the twelve eggs from which the Ancestors hatch, and the cutting of the umbilical cords of the infant Ancestors. After Jang Vang is elected "Elder Brother" because of his cleverness, the nestlings disperse, for

> A family with no children is an unhappy family,
> but if the children are too many, it's chaos. (122)

It seems that not only did the Miao find the population crunch a factor in dispersal, but so did the Ancestors. Thus, the Dragon goes westwards down the rivers and the Thunder God soars to the sky where he can watch over what happens on the earth. Meanwhile, Jang Vang finds an ancient ax in the overgrown foundations of the houses of the previous era's gods and begins to open the land westwards. Unfortunately, he runs into a centipede that is intent upon retaining its ancestral graves, suggesting that the Miao may not have been the first people to dwell in Southeast Guizhou (remnants of an ancient group called the Ka by the Miao still exist in the region). Though poisoned by the centipede, Jang Vang continues to clear and plow the land, feats of central importance to an agricultural people. Waterbugs and bees teach Jang Vang to do the drum dance, and the episode closes with Jang Vang, his buffalo, and a rake dancing and singing in the rice fields.

The following episodes of the *Song of Butterfly Mother* concern obtaining the ceremonial drums, sacrificial bull, ritual vestments, and wild beasts for the Ancestor Sacrifices. The drums are found in the mountains, and the bulls follow the rivers east to get their hair whorls (on their shoulders) and horns. The ritual vestments are obtained from the Han people. We find that Jang Vang's nine sisters marry, each one mistakenly taking an object necessary for an Ancestor Sacrifice when she leaves, ensuring that at each sacrifice the sisters return to officiate over some essential function, while incidentally stressing clan unity. Several of the sisters marry Han husbands. The dull-witted A Diu (Ah Diub) serves first as a maid in a Han household; the other sisters cause their parents hardship by forcing them to sell off land to cover court costs for the breakup of forced engagements to Miao men. The attitude towards the Han in the epics is ambivalent. The marriages are portrayed in a rather negative light, but it is the Han who supply the sacrificial vestments and metal goods. The mention of court costs indicates the presence of Han *yamen* offices in the Miao region, suggesting that the details of these marriages are fairly recent additions to these epics that certainly date from much earlier than the beginning of the nineteenth century, when significant numbers of Han people (called "Guests" in the epics) arrived in Southeast Guizhou (Wu and Qian, 103).

The final segment of the cycle is *The Great Flood*, concerning a dispute between Jang Vang and the Thunder God, who threatens to flood the earth. The Thunder God is tricked into delaying the inundation for several days, allowing Jang Vang enough time to grow a huge calabash. Rains fall for three days and nights, then hail for another nine. The floodwaters rise and nothing is left in sight but the floating calabash, duly reported to the Thunder God as a mountain by a series of bird and animal messengers until a chicken finally reports that all is clear. When the floodwaters recede, Jang Vang is left alone with the only other survivor, his sister. Though he knows it is wrong, his prospects are limited. His sister at first refuses, but he eventually manages to trick her into marrying him. The result of their incest is a misshapen ball of flesh, which Jang Vang in a rage hacks into bits with a sickle on a spruce chopping block. The bits are placed in nine manure buckets and spread over the earth, changing into untold numbers of people, none of whom can speak. The secret of speech is discovered by once again tricking the Thunder God, and the different languages are voiced. Once again the population is seen as excessive, and the people spread out in search of a better life. Though many Chinese researchers are fond of viewing the brother-sister incest motif as a survival of a former primitive marriage system, it is more likely a manifestation of an incest taboo, obviated by Jang Vang's wrath and the fact that incest is normally a taboo subject.

The last epic in the collection, *Westwards, Upriver*, is set in a legendary rather than mythic time and may be rooted in a probable migration of human ancestors westwards into Southeast Guizhou centuries ago. Certain themes of the entire cycle are repeated, particularly the killing of a nemesis (the eagle), mentions of agricultural techniques, and the Ancestor Sacrifices. Though thought by singers to be different from the mythic epics, the song is often sung as a continuation of *The Great Flood*.

Language and Formal Structure

The dialects that constitute the Miao language are in the Miao-Yao group of the Sino-Tibetan language family. Many dialects are not mutually intelligible (in ways similar to the situation with the Han Chinese dialects), and some are closer to the Yao language, which has sometimes made classification difficult. Like Standard Chinese, Miao is a tonal language. Sentences follow a subject-predicate-object order.

Unlike Chinese, however, Miao adverbs follow verbs, and adjectives follow nouns. Chinese researchers have labeled the linguistic areas where the epics circulate as the "Eastern Dialect Division" (subdivided into northern and southern groups), which includes eastern Guizhou province and the northern part of the Guangxi Zhuang Autonomous Region. Mutually intelligible dialects are still commonly spoken throughout the region, to the extent that even some local Han people are fluent in them.

Though Miao folklore mentions ancient written scripts, history records no evidence of a written language (aside from Chinese) prior to the early twentieth century, when missionaries such as Samuel Pollard devised Romanization systems. In the early 1950s scholars in China introduced the present system, though wide dialectical differences require significant regional modifications of the system. As is typical of epic traditions anywhere, the language style used in the epic singing is conservative and contains words and usages that may seem old-fashioned or obscure in modern vernacular speech. The lines are structurally compact and certain units of language (such as pronouns) can often be left out, understood by implication or context.

The Miao epic poems from Southeast Guizhou do not rhyme, and like most Miao songs in the region have five syllables in each line. A major structural element in the epics is the repetition of tone patterns, a device found in songs of other tonal languages in southwest China and in Chinese Classical poetry. In epic singing a tone pattern is repeated for an indefinite succession of lines, and changes in tone patterns are dictated by how quickly the singers run out of words that can fit a particular tone pattern, or by changes in content. In the system of Romanization used to write the local dialect used in the epics, the last letter in each word represents a tone in which the word is voiced. (As noted in the Key to Pronunciation for Eastern Miao Dialect Romanization, the marker itself is *not* pronounced as part of the word, for it only indicates the contour of the tone.)

There are many tone patterns used in Miao folksongs and epics. Shorter songs usually have more complex ones than the epics, and some patterns require that every tone in a line be repeated in succeeding lines. The following love song (in which the terms "sister" and "brother" represent lovers) gives examples of tone marks and a common tone pattern.

> *Bangx pud ghab jil det*
> Flowers open branch tree
> *Niangx ghaid ob lol leit*

Seasons one two come here
Dax ed xenb mongl xongt
Come sister marry go brother
Ax ed xenb jel ot
Not sister marry single

Translation:
Flowers blossom on the tree branches,
Seasons pass one by one;
If brother comes, sister marries,
If not, then sister is alone.

In the example, every word is part of the tone pattern. Sometimes, however, a singer may run out of words in a desired tone. In such cases certain tones can be substituted. For instance *b* tones can be substituted for *s* tones and *t* tones for *k* tones and vice versa. Thus if a word with a *b* tone is substituted as an *s* word, the word will be pronounced with an *s* tone, and so on. Parallelism and repetition are also important features of the songs, as indicated by lines 3 and 4 above. Measure words that help mark quantities of certain things (similar to a "loaf" of bread, or a "piece" of candy in English) often help to fill out the needed number of syllables in a line.

Because of the length of the epics, tone patterns used in them are less strict than in shorter songs. The following example is taken from the last stanza of *Westwards, Upriver*.

Lot ot laid niangx niangl
Old time [measure word] unfamiliar age
Mangx bib jus dail nal
We you (plural) one [measure word] ancestor
Jus laib naib lol diangl
One [measure word] grandma come birth
Jus gangb eb nix yil
One [measure word] water silver wash
Jus dlaf dob nox ghol
One [measure word] cloth blue color
Jus bens ngax hob gil
One [measure word] meat Thunder God dry
Jus jut ngax dliangb lol
One [measure word] meat ghost come

Translation:
> In the ancient times
> you and I were of the same ancestors,
> born by one grandmother;
> washing in the same basin,
> wearing the same indigo cloth;
> as one slice of meat sacrificing to the god of drought,
> as one string of the meat sacrificing to the wild ghosts.

In an epic singing event, opponents question and answer each other using the same tone pattern, though after an answer, a new tone pattern may be substituted. Repetition of many types is one of the most obvious features of the epics. In the example, the word *jus* provides unity to the lines, merging form and content. (Numbers usually appear at the beginnings of lines.) Formulaic phrasing includes repetitions of lines contrasting past and present ("If it were today . . .") and patterns comparing human and mythic ways of doing things ("If our parents were building a house . . ." with "When Fu Fang built the Seeds' house"). Formulaic phrases that essentially say the same thing ("Let's talk of making the Moons," or "Let's speak of making the Suns and Moons") often vary significantly, due at least in part to changes in tone patterns. Another feature is the appearance of similes in otherwise identical lines ("Every kind of Seed was born by Mud; / every kind of Seed was birthed by Mud").

In some instances, references to supernatural beings, customs, or places that seem once to have been meaningful, are now obscure, yet are still retained by the singers. Other examples of now unfathomable information are the references to the "Principles," seemingly an early social code, and to certain constellations mentioned in *Song of Gold and Silver*. The appearances of these obscure features are due to the conservative nature of the epic performance tradition (Foley, 138–9). Although each performance is a re-creation, that re-creation is composed mostly of traditional elements that circulate among the singers. Like cherished material objects from ages past, aspects of oral tradition are sometimes retained, although their earlier meanings are no longer understood. The obscure references may have rhetorical functions, however, as when a series of place names is needed to convey movement through a landscape. In some instances the appearance of such phrases may cause some audiences members to respond simply because the references have appeared once more in an epic recital.

Situation and Process of Performance

Examining the situation or context in which an item of oral tradition is performed and the process of unfolding performances can give us insight into the traditions themselves and what they mean socially to the cultures that engage in them (Bauman, 27–9). Though fewer people than in the past are carrying on the tradition of epic singing, the stories in *Butterfly Mother* are still regularly performed in a number of rural communities by singers as young as thirty who sing segments of the songs at a variety of social events. The following paragraphs outline some of the more typical performance contexts and aspects of performance of the Miao epics in the Taijiang area in recent decades (Bender, "Felling the Ancient Sweetgum").

Like welcoming songs, drinking songs, and love songs, the epics are sung antiphonally. Singing is usually done outside in a clear place where a crowd can gather. The four singers sit on benches at a small square table, each pair side by side. Listeners, who may vary in number from a handful to dozens, crowd closely around. Pairs of singers may be of the same sex or mixed. Some singers prefer to sing with or against singers of the opposite sex. Singers in a pair often hardly know each other, and few practice together regularly. Before singing, a pair may discuss briefly what they hope to sing, or discuss what pitch to begin in (songs are sung to one penta-tonic tune that varies by locale). Singers like to sing and listen to other singers to increase their understanding of the songs and add to their stock of questions. Very few singers know the entire cycle, which would take approximately ten days to perform.

Singers, who are otherwise regular people, are invited to sing at festivals, weddings, and house-raisings. Ritual specialists sing the songs at Ancestor Sacrifices. At song-festivals, up to ten groups of epic singers may perform simultaneously, and the milling crowds may exceed twenty thousand. After the harvest season a pair of singers may visit a neighboring village in search of opponents. As the singers enter a village they sing out a challenge. When opponents appear, the guests will begin the song exchange. If, however, the singers are invited to a village, the host singers will sing first.

When beginning, singers degrade their own ability to sing and to answer the opponent's questions. This prelude is answered in kind by the opponents. Then the two sides discuss (in song) what portion of the epics to sing. The goal of epic singing is to out-sing and out-query one's opponents during the story-singing process. Familiarity with the songs, a strong voice, a quick mind, physical endurance, and the ability to work closely with one's partner are all necessary qualities to win.

As the actual narration begins, side A will recite a segment of the epic to be performed and will sing up to a point when a question can traditionally be posed. Side B will repeat what Side A has already sung (this repetition usually does not appear in this book), answer the question with as many lines as necessary, and further the story until a point is reached when a "who, what, when, or where" question can be asked.

In a pair, one singer is the lead but both sing the same lyrics simultaneously. The usual procedure is to sing two lines and pause a few seconds before continuing. This gives the singers time to catch their breath, for the lead to recall or compose the next lyrics, and for the second singer to anticipate what the lead will sing. The question-and-answer style of singing is very important, for it is the stimulus of the questions and the support of one's partner that allow the singers to go on singing day and night. It is said to be very difficult for singers to sing long sections of the epics alone. While singing, singers often drink distilled rice wine from ceramic rice bowls and many smoke strong, unfiltered cigarettes. In the course of the narration, few, if any, gestures or facial expressions are used.

Singing will often last three days and nights. Such marathons are strenuous, and Jin Dan, the collector of the versions of the epics in this book and a singer himself, feared the all-night sings of his youth, sometimes sleeping all day afterward and often developing a hoarse throat. A usual recital begins with the singers eating and drinking in the morning. Afterwards, the singing starts and lasts an hour or so until more wine is required. There is then more singing, followed by lunch and more wine. Singing and drinking alternate until the evening, when the singers eat another meal—with more wine. Then the singing continues until 1:00 or 2:00 in the morning or dawn, often near a pot of burning charcoal, and with occasional refreshers of wine. When the epic singing finally ends, the guest singers will be escorted from the village with songs of farewell.

Knowledge of the epic tradition and singing strategies make for effective singers. The singers' stock of questions is of utmost importance, for the more questions a pair know, the better chance they have of defeating their opponents by asking a question that cannot be answered. Therefore, singers familiar with a song will try to lengthen it, and singers less familiar with it will try to sing something else. If singers get stuck, they may confer in whispers while the other side is singing, or they may be prompted by members of the audience, as listeners are all familiar with the songs. Singers who invent new content or new questions are not respected. If singers cannot answer a question, the askers must answer it themselves, while ridiculing the ignorance of the other pair. (It is interesting that when asked to sing a passage of an epic, some individual singers find it difficult to sing alone without being prompted by questions.)

The main storyline of the epics is known as the "bone." The lengthy passages of elaboration and repetition are called "song flowers." Many of these "flowers" take the form of lyrics that range from about eight to over twenty lines. Their use in the songs is very fluid and they can be inserted when and where the singers feel necessary during a performance. Though some of these lyrics have little or nothing to do with the content of the epics, they enhance performances and allow singers to display their verbal skills and knowledge of the tradition. Dozens of such "flowers" circulate among the singers, and constitute a special dimension of performance. A major reason that the epics can go on for days is the song flower elaboration. Only a few such "flowers" (as chosen by the initial collectors, Ma and Jin) are included in this text as emphasis is on the "bone" of the narratives. One example is in the first two passages of "The Brothers Divide," and several others appear in *Westwards, Upriver*. (For other examples, see Jin; also Bender, "Three Oral Poetries," 27–8, and "Hunting Nets," 51–2.)

Besides listening to regular performances, some younger singers may take a roast duck and some wine to an older singer, in search of instruction. At such times the older singer will sing the "bone," usually without the questions, even though it is the questions that the younger singers prize most. The epics in *Butterfly Mother* include a comprehensive stock of questions gathered from several singers throughout the region; more questions than any one singer would likely know. However, some questions have two answers, and it is a constant challenge for the singers to gain a complete knowledge of the epics, for failure to answer questions leaves one open for keen satire from the opponents. Some passages or references concern places, personages, and customs that even the singers find obscure, though for the most part the vocabulary of the epics is colloquial.

Though singers can remember a song by hearing it only once, inspiration (and wine) is as important as recall. If a singer is not in a good mood, he or she will not perform well, and if disturbed by a personal calamity, may not sing at all, sometimes for years. Few singers, however, sing more than several times a year. As mentioned above, both singers in a pair sing the same lyrics simultaneously. Close listening, however, reveals that the second singer will occasionally fail to follow the lead perfectly, though the degree of rapport between well-paired singers familiar with the songs can be quite amazing. Though lyrics vary from recital to recital, the emphasis is on telling the story correctly to a demanding audience of singers and to aggressive opponents who are always ready to play on the slightest weakness in knowledge.

Collection and Translation

The collecting of the epics began about 1952, soon after the founding of the People's Republic of China, during an era when folk traditions of ethnic minority groups all over China were being examined by teams of scholars and educated youth. The well-known Chinese linguist, Ma Xueliang, and a young Miao scholar and epic singer named Jin Dan (Jen Dang or Jenb Dangk in Eastern Miao dialect Romanization), were part of the collection effort in Southeast Guizhou. The singers that performed the epics were Ghe Hfu Dle (Ghet Hfuk Dlens), Ghe Dla Dang (Ghet Dlas Dangk), and Ghe Dang Sang Ma (Ghet Dangk Sangb Mal), from the village of La Ci.

The goal of collecting and editing the epics was to create a "complete" version of the epics in writing for an educated reading audience—which meant that the original oral version would inevitably be modified. In the process of transforming the transcriptions or oral text into "tradition-related" reading matter, the team first collected oral versions (in the early stages without the benefit of tape-recorders). Initially the texts were transcribed in the International Phonetic Alphabet but later the Romanized Miao script was employed. The transcriptions were then translated into Standard Chinese, and the epics placed into chronological order. As noted, the emphasis was on collecting the main narrative thread (the "bone") of the songs. Thus only a few of the numerous "song flowers" that vary between performances and do not contribute directly to the plot were included. (It is estimated that this text would have been about two-thirds longer if a normal range of "flowers" had been added.) The team also supplied extensive notes on customs, lore, and performance practices. They included short passages in Eastern dialect in the notes to give readers a sense of the original language of performance, a decision that was quite innovative for the times.

Given the immensity of the epic corpus, the editors also found it practical to arrange the individual texts in a chronological order that would invite readers to read the volume. Each major section (such as *Song of Gold and Silver*) is comprised of a series of songs that are considered part of a thematically-related group (though the divisions, like the names of each portion, differ somewhat between singers). Decades of political turmoil, however, delayed publication and it was necessary for Jin Dan to re-collect some of the material in the late 1970s and early 1980s. The work was finally published in 1983 under the title *Hxak Hmub: Miao Epic Poems* (*Hxak Hmub: Miaozu shishi*) (Ma and Jin).

I became aware of the epics in 1984 while teaching at Guangxi University, in the Guangxi Zhuang Autonomous Region, located just south of Guizhou. During the eventual translation process, I was able to consult directly with Jin Dan on matters regarding the text and to examine portions of Miao transcriptions of the epic. On my first visit in 1985, Jin Dan led me and my fiancée, Fu Wei, to various relevant areas in Southeast Guizhou to visit a silversmith, a blacksmith, a carpenter, and a weaver. We also examined farm tools, animals, rice fields, houses, shrines, trees, medicinal herbs, and dragon boats. We visited a large courting party where groups of young people sang love songs to each other, and drank, ate, and sang with the locals. I met Jin Dan again in Guizhou in 1992. Most recently, in the summer of 2005, I visited the upland village home of an epic singer in the village of Fangzhao and met other singers in Taijiang. Such experiences added an invaluable dimension to my understanding of the epics.

In the process of translating the Jin and Ma text, I supplied a new introduction, as well as section introductions, tailoring them to the needs of readers outside China. In the process, I incorporated many of Jin Dan's insights on epic performance and traditional Miao culture in the region. When necessary, I also revised, condensed, and added an occasional endnote.

Following Jin Dan's advice, I sometimes changed small features of the Chinese text to conform to the original epic style as performed in Miao. These alterations included changing the phrase "talk about" to "sing about" and sometimes replacing a proper noun with a pronoun. In some instances I added a few words for clarification and broke a long line into shorter segments or combined two short lines for better readability.

Some stylistic features are still challenging. Characters in the storylines are often introduced using pronouns before their actual names are used. Several voices are also used in the narration: an omniscient voice that seems to come out of nowhere, the voice of the actual singers (often in a self-referential mode), and voices of the various characters. I have used quotation marks for some of these voices, letting context distinguish between them. I have also capitalized the names of things such as Tree Seeds, Sun and Moon, and Gold and Silver, when it is apparent that they are being regarded as sentient, mythic beings.

A number of names and words of things that appear in the epics are written in the Romanization for Eastern Miao dialect. In some instances, common local terms for some items such as sticky-rice cakes, widely known as *baba*, or the musical instrument *lusheng* (known as *gix* in Miao), have been given in Chinese. With Jin Dan's help I have also added a few Miao names that do not appear in the Ma and Jin notes, and where possible, I have included Latin names for some of the more obscure flora and fauna.

As noted in the Key to Pronunciation and the Notes, the Miao words are written without the sometimes confusing tone marks, which appear as a consonant letter at the end of the words. For example, the culture hero/trickster figure Jang Vang is written Jangx Vangb in Miao script. The tone-marked versions of most Miao words appear in the notes or introductions, often in conjunction with the unmarked version (for instance, Hmu/Hmub).

As mentioned, in actual performance the epics are usually sung in an antiphonal question-and-answer format by two pairs of singers. The Chinese version only implies this arrangement. In this English translation the text has been divided into parts sung by "A" and "B" to approximate the alternating roles that would be taken by each pair of singers. Moreover, to aid readers in following the dynamics of the songs, *the questions posed by the singers have been written in italics*. It should be noted, however, that the convention of antiphonal performance has many sides in actual performance and is more complex than reflected in the present text. (For instance, singers may sometimes ask and answer questions themselves as well as insert song flowers—features represented only a few times in the translations.)

With these comments in mind, it is now time to turn to the epics themselves.

Part I
Prelude

Introduction

Each epic singing event begins with a prelude, a time in which the singers converse in songs to decide which portion of the myth epic to sing. The prelude gives the singers a chance to limber their voices, coordinate their singing with their partner's, and feel out the strengths and weaknesses of the opposing side. The prelude below is an example of what might be encountered if attending an actual singing event. Like all aspects of epic performances, however, preludes unfold somewhat differently each time one is performed, depending on the individual singers and the situation at hand. Similar discussions in song (or regular speech) always precede the singing of a portion of the epic, though for the sake of space, in this translation a prelude is only included for the first song, *Song of Gold and Silver*.

The prelude begins with the mention of a number of songs concerning various stages of creation and mythical beings. As in other mythic traditions, more than one stage or era of creation is recounted in the epics. The first concerns an era of giant beings, such as the well-known Bang Xang Ye (Bangx Xangb Yel), the original creator of many of the supernatural beings that figure in the epics. Butterfly Mother, from a later stage in the epics, is also mentioned. From her eggs hatch the culture hero Jang Vang (Jangx Vangb) and his sister, who eventually create the first real humans.

As they converse in song, the performers typically decide to sing about a time when "even insects had yet to be created, / and there were neither people nor ghosts." One group of singers then poses the question: "*Who was born earliest?*" The answer is that it was Grandpa Xong Jang (Xongt Jangx), the being who built a bridge in the heavens. The idea of celestial bridges and the use of small wooden bridges in rituals, figure in the cosmogony and ritual activity of a number of ethnic groups in southwest China. The mention of the bridge here may also be related to the custom of building a small bridge, such as those often found in front of Earth God shrines, at which some women kneel to ask the supernaturals for the ability to conceive children.

As a result of building this bridge, Grandpa No (Nos) is born. He, in turn, gives birth to Grandma No (Nos). She then births the metals, gold and silver, subsequently used to make the pillars that hold up the sky, and as mentioned in *Song of Gold and Silver*, to create the sun and moon. The names of the two mythic grandparents refer to sites where metals were once mined, giving us some insight into the relation between the local topography and the mythic world. Grandpa Xong Jang also builds a bridge by which Bang Xang Ye is born. This being's eyebrows turn into indigo plants, which humans later will "soak in a wooden vat," where the natural coloring "becomes more and more purple" and "People take it to dye clothing." Indigo-dyed cloth is still made and worn in more conservative communities of several ethnic groups in Southeast Guizhou, and is actively marketed in a variety of styles both traditional and modern in the tourist trade. According to the song (collected in the 1950s when indigo clothing was still standard dress), older people use the clothing to keep off the cold, while young people wear it when dancing the drum dance during premarital courting activities called *ye fang* (*yet fangb*). In this poetic way, traditional clothing is highlighted as a meaningful marker of the local ethnic culture.

Another bridge that Grandpa Xong Jang builds results in the birth of Hsen Ye (Hsenb Yel). His name sounds very similar to the Han Chinese word "immortal, transcendent" (*xianren*), which refers to a supernatural human endowed with long life and magical powers. Whatever the origin of his name, the being also builds a bridge to one side of the sky, by which Xang Liang (Xangb Liangx) is born. In the *Song of the Ancient Sweet Gum* this figure clears and tills the wastelands in preparation for the planting of the trees that cover the earth (one of which is the nest of Butterfly Mother).

Next we are told that Grandpa Xong Jang is again born by a blast of wind blowing down a river. Another such blast, blowing against some cliffs, gives birth to the "Grandma Who Supports the Sky" and the "Grandpa Who Holds Firm the Earth." Yet neither of them grow up, both falling down like "sticks of firewood." Thus there was "no water in the river to wash pots, / and no people around to light fires. / It was really desolate and lonely" (5–6). Though speaking of distant past epochs, there is an immediacy in the images of the daily basics of contemporary human life that resonates with listeners.

The singers then state that bridges of stone are the best, that only with such a bridge could the mythical grandma and grandpa be born. Yet because the one (unspecified) who gave birth to them "held her breath" and had not "panted," they were born anyway. But it seems that the singers have been not altogether honest, for they ask: "*But who was really born?*" To which question the answer is "An Egg" (6).

The egg is compared to the one from which the mythical culture hero, Jang Vang, later hatches in the *Song of Butterfly Mother*. But unlike that one, which took only three years to hatch, this egg refuses to hatch after "nine thousand springs and autumns" and then only after "seventy thousand years." When finally broken open, it results in five pieces, which are set in five places. The fragments turn into mythical beings. One god goes to support the sky and earth. Another makes mountains and rivers. Yet another is a sort of judge who later brings the people "the Principles," the mention of which is a reference to a now-obscure social code of the ancients, existing only in skeletal form in the epics. One piece of shell becomes a giant woman in the sky, who husks rice and measures the sky with her hands and feet. One last piece becomes the being that created fire.

Thus, in the process of naming and the mention of important details and themes in the epics, the prelude brings meaningful images to the minds of listeners that hold rich associations for those familiar with the stories and culture. Questions over the nature of the world—what holds up the sky, the origin of the physical and spiritual world, including humans and their practices (such as agriculture)—are implicit cultural concerns in the lyrics, all of which are suggested in a medium that demands displays of ability in the areas of singing, humor, knowledge, and endurance.

PRELUDE

A: If we're to sing, we'll sing the Ancient Songs,
   those twelve ancient songs,[1]
   those twelve songs that pass among the people of the world.

The most beautiful of the songs is "Niang E Sei";[2]
the most splendid is "The Birth of Butterfly Mother";[3]
the most enduring is "Bang Xang Ye";[4]
"Transporting Gold and Silver" is the richest;[5]
"Niong Ji Bong" is most terrible;[6]
"The Five Pairs of Parents" is most bitter. . . .[7]

We won't take a thousand roads.
Water won't flow in a hundred streams
—we won't sing any other songs.[8]
We've come to sing of the ancient times,
about the origins of everything in the Sky and Earth.

In the ancient ages of the past
the Sky and Earth had yet to be created—
even insects had yet to be created,
and there were neither people nor ghosts.
Most certainly there were neither we nor you,
for all of the myriad beings had yet to be born.
Who was born earliest?

B: It was he who came to create the myriad beings.
   And that was Grandpa Xong Jang;[9]
   he built a bridge[10]
   and by doing so bore Grandpa No,
   and gave birth to Grandma No as well.[11]

That clever, capable Grandma No
also bore Gold and Silver.

Thus there were Gold and Silver to make the Sky Pillars,
and to hang the Sun in the Sky,
and to set the Moon in the Sky.

Old Grandpa Xong Jang
went and built a bridge,
and bore Bang Xang Ye;
Bang Xang Ye's eyebrows turned into indigo plants,
that purple grass that grows on the hillsides.
When plucked and put to soak in a wooden vat
it becomes more and more purple.
People take it to dye clothing.
Old people wear the clothing to keep off the cold winds;
young people wear it to *ye fang*,[12]
wear it to a flat place to dance the drum dance,[13]
to make merry and enjoy themselves.

Old Grandpa Xong Jang
went and built a bridge;
the bridge was built high in the Sky
and Hsen Yen was born there.[14]
He built a bridge to one side of the Sky
and there Xang Liang was birthed.[15]
But who else also gave birth
to Grandpa Xong Jang?

A: A lone blast of wind came blowing down a river—
that blast of wind gave birth to him,
and thus Grandpa Xong Jang was born.

There was also a steady blast of wind
that blew against the river cliffs.
Who did it bear?

B: It bore Grandma Who Supports the Sky
and gave birth to Grandpa Who Holds Firm the Earth.

But neither of them grew up.
Without a noise or a gasp they both fell down
just like a couple of sticks of firewood.
So there was no water in the rivers to wash pots

and no people around to light fires.
It was really desolate and lonely.

A bridge is best made of stone.
Only with such a bridge could Grandma Who Supports the Sky be born;
only with such a bridge could Grandpa Who Holds Firm the Earth
    be birthed.

If the one who bore them had panted, they might have been spoiled;
but the bearer held her breath and they were born.
But who was really born?

A: An Egg was born.
   If it was the Egg from which Jang Vang hatched[16]
   it would open if sat on for three years.
   But this Egg's shell was too thick;
   after nine thousand springs and autumns,
   after seventy thousand years, it still didn't hatch.
   There was nothing to do but break it open.
   It was thus broken into five pieces
   and the five pieces were put in five places.

The first piece turned into Fu Fang,[17]
the second piece turned into Bu Pa,[18]
the third piece turned into Ye Xing,[19]
the fourth piece turned into Niu Dliang,[20]
the fifth piece turned into Hu Li.[21]
What did Fu Fang do after he was born?

B: He went to support the Sky and Earth.
   What did Bu Pa do after he was born?

A: Bu Pa really knew how to dig—
   he made the mountains and opened the rivers,
   dug them far and wide.
   What did Ye Xing do after he was born?

B: He gave the people the Principles.
   What did Niu Dliang do after she was born?

A: She measured the wide Earth.
   What did Hu Li do after he was born?

B: He brought the first sparks of fire.
   All the gods[22]
   had their own affairs,
   had their own tasks to do.

PART II
SONG OF GOLD AND SILVER

Introduction

The first song in this series is called *Creating Sky and Earth*. It outlines events from the distant times when the sky and earth were still in one piece, detailing the activities of the early mythic giants to divide them, measure the sky and earth so that they fit properly together, and prop up the sky with wooden pillars. These pillars soon collapse, and are replaced by ones of gold and silver. The time to prop the pillars, however, had been miscalculated and they had to be propped up again. Soon after things were steadied, mythical beings that include a tiny crab and a water buffalo (which figures in many ensuing sections) help make the waterways and paths by which metals can be transported to make the celestial bodies, detailed in the ensuing songs. The next song, *Transporting Gold and Silver*, dwells on the mythical acquisition of metals, which were given to make the ancient families wealthy:

> . . . how rich were the lives of the Ancestors!
> All houses were built with six posts,
> with crossbeams like drake plumes;
> their earthen-tile roofs were like pangolin scales
> and each home was filled with chairs;
> the halls shone in ruddy hues,
> just like the Dragon King's palace. . . .
>
> Houses were compared to see which were of the best design;
> when eating, people compared the number of chopsticks,
> and they compared their silk and satin clothes,
> to see who had the best of what!

It is noteworthy that the "prestige" items listed above (house posts, tile roofs, chairs, chopsticks, silk, and satin) are items of local Miao culture that seem to be elements of material culture borrowed from the Han (called "guests" in the songs) or nearby Tai-speaking peoples (especially the Dong [Gaem] ethnic group). Although uncommon in the Miao areas today, horses are mentioned a number of times in the epics. Although horses tend to be associated with the northern steppes of Asia, the animals did play a role in warfare and trade in southwest China from early times. The Yi ethnic group, former rulers of much of Western Guizhou, still raise many horses in the mountains of Southern Sichuan. Thus, certain elements of material culture in the songs point to a complexity of relations among the ethnic groups in this part of China that lends itself to further research.

The focus on the personified metals is very prominent in *Song of Gold and Silver*. Early on we are told that the metals, gold, silver, copper, iron, steel, and tin, were all born in the "the glittering sands of yellow pool banks," though later the singers declare that they have been deceiving their listeners. In fact, the singers now tell us, the metals were born in other places. But this too turns out to be false information. Finally, we find that, on Hxu Niu's (Hxub Niux) advice, the hillsides were burned to cause the rocks to crack, thus allowing the metals to "fall out." (Cogon grass [*Imperata cylindrica*], used for thatch and other purposes, is specifically mentioned as being in danger of being scorched if the process is not handled correctly. The grass, along with the medicinal herb *moxa* [*Artemesia vulgaris*], is mentioned numerous times in the songs. One use of moxa is as tinder for starting fires.) Eventually the metals are scooped up by Grandma No (Nos), after they have escaped from the gourd ladle wielded by the "Emperor of the East" and his one-eyed son. Grandma No cleans each metal's face with herbs and borax water. (One possible cleansing herb might be the fruit of what the Han Chinese call *yangtao* [*Actinidia chinensis*], used in some areas to polish silver.)

The question arises as to why the metals—if they have all come from one mother (the earth)—are so different? The answer given is that they suckled breasts located at various parts of Grandma No's body. Gold and silver sucked the breasts on her chest. Iron is dark, because it sucked the breasts on her knees. Poor lead became purplish because it sucked the breasts on her toes. Eventually the metals grow up and marry husbands or wives, the births of their various spouses also being detailed. Iron, for instance, marries a husband called "Pipe-Bellows," referring to a tool used in blacksmithing. (An earlier epic tells us that after the creator Bang Xang Ye died and was divided into pieces, his stomach changed into "Pipe-Bellows.") Silver, who marries Borax (born of Bang Xang Ye's teeth, which were discarded in water), later wants children, so she gives birth to "Neck Rings" (silver torques Miao women wear around their necks). Copper's children become the copper reeds inside the *lusheng* reed-pipes (*gi/gix* in

Miao). Lead's children are "Net Weights." The children of Steel are "Knife Blades," while those of Iron are "Hoe Head" and "Rake Tines."

Eventually, the parents of the metals die and are buried. Later the metals follow their sacrificial buffalo eastwards, where it is going to get the hair whorls on its shoulders painted and its horns fastened. (The journey of the sacrificial buffalo is recounted in greater detail in *Song of Butterfly Mother*.) But the metals are finally captured and brought back to the west in wooden boats to be made into the suns and moons, described in *Creating the Suns and Moons*. Numerous tools and materials of metal working are mentioned, including the various parts of a pipe bellows, charcoal, crucibles for melting silver, tongs, and hammers. Even an alloy is noted (a mixture of silver, graphite, and raw copper). Grandma Yu (Yus) separates the melded celestial spheres with scissors. The twelve suns and twelve moons are named after the Earthly Branches in the Chinese lunar calendar. The eldest one is named "First Earthly Branch," the second oldest is called "Second Earthly Branch," and so on.[1] They are all married to the various lunar months. The leftover bits of gold and silver are made into constellations. After great toil, the spheres are hung in the sky. Then, in the section *Shooting Down the Suns and Moons*, the earth begins melting from their heat and the excess spheres are shot down by the archer Hsang Sa (Hsangb Sax). He stands in a "Horse-Mulberry Tree" to shoot, and thereafter the tree is cursed by the remaining sun and moon to be forever stunted. Hsang Sa later kills his own son, after discovering the boy's prowess with the bow.

Song of Gold and Silver

Creating the Sky and Earth

A: In the murky depths of the past
   the Sky was stuck to the Earth
   and the Earth was stuck to the Sky.[1]
   Huangping was curdled in one piece,
   and Yuqing was curdled in one chunk,[2]
   just like an ingot of silver,
   or like a magical taro.
   The river water couldn't flow eastward,
   Gold and Silver couldn't be transported westward.
   Draught oxen couldn't rack their horns,
   and girls couldn't marry.
   It was sad, so sad.

   In those far-off ancient times
   the Sky was stuck to the Earth
   and the Earth was stuck to the Sky;
   when sitting, you had to curl your spine,
   and you'd bump the Sky if you raised your head,
   to say nothing of planting any grain crops.

   Anxious, so anxious,
   dawn to dusk was spent worrying;
   nightfall to daybreak was spent worrying.
   What was to be done?

B: Let's see who came to create the Sky and Earth,
   see who came to smelt them.
   In those ancient times, it was the Sky-creating Grandfather;
   in those remote times, it was the Sky-making Grandmother.
   They made a great crucible,
   then used it to smelt the Sky and Earth.

One casting gave two great pieces.
The white particles floated upward to the surface;
the black spots sank to the bottom.
This way they got one wide piece of Sky;
this way they got a great chunk of Earth.

But the Sky declared that it was wider,
and the Earth declared that it was bigger.
Both bragged that they were the widest or the biggest.
Thus the Earth hurriedly tried to rise,
and the Sky urgently tried to descend;
they collided at that ancient threshing ground
on the summit of the Five Peaks.[3]

A bow was drawn and a shot released;
a sword was raised and slashed murderously.
Who was slashed to death in the Sky?
Who was shot to death on Earth?

A: The dead in the Sky was Li Bo,
who was killed by the son-in-law of Grandfather Ha Liong.[4]
The dead on Earth was Li Qe,
who was killed by Grandmother Vong E's son.
A pair of brave husbands died
leaving behind two shrewish widows.
Each day the widows cursed each other;
as they bickered, they cursed.
In the struggle in the Sky, Li Bo was killed
by Grandfather Ha Liong's son-in-law;
in the struggle on the Earth, Li Qe was killed
by Grandmother Vong E's son.
But the Sky still claimed it was widest,
and the earth still claimed it was biggest.
Each went on declaring that it was the widest or the biggest.
Who was tall and stout?
Call him to come measure the Sky and Earth!

B: Grandmother Niu Dliang was tall and stout.
Her legs and arms were immensely long,
so she was asked to come measure the Sky and Earth.
Armspread by armspread she measured the East;[5]
stride by stride she measured to the West.

*Was the Sky bigger than the Earth,
or was the Earth bigger than the Sky?*

A: The Earth was slightly longer;
the Sky was a bit wider.
Since they were so nearly the same,
they should not have quarreled.

The Sky was like a great bamboo hat,
the Earth was like a vast winnowing basket.[6]
The Void still had one more layer of Sky.
What mother bore it?

B: In fact, it was a layer of black cloud
that floated from East to West.

Today, in our time,
Golden Pillars prop up the Sky,
and Silver Pillars hold up the Earth.
The Sky is steady as can be,
and the earth is firm as can be.

But in the murky depths of the past
the Sky was propped up by birch tree trunks,
and the Earth was held fast by *wubei* wood.[7]
The Sky lurched back and forth;
the earth rocked to and fro.
One day everything nearly collapsed six times,
so for seven times the people gathered their gourd ladles
and earthen pots and ran away.
Those people went to extremes—
they ran clear to the ends of the earth!

There was a Grandfather Je Sang Ngang
whose body was thick as seven iron barrel bands.[8]
He was capable of eating nine troughs of *baba* rice cakes
and was capable of eating nine palm baskets of raw fish;
he was as solid as a fellow could be.
He came along to prop up the pillars of the Sky;
he raised them higher and higher.
For ages he tried to steady the Sky, till his very arms ached.
But finally his arms ached so much that he couldn't raise

them any longer.
The Sky cracked open, the crack as thick
as the ridgepole of a grain crib.
It seemed that the whole works would collapse.

There was also a Grandma Yu.
With a steel pot on her head she entered the villages,
heartily crying out to all:
"Wait till the Sky Pillars are steadied, don't return till then!
Until they are steadied, don't come back!
If the Sky falls, someone might be crushed!"

Everyone loves brightness,
and the whole earth was bright as could be.
But if the Sky was going to fall, it was better
for everyone to escape.
Who would have liked to live in the dark?

A: The bats that fly around the beams at night
might like the dark, in fact.
At that time a bat did go out one midnight,
went as far as Hongjiang.[9]
There it filled up on mosquito larvae.
At each meal it had to have three courses,
so it took three meals of fried meat each day,
without even a shred of vegetable.

Everyone loves brightness.
Who would prefer darkness?

B: Well, that Silkworm, thick as a pole,
preferred darkness more than anything.
It enjoyed eating only in the dark,
and at each meal it ate three courses.
At three meals it ate only fish and meat,
without even a green cabbage leaf.
When the Sky collapsed,
who was crushed?

A: Grandma Yu was crushed.

B: *Where was she buried?*

A: She was buried on a riverside.
As she stretched out her legs, she knocked against mountains;
as she drew in her legs, she scraped against tea terraces.
Six mountains were leveled in this way!

Grandfather Je Sang Ngang was also crushed.
After dying, what did he become?

B: He became a cicada.
Such a huge man changed into such a tiny creature.

In our time, today,
Golden Pillars prop up the Sky,
and Silver Pillars hold up the Earth.
The Sky is steady as can be,
and the Earth is steady as can be.

But in the murky depths of the past,
the Sky was propped up with birch tree trunks,
and the earth was held up by *wubei* wood.
The Sky lurched back and forth,
the earth rocked to and fro.

A white chicken flew East and West, crying as it went,
a white-mouthed pig, rooting about in the mud,
had rooted up the pillars!
Anyway, it's said that a white-mouthed pig did it.
But in fact, a blast of river wind did it.
A great blast of wind blew the pillars down.
What family was rich enough
to replace the wooden pillars
with Golden Pillars to prop up the Sky?

A: The Yang Yu family was very rich.
After the *wubei* pillars were lost,
Golden Pillars were brought to prop up the Sky.
Let's see how the pillars were made;
just how were the pillars that support the Sky made?

B: It took twelve years to make one pillar,
and all together, twelve pillars were made;
those twelve pillars were used to prop up the Sky.

One pillar was taken to Leigong Mountain
and was set atop Leigong Mountain.[10]
Everything there suddenly became bright.
The rice stalks grew long and thick,
just like horse tails.

One pillar was placed at the capital,
and all under the Sky was brightened.
One pillar was placed at Jenyuan,[11]
and everything brightened there.
The rice stalks grew long and thick,
just like horse tails.

One pillar was set at Bie'e,
placed on the east face of Zhandang Mountain,[12]
so everywhere around Sword River was bright.
The rice stalks grew long and thick,
just like horse tails.

One pillar was set at Gedong.[13]
One pillar was set on the Clearwater River.[14]
One pillar was set on Censer Mountain,[15]
set to the west of Kaili.

One pillar was set in Jijiang.[16]
Jijiang was really a good place!
Each tile-roofed house had six posts,
and over one thousand families lived there.
Hundreds of young people gathered
at the west end of the village
and courted at the foot of a great tree,
singing songs in the shade,
enjoying themselves contentedly.

There were still four smaller posts
that were too short for pillars,
but too long for "short melon" beams.[17]
So, what were they used for?

A: They were used for a bridge
that was built on some sandy yellow earth.
Later, Niang E Sei was born,
and that girl was a real beauty!

Creating the Sky and Earth

After the Sky Pillars were all erected
the people's cries were louder than thunder.
Everyone bustled about, readying to move back home.
But the feet of the pillars suddenly cried out:
"Don't be in such a great hurry to leave!
Don't be in such a great hurry to leave!"
The tops of the pillars were aslant against the Sky!
In a flash, great black clouds came rolling!
It looked as if all the pillars were going to fall!

They hadn't chosen a good day when they first propped up the Sky.
What sort of day was chosen—
At what time were the pillars erected—
So that when they were propped up they fell down?

B: The day it fell was an unlucky day,
and the hour of day violated the taboos.
The proper times weren't used;
those used shouldn't have been chosen,
thus the pillars fell down when raised.
When the Sky pillars fell
who came as the Master Craftsman?
Who came to pick an auspicious day
on which to again prop up the Sky?

A: Yen Vong Bo was that craftsman;
Hxen Ju Bo chose the auspicious hour.[18]
When the day was correctly chosen
the Sky was propped up again.
A pillar snapped.
It was too short to use.
One of the pillars broke.
It couldn't support a crossbeam.[19]

What could be used to repair them?
What could be used to refurbish them?

B: Magic *Ja Fang Yang* medicine was brought to mend them;[20]
The juice of the Fruit of Immortality was used to weld them.[21]
The snapped pillar was made longer,
the broken pillar was restored,
and the Sky was propped up once again.

When the Sky Pillars were firmly in place
the cries of happiness were louder than thunder.
Everyone bustled about, ready to go back home.
Everybody found their own family
and went back to work, at ease.

In the murky depths of the past
the Sky was stuck to the Earth,
and the Earth was stuck to the Sky.

The riverbeds were only the width of a heel bone;
the river water ran quietly eastward.
Though maybe a leech could pass through
and tubeworms could wriggle East and West,[22]
the Gold- and Silver-bearing boats couldn't have passed.
A little crab was born by its mother.
It lived in this sort of place:
A place where only a hand span was between[23]
Sky and Earth.
It came down from the mountain rivers
to prop up the Sky and Earth.
Waters cascaded to the East,
and bits of firewood drifted by.
Who opened the waterways?
Who cut the mountain roads?

A: Hxu Niu opened the waterways;[24]
   Bu Pa cut the mountain roads.
   The riverbeds were made three arm spans wide
   so flotillas of fir trees could drift to the East.
   Thus there was water to transport Gold and Silver.
   How was the ax that cut
   the mountains and rivers made?

B: If it was a brush ax,
   then the handle would be made of birch
   and the blade of finely forged steel;
   one chop and the log would split into four pieces.
   But the handle of that mountain-opening, river-making ax
   was a muddy stream,
   and its blade was crystal clear water.
   That was the ax used to open the mountains and waterways.

How about Hxu Niu, who opened the mountains and waterways?
What was his body like?
What was his head like?
What were his four feet like?
What was his tail like?

A: His body was like a water buffalo's;
   his head was like a lion's;
   his tail was like a palm frond;
   his four feet were like iron-teethed rakes.

   If an ox is sacrificed to the Ancestors,
   it leaves behind its horns,
   leaves them in our parents' homes
   to hang on the center posts,[25]
   hang for the relatives to see.
   But when Hxu Niu went,
   where were his horns left?

B: They were hung in temples,
   and hung in every government *yamen*,
   where all the Miao and Han people came to see them.

TRANSPORTING GOLD AND SILVER

A: The high Sky was steadily propped;
   the wide Earth was firmly supported.
   In some places, rice could be husked;
   on the rivers, Gold and Silver could be moved.
   Now we'll sing *Transporting Gold and Silver*,
   tell something of how Gold and Silver were moved to the West.

   Gold was transported to give to the Ancestors,
   Silver was moved to give to the Ancestors;
   the Metals were given to make families wealthy,
   and how rich were the lives of the Ancestors!
   All houses were built with six posts,
   with crossbeams like drake plumes;
   their earthen-tile roofs were like pangolin scales
   and each home was filled with chairs;

the halls shone in ruddy hues,
just like the Dragon King's palace.¹

Each family was as rich as the other:
Houses were compared to see which were of the best design;
when eating, people compared the number of chopsticks,
and they compared their silk and satin clothes,
to see who had the best of what!
But all this happened later,
for then it was still the murky depths of the past.
Why was Gold to be transported?
What was the use of moving Silver?

B: Gold was transported to give to the Ancestors;
Silver was moved to give to the Ancestors;
to give to the Ancestors to make the Suns and Moons;
to make the Suns to hang in the empty Sky.
Where was Gold born?
Where was Silver born?
And where were all the other Metals born?

A: Gold was born beside the glittering sands of yellow pool banks;
Silver was born from the glittering sands of yellow pool banks.
The other Metals were also born from the glittering sands of
yellow pool banks.
The glittering sands of yellow pool banks
were birthed by what mother?

B: Five flats and six ranges bore them;
five hills and six ranges cradled them.
That's how the glittering sands
of yellow pool banks came to be.
Gold was not born in the glittering sands of yellow pool banks;
Silver was not born in the glittering sands of yellow pool banks.
If not, then where were they born?

A: Gold was born in Yu Je Pool,²
Silver was born in Yu Je Pool.
Which mother gave birth to Yu Je Pool?

B: Well, the Crab King took a pair of dustpans
and Hxu Niu took a pair of steel rock-drills,

and they came to build Yu Je Pool.
Who was the good-hearted one that built a six-post house
to encircle Yu Je Pool?

A: The good-hearted Spider made a six-post house
to encircle Yu Je Pool.

Gold was born in Yu Je Pool,
Silver was born in Yu Je Pool.
Beside Yu Je Pool were nine great roads.
The nine great roads went East and West.
The nine great roads formed a horse racing grounds.
Each of the roads had a name.
Which street was Gold born on?
Which street was Silver born on?

B: Gold was born on the Great Yellow Road,
and thus Gold glitters brightly.
Silver was born on the Gray Way,
and thus Silver is of a grayish cast.
Iron came from the Black Road,
and thus Iron is an ugly black.

But all this is untrue!
Yu Je Pool produced only fish and shrimps,
Yu Je Pool didn't produce Gold and Silver!
So, where were Gold and Silver born?

A: Gold was born at the Sacred Fairy Cliffs;
Silver was born at the Sacred Fairy Cliffs.
When the Fairy Cliffs collapsed,
Gold and Silver dropped down.

But this is untrue as well!
Gold wasn't born at the Sacred Fairy Cliffs,
Silver wasn't born at the Sacred Fairy Cliffs.
But then, where were they born?

B: Gold and Silver were born in a whirlpool.
They were born in the East, in the Fang Liang River.[3]

But this is also untrue!
Where were Gold and Silver really born?

A: Gold was born at Gha Nang Liang;[4]
   Silver was born at Gha Nang Liang;
   that's the place that produced Gold and Silver.

   And who was that clever, diligent one
   who birthed the white-mouthed cow
   that he used to plow the hillsides,
   tilling the hillsides to plant the Silver seeds?

B: Ghe Lu was the clever, diligent one[5]
   who birthed the white-mouthed cow
   that he used to plow the hillsides,
   to plant the Silver seeds in the furrows.
   And who was the clever, diligent one
   who birthed the bull with the white forehead
   then led it to plow the hillsides
   to cultivate the Gold seeds in the furrows?

A: Ghe Lu was the clever, diligent one
   who birthed the bull with the white forehead
   that he led to plow the hillsides
   to plant the Gold seeds in the furrows.
   Our parents plant grain crops,
   but who planted Gold and Silver?

B: Ghe Lu planted Gold and Silver.
   Our parents make small dikes for irrigation,
   but who made the road for Gold and Silver?

A: Ghe Lu made the road for Gold and Silver,
   finishing it smoothly so Gold and Silver could pass.
   As for the forests,
   our ancestors cultivated the fir trees;
   but who cultivated the Gold and Silver mountains?

B: They were cultivated by Ghe Lu.
   Every mountain cleft has a spring,
   every mountain peak faces the Sun.
   But in which mountain was Gold born?
   How was anyone to know?

A: Bo Ji Li was clever and brave.[6]
   He dived into the sea

and snatched away a Dragon's horn.
He huffed and puffed up to a mountaintop,
then blew the horn in wavering blasts, "lie-li, lie-li,"
that echoed down the mountain valleys, "wu-ai, wu-ai."
When Gold heard it,
Gold replied.
When Silver heard it,
Silver replied.
So it was discovered which mountain had Gold.
Every mountain has green grass,
every mountain village has families.
But what mountainside birthed Silver?
How could it be known?

B: Bo Ji Li was clever and brave.
He dived deep into the waters
and wrested away a Dragon's horn.
He scrambled to a mountaintop,
then blew the horn in wavering blasts, "ya-ii, ya-ii,"
that echoed through the mountain valleys, "ai-wu-ai."
When Gold heard the blasts,
Gold answered.
When Silver heard the blasts,
Silver answered.
So it was discovered which mountain had Silver.
Whose ideas were the shrewdest?

A: Hxu Niu's ideas were the shrewdest.
He cried out to all in every direction,
rousing the nine drum societies, shouting:[7]
"Each family bring a basket of charcoal,
which we will use to burn off the mountain cliffs.
There is much Gold in the mountain cliffs!
There is much Silver in the mountain cliffs!"
What day did they burn off the mountain cliffs?
What day were the mountain cliffs scorched?

B: On the Third and Fourth Earthly Branches,[8]
the mountain cliffs were scorched.
On the Seventh Heavenly Stem and the Ninth and Tenth Earthly Branches,
the mountain cliffs were burned.

The mountain cliffs cracked into nine pieces;
then Gold and Silver dropped down and fell into the water.
Gold and Silver couldn't be retrieved.

Gold lived on this side of the pool;
Silver lived on that side of the pool.
But who lived on the other sides,
and kept Gold and Silver company?

A: Duckweed lived on one side;
Borax lived on one side.
They kept Gold and Silver company.
What did Silver resemble when it was born?

B: When Silver was born it looked like a horse,
its back was white as could be.
What did Gold resemble when it was born?

A: When Gold was born it looked like a yellow cow,
its back was as yellow as could be.
When Iron was born, what was it like?

B: Iron looked like mud when it was born;
so black all over it was.
When Tin was born, what did it look like?

A: Tin was born on a hillside where *xini* grass grew,[9]
and its face was green as could be.
When lead was born, what was it like?

B: When born, it was like a cat,
its eyes so very blue.

When Gold and Silver were all taken out of the pool,
there were holes left behind by the Metals,
holes that were very deep.
Who found them?

A: The Sheep Dragon found them.[10]
It stretched out its tongue to lick,
then used its horns to ram;
as it rammed away, its horns curled,
as crooked as those of a cow.

When all the Gold was taken out,
and all the Silver was taken out,
their Mother let out a great cry.
Who saw her crying?

B: Winter Grass saw her crying.[11]
Winter Grass persuaded her not to cry out.
Still, she wanted to run out to find her daughters.
Who held her back?

A: Winter Grass held her back,
Winter Grass persuaded her not to go.
Who saw Gold and Silver taken out?

B: Father saw Gold taken out.
Mother saw Silver taken out.
But Father and Mother didn't dare to take even a pinch.

When Gold and Silver came out,
the Emperor of the East saw them.
He took a gourd ladle to scoop them up,
he used a gourd ladle to take them up;
so Gold and Silver became his.
But he really didn't get them,
for Gold and Silver drilled their ways into the Earth
and later changed into Silver ingots.
And who found the Silver ingots?

A: The Emperor had a son,
and this son had only one eye.[12]
With nine lanterns following him,
that son took nine hoes to go digging,
and thus got Gold and Silver.
When Gold and Silver were taken out,
it wasn't the Emperor who saw them.
So, who saw them?

B: It was Grandma No who saw them.
She ladled up Gold and Silver,
so then Gold and Silver became hers.
What did she use as a ladle?

A: She used her hands to scoop up Gold and Silver,
   then she put them in her pocket.

   When Gold was born, its face was shiny black;
   when Silver was born, its face was shiny black.
   Shiny black from head to toe,
   even the whites of their eyes were black.
   What sort of water was brought to wash them?
   What sorts of herbs were brought to doctor them?

B: That old woman, Grandma No,
   brought Ja herbs from the East,[13]
   which she rubbed on Gold's face,
   which she rubbed on Silver's face.
   She also used Borax Water to wash them.
   Silver's face turned white as a newly laid duck egg.
   Gold's face became as clean as a mountain meadow blossom.
   Gold's face was washed;
   Silver's face was washed.
   What about the embroidered wash towel?
   Where was it lost?

A: It was lost on a hilltop and later turned into a pangolin.
   Where was the dirty wash-water thrown?

B: It was thrown into a pig pen and later turned into saltpeter.
   Weren't the Metals born by one mother?
   But if so, why were they so different?

A: They were born by one mother,
   but each suckled only one of her breasts.
   Which breast did Gold suckle?
   Which breast did Silver suckle?

B: Gold and Silver suckled at her chest where the milk was plentiful;
   that's why Gold was beautiful, its face glowing so ruddily,
   and that's why Silver was so pretty, its face so white.
   But Copper suckled at a breast on her back.
   Milk didn't flow to there, so Copper's face became sallow.
   Iron suckled at the breasts on her knees.
   Milk didn't flow to there, so Iron's face became such a deep black.
   Tin suckled at the breast on the top of her head.

Milk didn't flow there, so Tin's face became green.
Lead suckled at the breasts on her toes,
Milk didn't flow there,
so Lead's face became purplish.
Steel suckled at the breasts under her arms.
Milk didn't flow to there,
so Steel's face became both black and blue.

When Gold and Silver were born, they both wanted stools to sit on.
If they were newborn babies, they wouldn't need to sit on stools;
they would just sit on their mother's knees,
rest protected on their mother's knees.
But what did Gold and Silver have for stools?

A: Gold and Silver had stones for stools.
As Gold and Silver grew up
their hair grew longer,
and they needed haircuts.
What was used to cut their hair?

B: If a baby is given a haircut,
the razor is one made by the Han people,
and given to the child's father to shave the baby's head.
But look at Gold and Silver's razor!
Who wielded that razor?

A: It was given to Gold and Silver's father
who used it to cut their hair.
The nine rivers washed in and out;
the ten rivers washed in and out,
breaking the mountains into nine pieces.
That was how the razor was gotten
that was given to Gold and Silver's father
to shave Gold and Silver's heads.

Grandma No was the strongest,
Grandma No's breasts were biggest.
No one's milk was better than hers.
She brought her milk to nurse Gold and Silver,
so Gold and Silver quickly grew up.
Who was Gold and Silver's uncle?
Who was Gold and Silver's aunt?

B: Later, when the Metals married
they received money from their nephews-in-law.[14]
Fu Fang was their uncle,
Mountain Bluff was their aunt.
Later, when the Metals married,
they received money from their nephews-in-law.

Gold grew up;
Silver grew up.
All the Metals married.
But where were their husbands from?
What were their husbands' names?

A: Silver married Borax;
Gold married Water Chestnut;
Copper married Ji Nang;
Tin married Pine Resin;
Lead married Pig Fat;
Steel married Yellow Earth;
Iron married Pipe-Bellows.[15]
How much dowry did the nephews-in-law give?

B: The nephews-in-law's money was given in ingots:
The Silver ingots were as big as knees;
the Gold ingots were as big as fists.

Silver's husband was Borax.
And who gave birth to Borax?

A: In very ancient times
Bang Xang Ye's teeth fell out.
He threw them into the river
and later they changed into Borax.
Silver married him,
and Silver was content.

Gold's husband was Water Chestnut.
And who gave birth to Water Chestnut?

B: In very ancient times
Bang Xang Ye's eyelashes
were lost in the spillway of a pond

and later turned into Water Chestnut.
Gold married him,
and Gold was content.

Copper's husband was Ji Nang.
He was born from the cliffs.
Tin's husband was Pine Resin.
And who bore Pine Resin?

A: Pine Resin was born by the great Earth,
and ever since pine trees have had resin.

Lead's husband was called Pig Fat.
And who birthed Pig Fat?

B: A girl who husked rice diligently
also raised pigs that were very big and fat.
By butchering a hog she got Pig Fat.

Steel's husband was Yellow Earth.
And who gave birth to Yellow Earth?

A: He was born by the mountain bluffs.
Iron's husband was called Pipe-Bellows.
And who gave birth to Pipe-Bellows?

B: In very ancient times, old Bang Xang Ye died,
his belly was left behind, and later it changed into Pipe-Bellows.
Iron married him,
and Iron was content.

Silver wanted children.
What were her children's names?

A: Her children were called Neck Rings.
Gold also wanted offspring.
What were the names of her offspring?

B: Her offspring were called Golden Flowers.
Copper also raised children.
What were her children called?

A: They were called Flute Reeds,
and they live inside reed-pipes;
when oxen are slaughtered, the reed-pipes
are taken out and played.
Lead also raised children.
What were her children called?

B: Her children were called Net Weights;
Net Weights people used to catch fish.
Steel also had offspring.
What were her offspring called?

A: Her offspring were called Knife Blades.
Iron also bore children.
What were her children called?

B: Her children were called Hoe Head and Rake Tines;
people used them to make a living,
so everyone could eat well and wear warm clothes.
Gold was also called Jen Li No;
Silver was also called Ni Li No.
All the Metals married
except for one Gi Li No,[16]
whose body was seventeen girths around;
her neck was as thick as a thigh.
Where did she go to get married?
Who became her partner?

A: She married in the West,
married Xang Bo Dai.[17]
Xang Bo Dai's family was very wealthy:
Their rice cakes were as big as water vats,
their popped corn was as big as duck eggs.
That fellow took Gi Li No to be his wife.

Gi Li No married in the West,
married Xang Bo Dai.
But who was their matchmaker?

B: Old Xong Tin sold silks and satins,[18]
went about everywhere selling filigree thread.
He met Gi Li No and had her promised to Xang Bo Dai.
And who were Xang Bo Dai's parents?

A: One was Ni Jen Sen;
one was Bo Ji Ghen.[19]
They gave birth to Xang Bo Dai.
This Gi Li No married in the West,
married Xang Bo Dai.
The son she bore was called White Copper.
Some say that Han people used it to make water pipes.
Some say it was used to make bullhorns
or reed trumpets.
When trumpets were blown in the streets,
the sound spread in all directions,
giving listeners a chill.

Everyone was married
except Vo Li No.
But who did she marry?

B: Her sisters had all married, then gone away;
so it was alright for this last girl to marry into her uncle's family.
So, Mountain Cliffs came to marry her.

Everyone was married,
and everyone was content.
But there was still Niu Gang Su.[20]
Her face was so pocked
that no one dared to love her.
Who would want to marry her?

A: Silver Crucible came to marry her,
so she and Silver Crucible made a family.[21]
The daughters were all married,
but what about their father and mother?
They were so old that they had already died.
Did they die from illness,
or were they bitten by poison insects?

B: They died of illness.
When Han people's parents die,
a fir coffin is used to hold them.
White cotton is used to wrap the corpse.
But when the Gold Crucibles' father and mother died,

what was used as the coffin?
What was used to wrap them?

A: The great Earth was their coffin;
the mountain bluffs were their grave clothes.

Everyone was married;
everyone was content.
While nursing, they thought of their mother,
but after marrying, they forgot their parents.
They left Mother alone by the rock piles,
abandoned Father beside an outdoor fire,
then they followed the flowing waters away.

"Sacrifice to the Parents before leaving!"
For only by sacrificing to the Parents,
could there be enough food and clothing.
What drum was used in the sacrifice?

B: If it was Jang Vang's drum,
the body would be made of yellow sandalwood.
A white chicken would walk through the cavity,
from this end, right out that end,
and an ox would be slaughtered as a sacrifice
to the Ancestors.[22]

"Come and see Gold and Silver's drum!"
What was it made of?

A: Mountain stones were brought to make it;
flowing water from mountain brooks ran through it;
and a locust was slaughtered as a sacrifice to the Ancestors.
Then Gold and Silver followed the waters away.
Gold and Silver went Eastward.
Who lived in the house they left behind?

B: The Earth God wandered to that place
and made a fire to warm himself.
So Gold and Silver's home was again warm as could be.
When Gold and Silver went Eastward,
the house foundations of the Parents were left behind.
And the fields of the Ancestors were left behind.

Who came to live there?
Who came to plow there?

A: The Hu and Xi snakes[23]
came to live in the Ancestors' houses
and came to till the Ancestors' fields.
On what day did Gold leave?
On what day did Silver leave?

B: Gold left on a fine day;
Silver left on a fine day.
But fish and shrimp left on a rainy day.

Gold and Silver wanted to go East.
Everyone followed the mountain valleys.
Which one followed the mountain ridges?

A: Steel went along the mountain bluffs
went along the mountain ridges.
The mountain ridges sounded with blasts of wind
that tore everyone's pants to pieces.
Mother scolded harshly,
scolded till her heart was icy cold,
just as if she were sweating ice water.
When Gold and Silver's Ox left,
who knew what it said?

B: If it were a bull for an Ancestor Sacrifice
it would go East to be painted with hair whorls;
it would go East to have its horns attached.[24]
When leaving it would tell the *gha gang* tree:[25]
"Grow up quickly!
I'm going East to be painted with hair whorls;
I'm going East to have my horns attached.
After I return I'll use you as a plow bow
and together we'll plow the fields.
In Autumn we'll store the grain in nine great cribs
to use in a sacrifice to the Ancestors;
for only by sacrificing to the Ancestors can we prosper."
What did Gold and Silver's Ox say?

A: It said to the Western Cliffs:
"Wait for me here,

I'm going East to find Gold and Silver.
Wait till I come back from the West,
then the two of us shall go create the Suns;
we'll create the Moons then hang them in the Sky."

Gold and Silver went to the East.
If it were a sacrificial ox that went out,
its hoof prints would be covered by pondweed.
No matter where one looked, not a trace could be found.
But what hid Gold and Silver's footprints?

B: The grass growing on the mountains
covered Gold and Silver's footprints.
As Gold and Silver's feet pressed down, the grass also pressed down.
But when they lifted their feet, the grass sprang up,
leaving the mountain pathways the same as before.
Not a footprint could be found.
Gold wanted to go East;
Silver wanted to go East.
Who on the mountaintop
had a waist bent like a bow,
and hair white as a horse's tail?
Who was it that saw Gold and Silver go?

A: Yang Yu rose early,
and was on a hilltop trapping *ge* birds.[26]
Seeing Gold and Silver leaving,
he dropped the box of bird lime[27]
and left behind the bait birds;[28]
he ran home as if flying
and picked up a horse knife.
Riding a spirited steed,
he cried out in a great voice to all:
"Gold is going East;
Silver is going East.
Quick, capture Gold and Silver;
don't let Gold go East;
don't let Silver go East.
If Gold goes, we'll suffer in poverty;
if Silver goes, we'll suffer bitterly.
Hurry, we must stop them!"

Gold followed along the rivers;
Silver went along the flowing waters.
But clever Yang Yu,
carrying a long-bladed knife
and riding upon a male tiger,
cried out to all:
"Hurry, hurry 'round!
Quickly, go quickly,
go stop our precious possessions.
If Gold goes, we'll suffer in poverty;
if Silver goes, we'll suffer bitterly!"
What road did Gold and Silver take?

B: No one knew.
"Go quickly to find a sorcerer to divine it!"
What sort of egg was used in the divination?

A: "Use a snake egg to divine!"
A snake egg can only divine for Jang Vang.
"Use a grouse egg to divine!"
A grouse egg can only be used to divine for tigers.
"Use an egret's egg to divine!"
An egret's egg can only divine for written words.
None of these eggs could be used to divine the road taken
by Gold and Silver.
But what sort of egg was used to divine?

B: A chicken egg was used to divine,
and it correctly told Gold and Silver's path.[29]
Yang Yu caught a *ge* bird.
Who went to steal a glimpse?

A: Jang Ju went to steal a look.
With a bow strapped on his chest
and a quiver of arrows on his back,
he saw that Gold and Silver were going East.

He aimed at Silver's head and shot,
but he missed his target.
Who did he hit?

B: His arrow struck Iron Brother.

Iron fell to the ground without a twitch;
so back at home he lived in the market.

Gold went to the East;
Silver went to the East.
When it grew dark, what was their lamp?

A: Glow Worms gave them light.
In the mountain valleys the Worms burned pine torches,
brightening both sides of the valleys
so that Gold and Silver could find their ways.
Who gave birth to those shining Glow Worms?

B: When Grandpa Xong made the Suns[30]
his hammer went "ding-dong"
and pieces of Gold fell down,
changing into Glow Worms.

The Glow Worms' lights brightened the way for Gold and Silver;
the Worms' lights shined as Silver and Gold went East,
slowly, step by step.
But no, that's all wrong!
The Glow Worms were to come later;
it wasn't they who gave Gold and Silver light.
But then who did light the way for Gold and Silver?

A: A nice, kindhearted mother gave birth to a fine son;
a cruel-hearted mother gave birth to an ugly son.
The Sky gave birth to Sky Fire,
and this firelight streamed down from the Sky,
brightening that place up.
It was Sky Fire who gave light to Gold and Silver.

Gold went East;
Silver went East.
Who lived in a river eddy?

B: Otter lived in a river eddy,
and he saw Gold and Silver go.
Clever Wild Sparrow[31]
made a house in a turn in a road.
He also saw Gold and Silver going East.

The clever Earth God who had
built a house beside the road also
saw Gold and Silver going East.[32]

Gold went East;
Silver went East.
They arrived at the border of the Emperor's realm.
Who was such a clever young man?

A: Spider was a clever young man.
He built a huge house with nine rooms,
each set with nine windows,
all around the Emperor's ceiling.

Gold and Silver went to the edge of the abyss.
Who used dogs to chase them?

B: Li Lang used dogs to chase them.[33]
Gold and Silver were frightened to death,
so they dropped to the bottom of the abyss.
Who saw Gold and Silver drop to the bottom of the abyss?

A: Clever Duck saddled and shoed his horse.
While climbing over the hills
Duck saw Gold and Silver fall into the abyss.

Gold and Silver entered a whirlpool at the foot of the cliffs.
Who came to meet them
and built a house for them to live in?

B: Otter came to meet them
and broke apart the rocks to let them live inside.
While Gold and Silver lived in the rocks,
what was their mosquito net?

A: If it were a mosquito net for people,
Mother would use her clever hands
to spin cotton for threads to weave the net
to keep off the July mosquitoes;
even a flea couldn't enter.

But how about Gold and Silver's mosquito net?
Who came to make it?

B: River Water used its clever hands
   to weave a net of green algae.
   It sent the net to Gold and Silver to hang up,
   so that fish and shrimp couldn't enter.

   Gold lived in the abyss;
   Silver lived in the abyss.
   What sort of stools did they sit upon?

A: If they were stools for people,
   they would be made of fir wood.
   But what were Gold and Silver's stools made of?

B: Gold and Silver's stools were made of stones.
   Gold wanted to wear clothes;
   Silver wanted to wear clothes, too.
   People's clothes are dyed with indigo,
   but with what were Gold and Silver's clothes dyed?

A: They were dyed with clear water.
   Gold wanted to do the drum dance;
   Silver wanted to do the drum dance.
   If it were boys who wished to dance,
   and if it were girls who wanted to dance,
   then the boys would play the drum and the girls would dance,
   or the girls would beat the drum and the boys would dance.
   The girls would wear embroidered shoes to dance,
   their shoes tripping lightly beneath them.
   Who beat the drum so Gold and Silver could dance lightly?

B: Pebbles beat the drum,
   Gold and Silver came to dance lightly;
   Gold and Silver wore Copper shoes to dance,
   and their Copper shoes shook and shimmered.

   If Jang Vang did the drum dance,
   he would drum and dance up in the mountain meadows.
   Where did Gold and Silver beat the drum?
   Where did Gold and Silver dance?

A: They beat the drum underwater,
   and they danced at the bottom of the abyss.

Gold and Silver lived in the abyss.
Gold and Silver cried out.
How did they cry out?

B: If a rooster crowed,
that rooster there in the corner of the house,
it would go "Cock-a-doodle-do,"
so all the girls would hear and get up early.
Where did Gold and Silver cry out?
Who heard Gold and Silver's cries?

A: Gold and Silver cried out at the bottom of the abyss.
Yang Yu heard them, and knew that Gold and Silver were living in the abyss.

When a rooster crows,
it's because the Earth God jerks the string,
making the bird go, "Cock-a-doodle-do,"[34]
causing its cries to issue from the chicken coop.
Who pulled the string
to make Gold and Silver cry out?

B: Water Dragon jerked the string
to stir Gold and Silver,
causing them to cry over and over,
till their cries issued from the cracks in the rocks.
Who went to choose an auspicious day?
Who went to weave a fishnet?
Who thought up a cunning scheme?
Who put the fish gate at the running water's mouth?[35]

A: It was none other than Grandfather Bo and Grandfather Xo.
Several old men then discussed it:
Some went to choose an auspicious day,
some went to weave fishnets,
and some thought up the cunning scheme of
putting the fish gate at the mouth of the running water
to catch Gold and Silver.
They didn't catch Gold and Silver,
so who did they catch?

B: They caught Otter.
The adults cried out for the pelt;

the children wanted the teeth;
but suddenly, Otter spoke:
"Don't kill me, don't kill me!
Let me speak.
There's a lot of Gold in the abyss;
there's a lot of Silver in the abyss.
The Gold pieces are big as pigs;
the Silver pieces are big as sheep,
and it's all in the abyss."
"Who can go catch them?"

A: "Crab King can go catch them.
He can dig up Gold;
he can dig up Silver."

Crab saw Gold as big as pigs,
and Silver fat as sheep.
Gold smacked its lips,
Silver ground its teeth.
Crab was a little afraid, and scuttled backwards,
using only his little legs to crawl,
for it seems he couldn't bend his body.
In despair he cried:
"The task is too big for me!"
What things were presented to persuade him?

B: He was presented with a slab of stone
that he took home to sleep on;
only then did he dig up Gold and Silver.

He dug at Gold and Silver's home,
and as he dug inside,
a piece of hillside slid down and
nearly crushed him to death.

Crab went to dig up Gold and Silver.
he had dug up half the bank
when some cliff fell down,
smashing Crab's feet.
What medicine could cure him?
What sort of water could mend him?

A: "Use salt as medicine.
   Use clear water to mend him."
   Thus his broken feet were soon as good as new.

   If you don't believe us,
   go to the waters sometime
   and catch a crab to cook;
   when you taste the salty flavor,
   you'll believe what we say.

   Crab Mother bore baby crabs,
   giving birth to an only son.
   Father agreed to let him go,
   but Mother did not agree.
   What sort of presents
   would make Mother agree?

B: "Send her five brooks;
   send her six ancient streams."
   So, now there are fish in the brooks
   for generation after generation,
   and crabs there as well.
   Today's crabs
   are all descendants of Crab King.
   What did Crab King look like?

A: He was as big as the floor of a grain crib;
   as big as the bottom of a wooden tub.
   Who gave birth to him?

B: Mountain boulders bear rocks;
   mountain soil bears sand;
   Crab King was birthed by stones and sandy soil.

   Crab bit at Gold and Silver's roots,
   and the lower two roots were broken;
   but two of the stems still grew too high.
   Who helped Crab to bite them?

A: It was Cormorant who helped him to bite them.[36]
   Were those two creatures born by one mother,
   or were they really born by two mothers?
   Why did Cormorant help Crab to bite?

B: Since both of them were really born by one mother,
they helped each other dig up Gold and Silver.

Crab went to dig out Gold and Silver.
The loose soil was easy digging,
but there were also some hard places.
A cave led to a hillside;
Gold and Silver were probably in that cave.
Who was to go to find them?

A: "Let Rat go and look."
Crab went to dig up Gold and Silver.
The hard spots were all dug out,
but there were still some loose places.
One path led to the mountain top;
Gold and Silver were probably there.
Who went there to dig?

B: "Let Rat go and dig."
Gold and Silver were all found.
How could they be captured?
What could be used to hold back the river water?
Could Gold and Silver be brought to dry land?

A: If it was today,
a bamboo mat could be used to hold back the water.
But at that time,
a Dragon's body was used to hold back the water.
The water was diverted into a river,
and Gold and Silver were left high and dry on the sandy banks.
Gold and Silver grew pale.

Gold was gotten;
Silver was gotten.
So now the Suns and Moons could be made.
Today, the Moon is very bright;
today, the Sun is very warm.
Each corner of the Earth is lit brightly,
and crops are raised in every field.

Before, the Moon's leg was crippled,
and the Sun was blind in one eye.

Thus, the four corners were not lit up brightly,
and the grain crops on the river banks couldn't ripen.
Who made the Sun?

B: It was Cold Winter who made it.
Today, the Sun is very nice;
Today, the Moon is very bright.
The Sun shines on the mountains,
and grain is grown in the valleys.
Before, the Sun was blind,
and the Moon had a crippled leg.
The Sun cast its shadow on the mountains,
and grain couldn't grow in the valleys.
Who made the Moon?

A: It was Cold Winter that made it.
Before, the Moon's leg was crippled,
and the Sun was blind in one eye.
The Sky was so black that girls couldn't marry,
and oxen couldn't rack their horns.
Who were those men who came to discuss it?

B: Grandpa Bo and Grandpa Xong,
Grandpa Qe and Grandpa Dong;
These few old men spent a whole night discussing it:
"Let's go to the East!
Get Gold and Silver to make Moons,
and make Suns to hang in the Sky.
Let there be brightness everywhere,
then girls can marry,
and oxen can rack their horns.
How could they transport Gold and Silver?

A: "Make boats to carry Gold and Silver."
One hundred big boats were made
to transport the hundreds and thousands
of Golds and Silvers to the West,
to make the Suns and Moons to hang in the Sky.

If it were today,
the trees would all be growing in the mountains.
But before, where did the trees grow?

B: They grew in the Heavenly Vegetable garden.
In the Heavenly Vegetable garden was a kapok tree:
"Just cut it to make the big boats."
Which clever person came to cut the tree?

A: The clever Yang Yu
went to the Sky to cut the tree,
cut it to make the big boats.
The root was used to carve bailers,[37]
the trunk became hulls;
the limbs were used as oars.
A saw was needed to cut the wood.
What did the saw look like?

B: It looked like saw grass,
and it sawed the wood into boards.
If it were today,
the boards would be laid on the hillsides
to be cured under the Sun's fire.
People would turn the boards with their hands,
and when the wood dried, it would be used to make boats.
That is today's way,
but before, where were the boards cured?

A: They were cured on the cliffs:
a pair of fairies who were whistling in the East
blew the boards dry with their breaths.

The boards dried quickly.
"Hurry and invite craftsmen to build the boats."
If it were today
and you needed to find a craftsman to build a boat,
one could be found in any village.
But before,
where were the craftsmen?

B: The craftsmen were all in Yu Ghang's family.[38]
Yu Ghang's father was a craftsman.
If it were today,
chisels are shaped like water buffalo's teeth;
rasps are shaped like dragonfly nymphs[39]
axes are like Father's instep.

Those are today's ways;
what did things look like then?

A: Chisels were like Dragon's teeth;
rasps were like Dragon's tongues;
and axes were like Dragon's horns.

The boats were ready to be made.
The clever craftsmen
in one hand held ink markers,
in one hand held bamboo brushes,
marking things here and there,
busy making big boats.
The boats were made.
But what did the bottoms look like?

B: The bottoms looked like swallow bellies.
What did the prows look like?

A: The prows looked like locust heads.
What did the deckhouses look like?

B: The deckhouses looked like ash dippers.[40]
And the pairs of oars,
what did they look like?

A: They looked like duck feathers.
There was also a pair of boat horseshoes.
What did they look like?

B: Well, the boats didn't really have horseshoes;
that's to say, they had push-poles.

The boats were made.
If it were today,
the boats would wear clothes soaked in tung oil;
clothes pressed so neatly,
so lovely when worn
that the boats would feel happy
and be willing to go East.
But that is today.
In the ancient times what did the boats wear?

A: They wore clothes made of the juice of the Fruit of Immortality,
   and their clothing was very neat;
   it looked so beautiful
   that the boats went happily to the West.
   The boats went to the river;
   the water was very clear.
   When the boats saw it they became a little frightened.
   The clever Yu Va[41]
   rolled his sleeves high on his arms
   and rolled his trouser legs to his knees,
   then jumped into the water for the boats to see,
   and said to the boats:
   "It's only *this* high
   where the water is deepest!"
   When the boats saw this, they were very glad,
   so glad they nearly jumped for joy!

   The boats arrived at the place of Gold and Silver.
   What were used as anchors?

B: Stones were used as anchors,
   and the boats were moored against the banks.
   Gold and Silver were now in leaves;
   before they had been in chunks.
   Where was the ax found that chopped up Gold and Silver?

A: Old Rooster was pecking in the dirt for food,
   pecking here and there,
   and found an old ax left by the Ancients,
   which was used to break apart Gold and Silver.
   Which clever one went to weave baskets
   and brought them to carry Gold and Silver
   to put in the boats' steerage?

B: Grandpa Xong was the clever one.
   He went to weave baskets,
   which he brought to carry Gold and Silver
   to put in the boat's steerage
   so that the Metals could be transported to the West.

   The searchers would not have returned without Gold and Silver;
   they returned only when they had gotten Gold and Silver.

Who rowed in the prow?
Who rowed in the stern?

A: Grandpa Yang Yu rowed in the prow;
   Grandma Yang Yu rowed in the stern;
   in one pull they rowed past seven gorges.
   It is said that the Silver boats were so heavy that
   it seemed they were going to sink.
   But in comparison, they weren't really heavy.
   The Tin boats—now they were really heavy!
   Their sterns sank slowly into the abyss;
   there in that place where Tin comes out,
   where the water tastes like pepper and ginger.[42]

   Without Gold and Silver the searchers wouldn't have returned;
   only after getting Gold and Silver did they return.
   They came to Changmenao,[43]
   where the mountain pass was narrow as a pestle bracket,[44]
   the river water could run through,
   but the boats going West couldn't pass.
   Who put things to rights?

B: It was Old Man Xiu Niu
   who came and broke apart Changmenao;
   so not only could the river water run through,
   but the boats could pass as well.
   The boats nearly jumped for joy.

   They went on and on,
   till they came to Pu Je Ngang,[45]
   where nine roaring rivers converged.
   The waves there were as big as grain cribs;
   where nine roaring rivers converged,
   and nine Thunder Grandfathers crowded together.
   When the boats saw that, they despaired:
   "If we had known this earlier,
   we wouldn't have come this way.
   Where we lived in the East,
   though there was less room than here,
   we were happier."
   Who thought up a way to drive off the Dragon?

A: It was Old Grandpa Xong
   who climbed over bank and cliff,
   who, on a mountain peak, drove in a copper stake.
   Thus, the Dragon returned to the river bottom,[46]
   and the Thunder Grandfathers went home,
   letting the boats go West.

   Going on and on the Metals
   arrived at Eagle's home.
   Eagle's mouth was as big as a basket.
   The bird wanted to eat Gold and Silver.
   Gold and Silver were in despair:
   "If we had known things would be like this,
   what would have been the point of coming?
   If life in the East was a bit harder, so what?"
   Why did Eagle want to eat Gold and Silver?

B: Before, when the boats were being made,
   and some persons went up to the Sky to cut wood,
   a timber fell down that crushed Eagle's sons and daughter.
   Because of that, Eagle wanted to eat Gold and Silver;
   it wanted Gold and Silver in payment for the lost lives.

   They could not go on until they shot Eagle.
   What did they use as a bow?

A: Their bow was made of wax-willow wood,[47]
   and the bowstring was made of green vines;
   they used a pellet of tin to shoot Eagle,
   and dropped the creature to the ground.

   The boats neared the Creation Site.[48]
   What was the Creation Site?

B: It was the place where they would make the Suns and Moons,
   so they called it the Creation Site.

   The boats came to the Waiting Place.
   What was the Waiting Place?

A: Since everyone was waiting there
   when Gold and Silver arrived,
   it was called the Waiting Place.

After all the boats arrived,
hundreds of the crafts lined the banks,
assembled in good order.
Such a wonderful sight!
Really wonderful!

Gold and Silver were taken to a flat place:
the piles of Gold and Silver were like water buffaloes;
it seemed like herds of cows were grazing on the hillsides;
everyone wanted to get some.
Which two called for everyone to assemble?

B: It was Yu Ghang and Li Qe.
They chose nine wives
and made seven marriage arrangements,
but all were unsatisfactory.
None of these marriages would satisfy them,
so up till now they are still bachelors,
and the three rooms in their homes are left empty.
They came and called to everyone:
"Move Gold to my house;
move Silver to my house.
Create Suns for me to see;
Make Moons for me to see."[49]

CREATING THE SUNS AND MOONS

A: Let's sing of creating the Moons,
of putting the Suns up in the Sky.
Who was the clever one?

B: Jeweler's Scales was the clever one.
Wearing an old style tunic,[1]
he came to weigh Gold and Silver.
What were the big pieces made into?
What were the middle-sized pieces made into?
What were the smallest pieces made into?

A: The thickest pieces were used to make the Moons,
used to put the Suns up in the Sky.
The middle-sized lumps were used to buy land,

buy land to give the descendants for growing crops.
The thin slivers were used to make necklaces,
to make bracelets, to give to girls
to wear at their weddings
so that fathers and mothers would feel secure.
Let's sing of making the Moons,
of putting the Suns up in the Sky.
Who went to measure the place?

B: Yang Yu went to measure the place.
He measured six feet to the East,
and measured six feet to the West;
and there was the center:
"Make the Moons right here!
Make the Suns to hang in the Sky!"
Who went to measure the sites?

A: Yang Yu went to measure the sites.
He measured East for three days,
and measured West for three days.
And there was the center:
"Make the Suns here!
Make the Moons here to hang in the Sky!"
What ruler was used to measure the sites?

B: If it was a tailor's ruler,
it would be made of yellow sandalwood.
But what sort of ruler could measure the sites?

A: Yang Yu's hands and feet were very long:
Every stride was of equal length;
every span of equal measure.
Such rulers measured the Creation Sites.

Let's look at the pipe bellows used in creating the Suns and Moons.
If they were a blacksmith's pipe bellows,
the wood for the pipe bellows would grow in the mountains,
and it would be cut down and bored through;
a plunger would be put through the pipe cap,
and on the vent flaps would be tied chicken feathers;
the handle would be made of buffalo horn.
Such is a blacksmith's bellows,

used to make rake and hoe heads,
   to give the descendants to open the wild lands.
   But what about the bellows for creating the Suns and Moons?
   What was used to make the bellows?
   Where did the wind come from?
   What was used to make the plunger?
   What was used to make the handle?
   What was used to make the hammer?
   What was used to make the charcoal?

B: "Use a valley to make the bellows.
   The wind will blow down from the Sky.
   Use the spine of a mountain as a plunger,
   and a high mountain as a handle.
   Use a boulder as a hammer,
   and use rich *da mu mong* peat as charcoal."[2]

   Let's sing of making the Suns and Moons;
   sing of hanging the Suns and Moons in the Sky.
   Whose spirit was captured?

A: Young Wind Boy was caught
   and put in the bellows;
   sounds of crying came from within;
   those sounds were used to create the Suns and Moons;
   to make the Suns and Moons to hang in the Sky.

   When they were made, the entire Sky would brighten.
   People would be able to play cards in their spare time,
   and scholars could review their lessons.
   People could wrest a livelihood from the land.

   The Suns were to be made;
   the Moons were to be made.

   Today, the Fire Sparks live in our villages;
   but in the very ancient times
   where did the Sparks live?

B: Down from the wide Sky fell five handfuls of Fire;
   for at that time, Fire came from the Sky.[3]

Let's sing of making the Suns and Moons;
sing of hanging the Suns and Moons in the Sky.
Who came to arrange the charcoal?

A: Short persons arranged the charcoal.
Who came to pump the bellows?

B: Tall persons pumped the bellows.
Who was a good fellow?

A: Xong Tin was a good fellow.
He came riding a stallion covered with fish scales
and shouted in every direction:
"Every family bring a basket of charcoal;
we'll take it to create the Suns and Moons;
to create the Suns and Moons to hang in the Sky,
so everyone can benefit."
Who was the capable one who carried the bellows?

B: Cold Winter was the capable one
who carried the bellows,
walking into villages looking for work.
Who talked with him?

A: Grandpa Bo and Grandpa Xong said to him:
"You threw together some silver, lead, and raw copper,
but you didn't get very good creation material.
So, we'll have to do it by ourselves, slowly."

Cold Winter replied:
"You claim that when I mixed silver and lead
with some copper the material was no good.
Well then, just do it yourselves, slowly!"

Singing of making the Suns and Moons;
singing of putting the Suns and Moons up in the Sky.
If the molten Gold and Silver were poured into holes in the ground,
all the moss would burn up;
if poured on the mountains, the trees would all burn down.
Where were Gold and Silver poured?

B: Gold and Silver were taken into a cave
where the wind was just right;

there the Metals slowly cooled—
it was a good place to make the Moons.

Singing of making the Suns and Moons,
singing of hanging the Suns and Moons up in the Sky.
If molten Gold and Silver
were poured into ponds,
every green thing would be scorched to death;
if poured on the hillsides,
all the cogon grass would be scorched to death.
Where was a good place to pour them?

A: They were taken to a stone trough.
Inside the trough it was very cool;
it was a good place to create the Suns.
Who made the crucibles for melting the Suns and Moons?

B: If they were crucibles for making silver jewelry,
they would be made by the Han people.
Today we melt Gold and Silver in crucibles
to make jewelry for the girls;
to give to the girls so they can marry.
That's how it's done today.
But what about the crucibles for making the Suns and Moons?
Who made them?

A: It was Grandma Yu who made them.
She brought them to create the Suns and Moons;
to make the Suns and Moons to hang up in the Sky.
What were the tongs patterned after?

B: A crab's claw was used as a pattern;
that's how the tongs were made.
What did the tong rivets look like?

A: The rivets looked just like leeches.
When leeches contracted,
they became rivets.

Singing of making the Suns and Moons;
singing of hanging the Suns and Moons in the Sky.
Who was the naughty one?

B: Silent Ghost was the naughty one.⁴
   Reaching out his hand from behind,
   he scooped up three handfuls of Silver,
   but it wasn't enough to fill a crucible.
   So he asked, "How can I succeed at the creation?"
   Who was the naughty one?

A: Silent Ghost was the naughty one.
   Reaching out his hand from behind,
   he scooped up three handfuls of Gold,
   but there wasn't enough to fill a crucible.
   So he asked, "How can I succeed in the creation?"
   Who was asked to trick the Silent Ghost?

B: "Ask Old Chicken to trick the Silent Ghost."
   Old Chicken tricked the Silent Ghost in a dark place,
   then everyone asked him to come out
   and create the Suns and Moons.

   Let's look at the five Silent Ghosts.
   Who was their mother?

A: Fire Tongs was kindhearted;
   sneaking a peek at the crucibles, it cried out:
   "Bo, has the Gold melted yet?⁵
   Qe, has the Silver melted yet?"
   Tongs reached out its hand to grab,
   and its five fingernails were burned:
   Those five fingernails turned into five Silent Ghosts.
   Who was the rich one?

B: The Earth God was the rich one.
   He sat resting on the grasslands,
   watching everyone make the Suns and Moons.
   But when he saw how the Suns and Moons were made,
   he lost his soul in fright.
   What was brought to use as wine?
   What was brought in place of ducks?
   Who was invited as the sorcerer to call back
   the Earth God's soul?

A: Wave foam was brought as wine;
   straw sandal bugs were brought in place of ducks;⁶

Ghe Lu was the sorcerer invited
to call back the Earth God's soul.
The Earth God's face returned to normal,
becoming as white as a duck egg.

B: *While Grandpa Xong was making the Moons,
and making the ancient Suns,
who was the kindhearted person who had nothing to do?*

A: Kindhearted Grandma Yu had nothing to do.
She ran outside the door
and back inside again;
ran out to look at everyone making the Suns and Moons.
She also wished to take part, just for fun.
Kindhearted Grandpa Xong called to her:
"Grown-ups need only look on,
we needn't help out.
Why don't you just do as you're told?
You just want to meddle,
to mess up our wonderful treasures;
then we won't be able to make the Suns and Moons."

Singing of making the Suns and Moons;
singing of hanging the Suns and Moons in the Sky.
Who was a little foolish?

B: Grandpa Xong was a little foolish.
He was Grandpa Bo's helper.
Grandpa Bo used the little hammer;
Grandpa Xong used the big hammer.
The hammers raised up past their shoulders;
the hammers rang "ding-dong, ding-dong."
Suddenly the head of one hammer fell off
and broke one of the creations on the ground.
Grandpa Bo could only shout in anger,
cursing Grandpa Xong for being so careless.
They had to make the broken creation over again,
patterning it after the former ones.

The Moons were already made;
the Suns were already made.
They piled them up together,

just like stacks of firewood;
just like putting greasewood by the cliff sides.[7]
The Suns were stuck together in one big piece;
the Moons were in one big roll.
Who came to unroll the Moons?

A: Grandma Yu came to unroll the Moons.
Unrolling the Moons was just like peeling an egg.
Who came to unfold the Suns?

B: Grandma Yu came to unfold the Suns.
Unfolding the Suns was like unfolding a piece of paper.

Twelve Moons were created;
twelve Suns were made.
But some scraps were left over.
Who came to cut them up?

A: Grandma Yu came to cut them up.
Her hands were so clever
that she cut out the Suns and Moons
as if she were making paper flowers.

The Moons were cut out;
the Suns were cut out, too.
Only a little triangle of scrap was left over,
just like a little red envelope
for sending gift money at festivals.
Whose family was it sent to?

B: It was sent to the Chicken King's family;
left for the Chicken King to use;
the Chicken King put it on his head.
Where were the scissors put?

A: They were put in Niang Ni's house for her to guard.
Down to recent generations,
families without children may take a pig and a chicken
to sacrifice to the scissors used to cut out the Suns and Moons;
those doing so can bear children.
Anyone doing so can have sons and daughters.[8]

The Moons were made;
the Suns were made.
But the Suns were still not so round,
and neither were the Moons.
Who was the clever one?

B: Yang Yu was the clever one.
He picked up a stone
and threw it into the water,
stirring ripple upon ripple,
round as sifting screens;
he took the ripples as a model,
and thus made the Moons round,
and thus made the Suns round.

The Moons were created;
the Suns were created.
But the tools had to be sent off.
What became of the pipe bellows?

A: The pipe-bellows were sent to the mountains;
later, they became Bong Yu Lio,[9]
and also became Bong Yu Nin.[10]
Where were the hammers sent?

B: They were sent into an abyss,
and later became tortoises.
Where were the tongs sent?

A: They were sent to the corners of the paddies,
and later became crabs.

The twelve Suns were made;
the twelve Moons were made.
Once made, they were ready to be weighed
to see how heavy they were.
What did the scales that weighed the Suns and Moons look like?

B: If they were scales for weighing common gold and silver
they'd have a horse bone as the arm,
silk strings on the pan,
and copper rivets.

Such are scales for weighing ordinary gold and silver
in the market.
But what did the scales for weighing
the Suns and Moons look like?

A: The yard was made of *gangfu* wood;
the strings were made of spider web;
the pan was made of leaves.
Such were the scales used to weigh the Suns and Moons.
Each creation was equally large;
each creation was equally heavy.

The twelve Moons were made;
the twelve Suns were made.
After they were made, they were named.
By what names were they called?

B: The eldest was called the First Earthly Branch;
the second was called the Second Earthly Branch;
the third was called the Third Earthly Branch;
the fourth was called the Fourth Earthly Branch;
the fifth was called the Fifth Earthly Branch;
the sixth was called the Sixth Earthly Branch;
the seventh was called the Seventh Earthly Branch;
the eighth was called the Eighth Earthly Branch;
the ninth was called the Ninth Earthly Branch;
the tenth was called the Tenth Earthly Branch.[11]

Some were used to make houses;
some married young girls;
some went to build storehouses;
each had its own task.
But there were still two little brothers
who were very young and incapable of doing anything.
They were called the Eleventh and Twelfth Earthly Branches.
Two creations were very long.[12]
Who came to ask for them?

A: April came to ask for them;
May came to pick them up,
and so the two longest branches were taken away.
Two creations were very heavy.
Who came to ask for them?

B: June came to ask for them;
July came to pick them up,
and so the two heaviest ones were taken away.
Two creations were very short.
Who came to ask for them?

A: September came to ask for them;
October came to pick them up,
and so the two shortest ones were taken away.

The Suns were made;
the Moons were made.
The Moons' skins fell off;
the Suns' skins fell off.
The skins fell down upon the pipe bellows
and collected into piles.
What did they later become?

B: Later they became hail,
that now causes people's feet to freeze.
The Moons' skins fell off;
the Suns' skins fell off.
The skins fell down under the pipe bellows.
What did they later become?

A: They became ice and snow,
so cold that people's feet freeze stiff.
Which one carried the pot?
Who carried the tripod to scorch the site?

B: Frost carried the pot,
carried the tripod to scorch the site,
burning the grass off the mountains
so the mountains turned a deep red,
red as chestnuts from a chestnut tree.[13]

Still, there were the Glow Worms,
with their little glowing lights.
Who bore them?

A: When Grandpa Xong made the Suns
and hung the Moons in the Sky,

Gold pieces fell down to the ground
and turned into Glow Worms
that gave off glowing light.

Still there was a group of Stars
that came out only very late at night.
Who gave birth to them?

B: When Grandpa Xong made the Suns and Moons
and hung the Suns and Moons in the Sky,
he had a little Gold left over
that couldn't be used for big things;
so he took it to make those Stars.

There were also Sai Gha[14]
and Tong Hsen.
Who gave birth to them?

A: Grandpa Xong made the Suns and Moons,
made the Suns and Moons to hang in the Sky.
He had a little Gold left over,
but not enough to make any Suns or Moons;
so he took it to make Sai Ghai,
and used it to make Tong Hsen.

There was also a pair of Tiger Sisters,
who came out only in the darkest of night.
Who was their mother?

B: They were changed from the Silver Hammers.
There was also a pair of Duck Sisters,
who came out when night was already deep.
What did they look like?

A hoe head was used as a pattern,
and thus the two sisters were created.

There was also a Woodcutter,
just like that Woodcutter up in the Sky.
By which mother was he born?

A: There was a little Silver left over in the Silver Molds,
so it was taken to make the Woodcutter.

There was also a Bailing Bucket,
used to measure rice in the Sky.
What did it change from?

B: It changed from a Silver Mold.
There was also the Milky Way.
How was it made?

A: Grandpa Xong made the Suns and Moons;
made the Suns and Moons to hang in the Sky.
When he exhaled, his breath rose to the Sky,
where it changed into a silver river.

There was also a wisp of red cloud
that floated East and West.
How was it made?

B: When the Sky pillars were being made,
a puff of smoke had floated up to the Sky,
then changed into a red cloud
that floated East and West.

After the Suns, Moons, and Constellations were all made,
they had to be carried to the Sky.
But if we are going to sing about carrying the Suns and Moons,
then we must say something about the Hail, Frost, and Snow!
How were the Hail, Frost, and Snow carried to the Sky?

A: Old Man Bong Yong[15]
ate nine troughs of *baba* cakes,
ate nine baskets of raw fish;
so his body was strong and stout.
His power was so great that
he put the Hail, Frost, and Snow up in the Sky.
He carried it up to Dlong Lia Lio,[16]
right up to Dlong Ha Ba.[17]
And who, in a great voice, scolded Bong Yong?

B: In a great voice, Old Man Thunder scolded Bong Yong:
"You really are strong
to carry all that Hail, Frost, and Snow,
but carry it somewhere else!

Don't bring it to our village;
our village has no room for it,
no place for that Hail, Frost, and Snow."
Who also called to Bong Yong?

A: Grandma Niang Ni also called to Bong Yong[18]
"Don't carry them anywhere else;
carry them to me.
I'll put them in my trunk."

Hail was a clever one;
he lived in the western end of the house.
No dust could float near him,
so his face was always white.
And where did Frost live?

B: Frost lived in the inner room;
no dust could float there either,
so Frost's face was always white.
And where did Snow live?

A: Snow lived in the sitting room;
dust couldn't float there,
so his face was also white.

Clever Hail!
He lived in the western room;
in March, he fell down.
And when he fell, what followed him?

B: Diseases followed him down.[19]
Frost lived in the inner room.
What time did Frost fall?

A: When he fell, it was October,
and Drought followed him.
When Frost came,
many fields dried up;
many wells ran dry.

Snow lived in the sitting room.
When he fell, who followed him?

B: He came near the end of the year.
   Thunder broke open the western Skies,
   and Rain followed the Snow down;
   and the paddies were again filled with water.[20]

   Hail, Frost, and Snow were carried away,
   so now it was time to carry the Suns and Moons to the Sky.
   Who brought a duck?

A: Grandma Niang brought a duck.
   Who brought a crock of wine?

B: Grandma Hang brought a crock of wine.
   They went up to discuss matters with the Sky,
   and afterward, the Suns and Moons were carried up there.
   Who was an able man?
   Who was a strong man?

A: Yu Ghong was an able man;
   Li Ghong was a strong man.
   They ate rocks,
   and they ate steel.
   Their bodies were strong and stout as could be—
   they could carry the Suns and Moons to the Sky.

   But when Yu Ghong was asked to carry them,
   he wasn't willing.
   When Li Ghong was asked to carry them,
   he also wasn't willing.
   Who could be found to carry the creations?

B: Old Man Bong Yong
   ate nine troughs of *baba* cakes,
   ate nine baskets of raw fish,
   so his body was strong and stout,
   and his power was great.
   He carried the Moons to the Sky;
   he carried the Suns to the Sky.

   He carried them to Li Gi Saddleback;[21]
   he carried them East of Li Vang Saddleback,[22]
   all the while figuring that the Suns were a good thing.

Who would have known that they were really balls of fire?
When they became hot, they were like furnaces,
and they scorched half of Bong Yong's face.
Bong Yong shifted them to his other shoulder,
reversing the load on his carrying pole.
But the Moons fell into the mountain valleys;
the Suns fell into the mountain valleys.
The Suns broke into nine pieces;
the Moons broke into seven leaves.

Tung oil is used to coat umbrellas;
lacquer is used to paint chests.
The Suns and Moons were dropped and broken;
what water was used to mend them?

A: Juice of the Fruit of Immortality was used to mend the Suns and Moons,
to mend them as good as new.
Again, Bong Yong was invited to carry the Suns and Moons,
but this time, Bong Yong was unwilling.
Who came to carry them?

B: It was the clever Earth God.
He fastened the rivers and streams on his neck
and carried the wells on his head.
Little Stars were tacked to his sleeves,
Big Stars were held in his hands;
he hoisted the Suns and Moons onto his shoulders,
and carried them up to the Sky.

Arriving at the Stony Mountains,
the way became slippery with moss.
He took one step and slipped;
the Suns went rolling into a pond;
the Moons rolled into a pond.
The Suns were covered with mud;
the Moons were covered with mud.
Who came to wash the Suns and Moons?

A: Xang Ong and Vi Hxe[23]
washed the Suns and Moons,
washed the Suns and Moons clean.

Once again the Suns' faces were white as could be.
Once again the Moons' faces were white as could be.
As before, the Earth God was asked to carry the creations,
but the Earth God was unwilling.
The Suns were as big as mountains;
the Moons were as big as mountains.
Who came to put wheels on them?

B: Niu Xang came to put wheels on them,
and used the wheels to pull the Suns and Moons,
to pull the Suns and Moons up to the Sky.
Old Man Thunder opened the back door,
let down a rope from the Sky,
and pulled the Suns up to the Sky,
and pulled the Moons up to the Sky.

The Suns went to the Sky;
the Moons went to the Sky,
*Who knows which clever one
had legs that seemed to grow wings?*

A: It was the clever Earth God
whose legs were like wings.
He climbed up quickly to talk things over,
to discuss fastening the Suns and Moons firmly,
so they wouldn't move around.

The Suns were going to the Sky;
the Moons were going to the Sky.
*When arriving at the mountain forest,
who brought a horse knife?*

B: The good-hearted Sky Dog
brought a horse knife
and cut the path clean as could be,
to let the Suns and Moons go on to the Sky.

As the Suns and Moons went on to the Sky,
they saw what seemed like a cloud ahead.
But who could have known it was a rocky cliff?
The Suns couldn't go further;
the Moons couldn't go on.

"Just nail them there!"
But the nails wouldn't go in!
Who took a sledge to hammer them in?

A: Grandma Yu brought a sledge to hammer them in.
　　The spikes she hammered could have held big dogs!
　　Thus she fastened the Suns;
　　thus she fastened the Moons.
　　Who was the clever one?

B: Grandma Yu was the clever one.
　　She took an embroidery needle in hand,
　　and used it to prick the Sky;
　　she pricked the holes one by one
　　in which she set the Stars.
　　Who came to sweep the Sky?

A: Grandma Yu took a broom
　　and swept clear a path for the Suns, Moons, and Stars to follow.
　　Who raised a white-mouthed cow?

B: Grandma Yu raised a white-mouthed cow,
　　and plowed the Sky flat
　　so that the Suns and Moons could go freely.

Shooting Down the Suns and Moons

A: Now let's see about shooting down the Suns,
　　sing of shooting down Moons.
　　The Suns and Moons were all up in the Sky.
　　They were told:
　　"Come out at dawn by turns;
　　go in at dusk by turns."

　　The Suns were a little hard of hearing,
　　so they misunderstood.
　　In the mornings they all came out at once;
　　in the evenings they all went in at the same time.
　　They shone until the ground and mountains were melting.
　　The Earth looked like a bubbling cauldron of vegetable soup,

and the mountain cliffs seemed like goo.
Two young persons were melted up,
and all the mountain boulders were melted up.
How could things go on this way?
One glimpse of that and Hsang Sa was furious.[1]
What was the use of making so many Suns?
He wanted to kill the Grandfathers who had made the Suns and Moons.

Grandfather Bo and Grandfather Xong,
Grandfather Qe and Grandfather Dang,
tried to clear things up with Hsang Sa, saying:
"Blame the Suns for being deaf;
when they come up,
they all come up in the morning.
When they go down,
they all go down in the evening.
You go and shoot *them*, alright?"

Hearing this, Hsang Sa calmed down
and walked off with great strides.
He wanted to shoot down the Suns and Moons;
he wished to shoot down the Suns before breakfast,
he wished to shoot down the Moons before dinner.

On the cliffs two youths were busy clearing land for fields.
The two asked Hsang Sa:
"Old Fellow, Old Fellow,
where are you going in such a hurry?"
"I'm going to shoot down the Suns!"

The two said to Hsang Sa:
"While clearing the fields,
we found an arrow;
on the shaft are eleven burn marks,
on the head are eleven steel barbs.
You take it and use it!"

Hsang Sa wanted to shoot down the Suns and Moons,
so he stood on the prow of a boat;
but the boat rocked back and forth;
it was hard to aim from the boat.
Hsang Sa climbed up to the cliff tops;

but on the cliff tops he couldn't stand steadily,
it was too hard to aim straight from the cliffs.

Hsang Sa climbed up a Horse-Mulberry Tree;
the Horse-Mulberry huffed as it grew taller,
until it was half as high as the Sky.[2]

Hsang Sa hurriedly got out his bow;
Hsang Sa hurriedly mounted an arrow.
He aimed at the Suns' heads,
and drew on the Suns' hearts:
The Suns and Moons all fell down!

Eleven Suns were shot down;
eleven Moons were shot down;
leaving only one Sun behind,
leaving only one Moon behind—
those two cried and yowled
as they ran to Du Li's house.[3]

Shaking with fright, the Sun and Moon hid in Du Li's house—
they didn't dare to go out.
What was to be done?

B: Grandpa Bo and Grandpa Xong,
Grandpa Qe and Grandpa Dang,
came to talk it over,
came to invite someone to call to the Sun,
came to invite someone to call to the Moon.
Who was invited to go and cry for them?

A: Rooster was invited to cry out.
Rooster crowed,
and the Sun poked his head out to look around;
the valleys and cliffs became bright
and the whole Earth was alight.
Old folks and young all set out to the mountains to work,
to open land for their descendants,
to raise food for their parents.

When Rooster crowed,
the Sun came out.
How was Rooster thanked?

B: He was thanked with a coin and two bits of gold,
   with an ounce and two coins of silver;
   a golden official's hat was made for him to wear.
   The more Rooster crowed, the happier he was.

   When the Sun came out, who welcomed it?
   When the Sun went in, who sent it off?

A: When the Sun came out, the Sunflowers welcomed it;
   when the Sun went in, the Sunflowers sent it off.
   The Sunflowers gazed at the Sun each day.

   The Sun and Moon were wounded.
   Who was invited to wash their wounds?

B: The Sky Dog was invited to wash their wounds.
   It was promised fifty *jin* of ground grain;[4]
   but after their wounds healed,
   the Sun and Moon didn't give the promised grain.
   So, in years of good harvests, the Dog eats grain;
   but in years of bad harvests, it eats the Sun,
   eats the Moon to fill its hungry belly,
   for only when full has it strength to walk.

   Which mother gave birth to this Sun- and Moon-eating Sky Dog?

A: It was born by the Silver Mold Bottom.
   The Mold Bottoms bore the Sky Dog that has two rows of teeth
   and is able to eat the Sun and Moon in the Sky.

   Hsang Sa went to shoot the Suns and Moons,
   went out for eleven years, nearly twelve years.
   He shot down eleven Suns;
   he shot down eleven Moons.
   Returning home, he asked his wife:
   "Where is our child?"

   "It takes ten years to raise a pig,
   ten years for a child to grow.
   Our child went out to shoot geese,
   to shoot turtledoves for dinner.
   Didn't you meet him on your way home?"

On his way home Hsang Sa had seen a boy:
"What are you up to, lad?"

"I'm here to shoot geese."

"Let's see you shoot."

"Grandfather, where do you wish me to shoot?
If you say to shoot out an eye, I'll shoot out an eye;
if you say to shoot a leg, I'll shoot a leg.
Whatever you say, I'll shoot it."

"Alright, shoot out an eye!"

The boy drew and released his bow,
hitting an eye dead center.
Hsang Sa then drew an arrow,
shooting the boy to death:
"This place has me,
so it can't have you!"

Later, Hsang Sa's whole family changed into Stars.[5]
Now the child comes out at dusk
and the mother after dark;
but only at cockcrow does the father come out
to chase after them.

Hsang Sa's whole family died,
so the Sun was as happy as could be.
But people felt sad about the deaths,
and gazed at the distant Stars with tears in their eyes.

Hsang Sa's whole family died,
and there was no one to care for the horses;
so later, they turned into snout-moth larvae
and ran to the paddy banks
to eat up Grandma Gha Liang's rice.[6]
There was also no one to care for the swans;
so later, they turned into aphids
and ran outside to eat Grandma Gha Liang's vegetables.

Part III
Song of the Ancient Sweet Gum

Introduction

Song of the Ancient Sweet Gum concerns the birth of seeds of various tree species, in particular those that are thought to grow into a giant sweet gum. The seeds are borne by Fu Fang (Fux Fangb) and raised in a house (which the singers claim represents Ghe Lu [Ghed Lul], the Earth). House-building practices are described in detail, contrasting Fu Fang's techniques with those of humankind's direct mythical ancestor, Jang Vang, or actual human ancestors (either "our Parents" or "Mother"). The following excerpt refers to the custom of placing a square of blue or red cloth on the center beam in the frame of a newly constructed house. Inside the square are placed a pair of chopsticks, made of Chinese toon wood, along with cotton bolls, tied on with raw hemp. Copper coins are nailed into the corners of the cloth. Variations of this custom, which serves to protect the home from calamity, are widespread in China.

> If Jang Vang were making a house,
> he would wrap a piece of cloth on the center of the beams
> and add a pair of chopsticks;
> both ends of the chopsticks would be tied with hempen thread,
> and two ingots of silver would be wrapped inside the cloth . . .

The mythical Grandmother Niu Xang (Niux Xangb) accidentally burns down the Seeds' house. The fire frightens away "three Han people" and "three brothers of the Dong people." While this event refers to actual ethnic groups, the meaning of "three" is obscure and may mean simply "many." The fire also destroys three sets of ancient rites and rules (now obscure), as well as "the Ancient paper." The Seeds then go east (always the route of escape in the myths), back along the rivers into Hunan province, an area that may have been a previous homeland of the Miao now in Southeast Guizhou. They are pursued by Xang Liang (Xangb Liangx), who returns them to the west and then goes about clearing the earth to plant them.

Agricultural implements and practices basic to clearing and preparing the land for rice farming are described in detail in *Plowing and Harrowing the Earth*. Among the items and customs are making the plug placed through the nose of a draft buffalo, a plow made of various types of wood, a plowshare "made by the Han people," ox-yokes, harrows with eleven teeth and ten iron bands, harrow harnesses, and so on. All of the items reflect actual tools in use today throughout the region where the epics circulate.

When Xang Liang completes the plowing, all the tools must be sent to certain locations (as happened with the tools used to make the suns and moons). The plowshare is placed on a mountain peak, where later it changes into the singer of the praise songs in the sacrifices to the mythical ancestors. The rest of the tools are thrown beside the garden, at the base of a cliff, beside the dike of a rice field, and so forth. In their respective places, they turn into snakes, birds, mud eels, or insects. The harrow, for instance, turns into a "little dog harrow" and is buried crossways in the road. This seems to relate to the custom of making and burying a tiny bamboo harrow during sacrifices aimed at warding off harmful spirits. In another instance, the plow ox turns into a large rock, upon which hemp was supposedly beaten to make paper. Because the rock got tired of being struck, legend says, it ate all the books and paper, offering an explanation for why the Miao in this area historically did not have their own written language.

Once Xang Liang completes the task of planting trees on the mountainsides, he also plants various trees beside a pond where he is raising fish. One of these trees is a sweet gum, which attracts young people who are courting as well as cranes, which feast on the fish and drop their scales in the tree branches. Xang Liang accuses the sweet gum of stealing the fish and a trial is held (similar to the trial of the great eagle in *Westwards, Upriver*), to which several wise men (*lu* [*lul*]) are invited to defend the tree, which cannot speak for itself. Ultimately the tree is found guilty and cut down:

> When the Sweet Gum was cut down,
> it turned into a myriad of things.
> The sawdust chips turned into fish;
> the woodchips turned into honeybees;
> the heartwood bore butterflies;
> the buds turned into flying moths;
> the knots turned into owls . . .

SONG OF THE ANCIENT SWEET GUM

THE SEEDS' HOUSE

A: Now to sing *Song of the Ancient Sweet Gum*,
   talk of the ancient Tree Seeds.
   The branches of that ancient Sweet Gum grew and grew,
   till their tips touched the edge of the Sky.
   The leafy branches spread out wide:
   thousands of mountains shared their shade;
   their coolness was given to ten thousand valleys.

   From those ancient Sweet Gum Seeds,
   the Gum Tree grew so tall and straight
   that its leafy branches entered the blue clouds,
   shading the whole Earth.
   Who was the mother who bore it?

B: Mother Rusty Water bore it.[1]
   That ancient Sweet Gum Tree, ha.
   What kind of dirt did its roots eat?
   What kind of water did the buds drink?

A: The roots ate rich black mud,
   the buds drank misty rain.

   That ancient Sweet Gum Tree—
   what sort of food did its roots eat?
   What kind of soup did its buds drink?

B: The roots ate fertile sludge;
   the buds drank dew and rain.
   The Sweet Gum was Rusty Water's child,
   but who bore Rusty Water's father?

A: When Grandfather Bang Xang Ye died,
his leftover blood gave birth to Sulphur Water's father.

There was also Rusty Water's mother.
Who gave birth to her?

B: The mountains collapsed sixteen times,
the floods rose to the Sky sixteen times,
burying the ancient Fir Trees in the deepest realms of the Earth;
that caused Rusty Water's mother to be born.
There was also Maize.
Which mother bore it?

A: Mother Mud bore it.
There was also *Ge* Vine.
Which mother bore it?

B: Mother Mud bore it.
There was also the Thornball Tree.
Which mother bore it?

A: Mother Mud bore it.
Each kind of Seed was born by Mud;
every kind of Seed was born of Mud.
But who doesn't know that?
In those ancient ages,
from which direction did the Seeds fly?
And in which direction did they put down roots?

B: They flew from the East,
and put down roots in the West.

If it were today,
every kind of tree would grow on the hillsides,
and the various trees would grow in the valleys.
The wild mountains would be covered in emerald green.
But that is today,
and who doesn't know that?
But in those ancient ages of the past,
each kind of Seed was in the East,
every kind of Seed was in the East;
they all lived in Ghe Lu's house[2]
in the eastern place called Wentian Province.[3]

The Seeds grew like piles of firewood,
like stacks of pine sapwood on the cliff sides,
piled layer upon layer.
The bottom layer was Rusty Water,
so today, we have Rusty Water Seeds,
and Rusty Water flows from the lowest layer of the ground.
The middle layers were stone,
so today, we have Stone Seeds,
and most are buried in the earth.
The top layers were Eagles,
so today, we have Eagle Seeds,
and Eagles soar through the Sky.
That house of Ghe Lu's,
which mother made it?

A: Mother Fu Fang made it.
   And Nang Te's house,[4]
   which mother made it?

B: Fu Fang was the "mother" who built it.
   There was also a house up in the mountain forests.
   Which mother constructed it?

A: Mother Wild Pig constructed it.
   There was still one house
   at the head of the shoal.
   Which mother built it?

B: Mother Whitefish built it.
   The Seeds lived in Ghe Lu's house,
   the house Fu Fang had built.
   Now let's see how Fu Fang made the house,
   made the house for the Tree Seeds to live in.

   If Jang Vang were making a house,
   he would use blue fir,
   blue and red fir to make a house,
   a house for Mother to live in.
   But looking back on Fu Fang,
   what did he use to build with?

A: Iron hammers are stronger than wooden mallets.

With one stroke the mountain stones flew;
the stones were taken to build with.
Thus he built a house in which those ancient Tree Seeds could live.

As for Fu Fang building the house,
well, if it were our mother and father,
the girls would weave the ink lines,
the Han people would make the ink markers,
and with the strings and markers,
the house could be built.[5]
But looking back on those ancient times,
who made the ink markers?
Who wove the ink lines?

B: The ink markers were made by the mountain hollows;
the ink lines were woven by spiders.
With such lines and markers,
Fu Fang could build the house.
If our parents make a house, ah,
a great tree will be the center pole,
and a thick-stranded rope will be made.
But that's our parents' affair.
But looking back on Fu Fang,
what was his measuring pole?

A: A tall mountain was the center pole;
a great river was the ink line.

If our parents were making the house, ah,
a carpenter would be invited to the home;
he would race behind the house
and choose a straight bamboo,
and that would be the measuring pole[6]
used to build the house.
But that's our parents' affair.
But looking back on Fu Fang,
where did he get his measuring pole?

B: His pole came from the home of the water dragons
and was fashioned from the horns of a male dragon.
Thus he got his measuring pole to make the house.
He made Nang Te's house,

in which he put the Tree Seeds
and let those ancient Gum Seeds live there.

If our parents make a house, ah,
the carpenter they invite is a master craftsman;
throughout all the villages are houses that he has made.
Who was the master craftsman
that made the house for the Seeds to live in?

A: Xiu Niu was the master craftsman
who helped Fu Fang build the house
for the Seeds to live in.

If Mother makes a house, ah,
the neighbors will bring hammers to pound;
brothers will bring beams to set in place,
but that's Mother's affair.

But looking back on Fu Fang,
who brought a hammer to pound?
Who brought beams to set in place?

B: Wang Wu took a hammer to pound,[7]
Ghe Lu brought beams to set in place.

When Jang Vang built a house, he did as follows:
Jang Vang had many sisters.
One elder sister was married to Vong E;[8]
Vang and Vong were close relatives;
Vang and Vong were brothers-in-law.
Vong carried a quivering bamboo pole.
On this end was a basket of glutinous rice,
on that end was a jug of wine.
Two silver coins were wrapped in the money pouch;
"ka-boom-crack-crack," firecrackers exploded,
shaking the earth till the mountains trembled
and clouds of smoke filled the Sky.
Congratulations were sent to Jang Vang for building the new house,
but that was Jang Vang's affair.

Looking back on Fu Fang,
he had no elder sisters,

he had no younger sisters.
Who was it then
who came to congratulate him for building the new house?

A: The clever, kindhearted Water Dragon came,
carrying a quivering bamboo pole.
On this end was a basket of glutinous rice,
on that end a jug of wine.
Two silver coins were tucked away in his belt;
"ka-boom-crack-crack," firecrackers exploded,
shaking the earth till the mountains trembled
and clouds of smoke filled the Sky.
Thus he sent his congratulations
for the new house that Fu Fang had made.

That clever, kindhearted Water Dragon
sent his congratulations for the new house Fu Fang had made.
But when the clan family tree was checked,
and the dragon was asked his grandfather's name,
it was discovered that his grandfather was not of Fu Fang's clan.[9]
When asked about his aunt,
it was found that she was not of Fu Fang's family.
The sources of the river water weren't the same;
the Dragon and Fu Fang were not born of the same mother.
They were like two different trees
whose roots had gone astray;
they were not of the same blood.

When Fu Fang was building the new house,
he had gone to the Water Dragon's place,
wanting a horn for a measuring pole;
thus he had made friends with the Water Dragon,
and that was their only relationship.

If Jang Vang were making a house,
there would be many sisters;
the girls would get up early,
get up early to cook.
They would carry pots of rice and bowls of food
for Jang Vang to eat when putting up the new house,
but that would be Jang Vang's affair.

> But looking back on Fu Fang,
> he had no sisters.
> *Who came to help?*

B: Niu Xiang was good-hearted.
   She got up early to steam rice and make soup;
   she carried pots of rice and bowls of food
   to give Fu Fang as he put up the new house.
   Fu Fang toasted her with three bowls of wine.

   If Jang Vang were building a house,
   he would use rice straw to make ropes,
   twist a pair of strong, tight ropes,
   and take them to secure the rafters
   and to pull the beams upward,
   but that would be Jang Vang's affair.

   But looking back on Fu Fang,
   what did he use for rope?

A: He went to the mountainsides
   and brought back Yellow Mud to twist,
   and twisted a pair of thick, strong ropes,
   and used them to secure the rafters
   and to pull the beams upward.

   If Jang Vang were making a house,
   he would wrap a piece of cloth on the center of the beams
   and add a pair of chopsticks;
   both ends of the chopsticks would be tied with hempen thread,
   and two ingots of silver would be wrapped inside the cloth as well.[10]
   But that would be Jang Vang's affair.

   But looking back on Fu Fang,
   he used Earth to wrap the beams,
   and the pair of chopsticks were made of stones;
   both ends were wrapped with thread made of spider web.
   The two "silver ingots" hidden inside
   were pieces of stone.

   If this were our parents' home,
   there would be seven posts,

and earthen tiles would cover the roof.
A house built for our parents to live in
would be tight against wind and rain.
Looking back on the Seeds' house,
what was used as a roof?

B: Trees, flowers, and grasses covered the hills;
trees, flowers, and grasses in myriad variety;
cogon grass was used as a roof,
so the hills were as green as could be.
When Fu Fang finished his house,
who came to dance the drum dance in celebration?

A: Xong Tin's grandmother came carrying a child,
and did the drum dance at the foot of the building;
so the foundation was stamped very hard.

As for today,
The West has all sorts of seeds;
The West has all kinds of seeds.
But that's today,
why talk about it?

B: Looking back on those hazy years,
that was when all sorts of Seeds were in the East;
that was when all kinds of Seeds were in the East;
all living in Ghe Lu's house,
in the Eastern province of Wentian.
Fearing the Seeds would run away,
Fu Fang made a barricade that surrounded the house.

Niu Xang set the house on fire by accident;
the Seeds shrieked and cried—
it was an uproar inside!
Where did Niu Xang get the fire?

A: If it had been Jang Vang,
he would have used old fir roots to drill and drill,
and used carambala vines to twist and twist:[11]
twist, twist, drill, drill to get a spark.
He would also have gotten some flint to strike with
and put some mugwort tinder to one side,

and puff, puffed the sparks alive.
That's how Jang Vang would have gotten fire.
But looking back on Niu Xang,
where did her fire come from?

B: Dead Grandpa Bang Xang Ye's eyes turned into lamps and fires;
his eyelashes turned into cogon grass;
that's the way Niu Xang got fire,
but that all happened later.
That ancient kind of fire,
who gave birth to it?

A: Good mothers bear good sons;
terrible mothers raise rotten sons.
The Sky gave birth to Niu Hxi Du,[12]
one bolt fell from the Sky,
and it was gotten, that ancient kind of fire.
Why did the Sky Fire fall down?

B: While Grandmother Niu Xang was grinding grain,
she grabbed the edge of the Sky in one hand.
The Sky wobbled back and forth,
and down fell five balls of fire,
which ignited the Seeds' house.

Niu Xang accidentally started a fire
and burned up the Seeds' house,
melting three horse legs,
frightening away three Han people,
accidentally losing three kinds of Rites,
losing three kinds of ancient Rules and Rites.
The fire in the Seeds' house
frightened away three brothers of the Dong people.
Three Principles were lost by accident,
three ancient Practices were lost.[13]

Niu Xang accidentally burned down the house.
Everyone ran ahead,
but who ran back?

A: Tiger ran back,
Old Man Tiger,

whose body was scorched by fire,
whose whole body was scorched, stripe by stripe.

The Seeds' house was burned up,
so everyone ran ahead.
But who ran the other way?

B: Old Cat ran back the other way;
that clever Old Cat,
whose whole body was burned
till it became tabby-spotted.

Seeking the Tree Seeds

A: Grandmother Niu Xiang started a fire by accident
and burned up the Seeds' house.
How many days did the fire burn?
How many nights did the fire rage?

B: It burned for thirteen days;
it raged for thirteen nights.
The fire burned from the Third to the Fourth Earthly Branches,
and coming around again to the Third Earthly Branch,
it finally died out.
Who brought water to put it out?

A: The Thunder God carried water buckets,
brought water to douse the fire.
Each of the four directions was under water:
The "Principles" Seeds were submerged,
the Tree Seeds were submerged,
the Paper Seeds were submerged;
the Tree Seeds were in one direction,
the Paper Seeds in one direction,
the "Principles" Seeds were in another direction.

Tong Yang could read and write;[1]
he knew about the ancient Paper.
Xang Liang knew of the Sweet Gum Tree,
knew about the ancient Sweet Gum Seeds.

Hsen Yi understood the "Principles";
he was familiar with the ancient Rites.
The White-necked Cow knew the fruits,
knew every sort of fruit there was.
What was he invited to do?

B: He was given a necklace to wear,
then raised his finger and pointed:
"The Tree Seeds are in that pile!"
Thus the Tree Seeds were found.
Who was the horse dealer?

A: Xong Tin was a horse-dealing man.
When his horsewhip cracked, "pop,"
the Seeds ran off in fright,
shooting up to the nine clouds.
Xong Tin chased a hog to sell;
when his whip cracked, "tat,"
the Seeds were scared witless;
they huffed and puffed up to the ninth level of the Sky,
and the Seeds lived beside the Sun,
with the Moon as a close neighbor.
Three kinds of Seeds were mixed together in one place.
How could they be told apart?
In which pile were the Sweet Gum Seeds?

B: The Sweet Gum Tree Seeds were yellowish.
In which pile were the Pine Seeds?

A: The Pine Seeds were crimson.
In which pile were the Fir Seeds?

B: The Fir Seeds were grayish.
So all the Seeds were identified.
But there was still *that* bunch inside.
What were they?

A: That bunch of Seedlings was born by the Ironwood Tree,
five or six Seedlings in a clump.
There was still that cluster in the West,
what was that?

B: They were Bamboo Shoots,
    tender-tipped Bamboo Shoots in a great pile;
    the Shoots were born in the West Garden.
    If children spied those Shoots,
    the kids' hands and feet would wave and their feet would dance;
    they would be so happy.

   When the Seeds went to the Sky,
   they lived there for three whole years,
   and being idle, they became dull,
   they didn't know how to do anything.
   Who was the clever one
   who slowly opened the Sky Door
   to let the Seeds come down from the Sky?
   Whose clasp knife was sharp?[2]

A: Brother Wind's clasp knife was sharp;
    he went to the Sky and cut apart the Seeds' roots,
    and the Seeds floated down,
    twirling just like spinning wheels.
    Who carried the hoe?

B: Brother Wind carried the hoe,
    carried the hoe to clear a road so the Seeds could go,
    and thus the Seeds rolled down from the Sky.

   The "Principles" came down lightly,
   the Written Words came down slowly—
   the Seeds came down with a "bop."
   "Plop," they fell in a big cluster into a deep pool,
   a pool nine thousand feet deep.[3]
   The Seeds sank slowly into the deep pool,
   then grew roots and sprouts.
   The roots were as thick as chisels,
   and clung tightly to the rocks.
   Who came and nibbled off the roots?

A: Water Rat went deep into the abyss;
    Water Rat nibbled off the roots,
    and thus the Seeds floated to the surface.

   Water Rat went to nibble at the Seeds' roots
   and nibbled off the small ones.

But some of the Seeds held on too tightly,
and Water Rat couldn't nibble them free.
Who went to nibble them free?

B: Gadflies like the smell of horse urine
and follow the stench of cows.
Otter liked the smell of fish,
and searched for fish along the rivers.
Otter saw the Seeds
and said they were grass carp;
he chomped wolfishly,
and the Seeds floated to the surface.
*Who was the clever one
who made a plow to till the land
for plowing West to East?*

A: In winter, snow fell;
in midsummer, hail fell,
causing nine great floods to rage to the East
and the nine great rivers to form into one.
The nine great waters converged in one place,
submerging the mountain boulders;
each as big as a grain crib.
"Oh, the surging billows!
Each as big as a corral."
The Seeds washed toward the East,
amassing upon a sandbar.
*Who wove nets with large holes?
Who wove nets with small holes?*

B: The rocks of the cliffs made big-holed nets;
tree branches and grass made small-holed nets;
mountains and waters surrounded the Tree Seeds,
and the river water let them flow downstream.
It didn't allow them to go East;
they had to go West, no matter what.

But the Tree Seeds were unwilling to go West,
so they made off for Nang Liang.[4]
Thus it was necessary to find a dog to chase them,
and only a hunting dog would do.

Give a hunting dog a mouthful of rice and he's happy;
he'll go chasing through the high mountain forests,
barking as he runs, snapping as he goes,
snapping the hairs right off the game;
that's how it is with a hunting dog.

With hunting dogs,
a bitch raises puppies,
and as they grow, they chase wild game.
But who gave birth to the Seed Chasing Dog?

A: He was born in the Sky.
If he could catch the Seeds,
how was he to be rewarded?

B: He would be invited to live beside the fields,
invited to live in the corner of a field,
where he could eat the crops as he liked.
Today, in good years, he doesn't even want the food;
but in bad years, he comes to harvest.[5]
Though the people's bellies are empty,
the Dog grows fatter and fatter.

The Seeds were on the opposite bank;
what sort of boat could cross?

A: A rice-straw boat could carry across an insect;
a fir boat could carry across our parents;
but a boat of wave foam carried the Seeds across,
bobbing them across the river.
The Seeds floated up against the other bank,
onto a wide sandy beach
where everyone came to grab them.
Everyone clutched them to their waists,
but no one could get them upon their shoulders.
Old Grandfather Xang Liang was clever and stout;
he grabbed the Seeds to his waist,
then hoisted them to his shoulders.
He said that the ancient Tree Seeds were his,
and so the ancient Seeds belonged to him.

Since the Seeds were wet, they had to be dried.
So let's see how the Seeds were dried.

If it were grain to be dried,
a woven bamboo tray would be the drier,
and Mother would turn the grain by hand,
and once a day, husk it in a husking treadle.
Where were the Seeds dried?

B: The Seeds were dried on slabs of stone,
and Grandfather Xang Liang turned them by hand;
when dry, he took them to pound in a husking treadle.
Let's look once more at the husking treadle.
If it were a rice-husking treadle,
it would be used to husk rice to feed the younger generations.
The beam of the treadle would be made of pine,
and the frame would be of pine;
the iron pestle would be cast by the Han,
and the mortar would be made of stone.
That's how grain is husked.
But looking back on how the Seeds were husked,
what was used as a treadle?
What was used as the sifter?

A: Mountains were used as the husking treadle,
flat lands were used as the sifter.
As the husker removed their skins,
the sifter shook bits of Seeds.
The Seeds' faces were white as could be,
and they happily went on Westwards.

If it were Mother,
she would invite a young girl,
hire some part-time help to husk the grain.
Who did Xang Liang invite?
Who was hired to husk the Seeds?

B: He invited his wife to do the husking.
When Mother hires part-time help,
she invites a girl to come to husk.
For three scales of grain,
the girl will be willing to husk.[6]
When Xang Liang invited his wife to husk,
what did he give her so she'd willingly husk?

A: He gave her a fan,
   a fan with two wooden handles;
   with one wave of the fan, she could fly to the Sky.

   If rice was being husked,
   the chaff and broken bits would be fed to the pigs,
   the big, thick grains would be fed to the children.
   That's how it is when rice is husked.
   But looking back on the Seeds,
   what did the rough chaff turn into?
   What did the broken bits become?

B: The rough chaff turned into Mosquitoes,
   the broken bits became Ants;
   the strongest pieces were taken as seed,
   and they became the most ancient Seeds.

   After the husking was finished,
   the tools had to be sent away.
   The sifter and husker had to be sent away
   before the Seeds could return to the West.
   Where was the husking pestle sent?

A: It was sent to a mountain saddleback.
   What did it turn into later?

B: It turned into a Turtledove,
   and cooed, "Gu-gu, gu-gu-ti."

   There was also a treadle beam.
   Where was it sent?

A: It was sent to the corner of a field,
   where it later turned into a *didi* bird[7]
   and cried, "didi-didi!"

   There was also a sifter.
   Where was it sent?

B: It was sent to the West.
   What did it turn into?

A: It turned into a wisp of cloud
   that floated East and West.
   Thus in winter the snow drifts down in great flakes.

   The tools were all sent away.
   Now it was time to carry the Seeds.
   What shape was the basket?
   What sort of carrying pole was used?

B: The basket was like an earthen crock;
   the pole was like a duck feather.
   Using a chestnut burr as a model,
   all sorts of baskets were made to carry the Tree Seeds
   for taking them back to the West.

   Xang Liang carried the Sweet Gum Seeds,
   transported those Seeds back to the West.
   But halfway back, he turned a corner too quickly
   and fell "plop" flat on his back!
   The Seeds in the baskets scattered everywhere,
   and some went into a cleft in the ground.
   Xang Liang quickly used both hands to scoop them up.
   But what did he see beside the cleft as he scooped?

A: He saw a pair of big, poisonous snakes
   whose fangs were bared, ready to bite him!

   The ancient Sweet Gum Seeds were going West, really going.
   They came to a steep, dangerous cliff,
   and at its foot was a deep, muddy pool.
   On the cliff tops was a deep, dark forest:
   Ancient trees densely covered both slopes,
   and aged vines twined through both valleys.
   It was hard for the river to flow East,
   and hard for the Seeds to go West.
   The Seeds moaned sadly:
   "If we had known this before, we wouldn't have come;
   we would have stayed in our Eastern lands;
   life there was hard, but it wasn't dangerous."
   Who was it?

B: It was Old Xiu Niu,
   who hammered out a chisel shaped like a fish mouth,

then chiseled through Horse-Mouth Cliff
   to the East he also chiseled out Monkey-Mouth Cliff.
   He cut a channel to let the water flow East,
   chiseled a road on land for the Seeds to go West.
   The Seeds were happy as could be:
   "We're going West for a carefree life!"
   Who grabbed his hand?
   Who whipped him?

A: Brother Wind grabbed his hand;
   Brother Wind whipped him,
   whipped him to the top of the dangerous cliff.

   The Seeds were coming, really coming.
   Who was it,
   who was it who came to speak with the Seeds?

B: It was a pair of flying children;
   they fluttered up to a mountaintop;
   and that pair could really fly.

   Fluttering over the mountaintop,
   they said to the Tree Seeds:
   "Yellow earth is in the East,
   deep as a horse's neck;
   black soil is in the West,
   deeper than a horse's head,
   deeper than a water buffalo's belly."

   The Seeds were happy to hear it:
   "We're going West to live a carefree life!"

   The Seeds were coming, really coming.
   They came to the side of a hill.
   Who was so clever and nimble-fingered?

A: Icicle was clever and nimble-fingered.
   His nimble fingers hammered out an iron rock drill,
   hammered out an iron chain of six links,
   then chained the Seeds to the hillside.
   The Seeds couldn't have moved even if they had wanted to.
   Who was clever and kind?

B: The Sun King in the East
   was clever and kind.
   He cut apart the six links in the iron chain.
   Thus the Seeds could go on Westwards.

   Coming to a mountain saddleback everyone sat together:
   Heads, faces, and feet, all in a line;
   really a lovely sight.
   What stool did the Seeds sit on?

A: They sat on slabs of stone.
   Let's look at those Sweet Gum Seeds
   that wanted to go West to lead a carefree life.
   Well, they were coming, really coming!
   They came to a three-way saddleback,
   they came to the head of a three-forked range.
   The way was covered with moss,
   and it was slippery going;
   one misstep, and you'd go head over heels.
   The Seeds were very sad:
   "If we had known this earlier, we wouldn't have come,
   we would have stayed in our Eastern lands;
   even if it was narrow and life was hard,
   we'd rather bear that, than this!"

   Old Man Sun said over and over to the Seeds:
   "Wait a while till I come out,
   then you can go on!"

   The Tree Seeds came to the three-forked range.
   Though the mountains had plenty to eat,
   they had no clothing to wear,
   and their backs were bare.
   What clothes were they given?

B: If it were a girl's blouse,
   threads would be woven on a fir loom,
   a bamboo needle would move among the threads,
   weaving the threads into cloth for clothing;
   how beautiful the girls are when they wear their new clothes!
   As for the blouses for the Mountain Range,

what was the loom?
What was the thread-tamping needle?

A: The clouds were the loom,
    and the misty rain was the needle.
    Thus the threads were woven into cloth for new clothing,
    the green-clad mountains were so beautiful!

    Coming, they were really coming.
    Hill by hill, one saddleback after another,
    till they came to the mountain for sacrificing
    to the Ancestors,
    till they came to the mountains
    of Xang Liang in the West.

    The high mountains looked like duck eggs,
    and it was hard to walk or stand.
    The Seeds were very upset.
    Again and again they turned to look back,
    hoping to see the East lands of their parents.
    Their eyes were full of tears.
    Who was clever and capable?

B: Xang Liang was clever and capable.
    He came to plow the mountains and harrow the wide earth.
    Seeing him, the Seeds were happy.

Plowing and Harrowing the Earth

A: Come see Xang Liang plow and harrow the land.
    In the murky depths of the past,
    the mountains were the wild pigs' mountains;
    the valleys were the wild pheasants' valleys.
    What did Xang Liang take to sell?

B: He took fern roots to sell,
    and bought the wild pigs' mountains.
    He got hazelnuts to sell,
    and bought the wild pheasants' valleys,
    bought the land to plant the Trees.

Plowing and Harrowing the Earth

Come see Xang Liang plow the land.
If Jang Vang were plowing,
he would till the fields and plow the land for his Grandmother,
and to support those Six Old Grandfathers.
His water buffalo would be bigger than a cow,
and Jang Vang would lead it to plow the fields,
but that's how it would be with Jang Vang.
But looking back on Xang Liang,
how big was his ox?

A: His ox was like a toad.
    He kept it in a bamboo basket.
    Lightly picking up the ox,
    Xang Liang carried it to plow the land.
    But he couldn't plow over the hills,
    and the mountains couldn't be tilled.
    Since the land couldn't be plowed,
    Xang Liang was so angry that he killed the ox.
    He ate the ox until only its bones were left;
    chewed on the jaws until only the skull was left.
    Later, he threw the bones into the forest.
    A day and a night passed,
    what did they turn into?

B: They turned into Kho Hxen.
    The big hat on his head was hard to wear;
    his mouth spoke endless gossip;
    his descendants loved to cause arguments:
    His family was the most evil of all.[1]
    You said Xang Liang's ox was like a toad,
    but that's not so.
    His ox was as big as a grain crib,
    for his ox was Xiu Niu.
    Xang Liang led it to plow the land,
    to rake flat the mountains in order to plant the Sweet Gum Trees.
    If Jang Vang were tilling the fields,
    Jang Vang would buy an ox.
    Since his family had money,
    he would just take some silver
    and go buy an ox.
    But that's how it would be with Jang Vang.
    But look at Xang Liang.

Xiang Liang wanted to buy an ox,
but where would he get the silver and gold?

A: A girl named Gi Ni Wen
   planted an Emerald Cypress Tree;
   its roots pierced the Earth,
   and its branch tips reached the Sky.
   The tree was covered with white blossoms
   without a single leaf;
   its fruit was as big as cooking crocks,
   and the fruit was silver.
   The girl picked some of the fruit and sent it to Xang Liang.
   Xang Liang took it to buy an ox,
   to buy an ox to plow the mountains.

   A girl called Gi Jen Ni
   planted an Emerald Cypress tree;
   its roots pierced the grassy ground,
   and its branch tips entered the Sky.
   The tree was covered with yellow blossoms
   without a single leaf;
   its fruit was the size of rice steamers,
   and the fruit was gold.
   The girl picked some of the fruit and sent it to Xang Liang.
   Xang Liang took it to buy a water buffalo,
   and to buy a cow to till the hillsides.

   If it were Jang Vang,
   he would go to the market in Bohu,[2]
   and to Cong'an to buy the ox,[3]
   to buy an ox to plow the fields,
   but that's how it would be with Jang Vang.
   Looking back on Xang Liang,
   what market did he go to?

B: He went to the market in Nantu,
   and in the market bought an ox,
   which he led to plow the fields.

   If it were Jang Vang,
   buying an ox would require a go-between.
   Liong Hlie was Jang Vang's brother-in-law,

so he would be the go-between in the deal.
   When Xang Liang went to buy a cow,
   who was the go-between?

A: Grandpa Xong Tin was very clever,
   so he acted as the go-between in the deal.
   Xang Liang got his ox,
   then led it to plow the hillsides,
   harrowing flat the land to plant the Trees.

   If it were Jang Vang,
   he would take the ox home
   and put it in a pen made of hemp and chestnut,
   then bring cogon grass to feed it;
   the longer he raised it, the fatter it would grow,
   its muscles growing thick as could be;
   it would be like raising a rat or a sparrow.
   Looking back on Xang Liang,
   after he bought the ox and took it home,
   where did he keep it?
   Where did he feed it?

B: He kept it in the wild mountains,
   fed it with earth and mud;
   the longer he raised it, the fatter it grew;
   its muscles were as big as could be;
   it was just like raising a sparrow or a rat.

   Xang Liang spent how much money,
   spent how much silver to buy it?

A: Xang Liang spent a thousand pieces of silver,
   bought an ox with a thousand ounces of silver,
   bought it to plow the hillsides.
   After the fields were plowed,
   flowers, grasses, and trees grew easily.
   The hillsides were tilled smooth
   so the wind could come and go;
   the cogon grass grew in endless clumps,
   and flowers filled the mountain saddlebacks.

   If it were Jang Vang,
   after he brought home the ox

his many sisters
would bring a jug of wine
and an old hen duck,
quacking all the way,
to toast Jang Vang's ox.
After the toasts,
the ox's eyes would be red as blood.[4]

Xang Liang went to buy an ox
and brought it back home;
but he had no elder sisters,
and he had no younger sisters.
So who was it,
who acted as his sister?

B: Magpie acted as his sister
and brought him a jug of wine,
as well as an old hen duck,
its quacking rustling the trees,
brought them to toast Xang Liang's ox,
till the ox's eyes were red as could be.

If it were Jang Vang,
after taking the cow home,
he'd use a piece of *wubei* wood
to poke through its nose;
then Jang Vang would pass a rope through the hole
and lead the ox to plow the fields.
As for Xang Liang,
when he took his ox home,
what did he use to pierce its nose?

A: A male Dragon's horn was the instrument
that was poked through the ox's nose;
then Xang Liang passed the rope through the hole
and led the ox to plow the mountains.
After plowing the fields,
flowers, grasses, and trees grew easily;
when the hillsides were harrowed smooth,
the wind could come and go;
the cogon grass grew in endless clumps,
and flowers filled the mountain saddlebacks.

If it were Jang Vang,
he would use a plow to till the paddies.
The plow beam would be made of willow,
the share shaft made of mulberry;
the share would be made by the Han people,
that would be a plow for tilling paddies.

As for the mountain-tilling plow,
the beam was a rolling mountain range;
the share shaft was a high mountain peak,
and the share was made of stone slabs.

If it were Jang Vang,
he would need an ox yoke to plow the paddies.
In Winter, fierce winds would blow from the East,
putting icicles on the branches,
causing the branches to curve;
curved branches would be used for ox yokes;
slung on the oxen's necks;
the oxen would huff along,
plowing the fields to support the Parents,
and to support the Six Old Grandfathers.[5]
But Xang Liang,
when he went to find an ox yoke to plow the mountains,
where did he go to look?

B: The Thunder God slept on top of the horse pen,
Xang Liang lay down by a rock pile;
as the Thunder God rumbled,
Xang Liang raised his head,
then leaped onto a horse's back and rode off,
whipping and flailing the horse along,
whipping and flailing the mountains as he went:

With one whiplash he made the valleys,
the mountain valleys as deep as could be,
the mountain peaks as high as could be,
the mountain ranges rolling like a horse's neck.

That was how he got his ox yoke.
He placed it on Xiu Niu's neck,
then Xiu Niu puffed along,
as Xang Liang plowed the mountains to plant the Trees.

If it were Jang Vang,
he would need a harrow to rake the fields,
so he would twist rice straw,
twist it into a harrow harness,
then lead the ox to rake the paddies.
That's how Jang Vang would do it.
As for Xang Liang,
what did he take to twist?

A: He took yellow earth to twist,
and twisted it into a harrow harness.
Xang Liang then used the harrow to rake the hillsides.

If it were Jang Vang's harrow,
it would have eleven teeth,
and ten iron bands set close together between them,
but this would be Jang Vang's harrow.
But looking back on Xang Liang,
how many teeth did his harrow have?
And how many bands were there?

B: His harrow had one thousand teeth,
and one thousand iron bands.

The tools were all ready,
and it was time to plow the land.

If it were Jang Vang,
the tilling of the paddies
and the plowing of the fields
would be done to support his parents.
Plowing to the East he would make nine furrows,
and get nine baskets of crucian carp.[6]
Plowing to the West, he would make nine rows,
and get nine baskets of yellow eels,
that's how it would be with Jang Vang.

But looking back on Xang Liang,
when he plowed Eastward, making nine furrows,
what did he get?

A: He got nine baskets of wild rats.

Plowing to the West he made nine furrows.
What did he get?

B: He got nine baskets of sparrows.
If it were Jang Vang plowing the paddies,
he would plow Eastward nine times
and break nine plow beams;
he would plow Westward nine passes,
and break nine plow shafts.
Jang Vang would be very angry.
Who would it be?

A: It would be Grandpa Xong Tin.
Who would say to Jang Vang again and again:
"Don't be upset, brother;
go to the market and buy some new tools!"

But looking back on Xiang Liang,
when he plowed to the West,
what did he break?

B: He broke nine mountain peaks.
When he plowed to the East,
what was broken?

A: He broke nine mountain summits;
Xang Liang was so happy!

If it were Jang Vang plowing the fields,
when he lowered the harrow, the water would muddy;
when he lifted up the harrow, the grass would float up.
That's the way it would be with Jang Vang.

But looking back on Xang Liang,
what happened when he lowered the harrow?
What happened when he raised the harrow?

B: When he lowered the harrow, he made hills,
made chain after chain of mountains.

If Jang Vang were plowing the fields,
his many sisters would catch fish and shrimp behind him,

and draw near the cow to catch tadpoles.
But Xang Liang had no sisters.
Who came to follow him to catch the fish and shrimp?

A: The clever magpie came to follow him to pick up
the fish and shrimp
and drew near Xiu Niu to catch tadpoles.
If Jang Vang went to plow,
he would plow till nearly evening,
till when the Sun hangs like a brass drum in the West.
Jang Vang would cook some carp,
cook some fish for dinner.
That's how it would be with Jang Vang.
But looking back on Xang Liang,
when plowing the mountains, he'd plow till nearly evening,
till when the Sun hangs like a brass drum in the West.
What did Xang Liang eat?

B: Xang Liang cooked toads,
cooked green snakes for supper.

If Jang Vang went to plow,
he would plow till nearly evening.
Duckweed would float near the dikes,
and fish would swim in the middle of the paddies.
But that's how it would be with Jang Vang.

But looking back on Xang Liang,
he plowed and harrowed the land to plant the Tree Seeds,
plowed till the Sun was in the West.
Where did the duckweed float?
Where did the fish swim about?

A: The duckweed floated near the mouths of the saddlebacks,
and the fish swam about the sloping hills.
And later, what did they turn into?

B: The fish turned into pangolins,
and the duckweed turned into *xini* grass.
If one is unlucky enough to meet a pangolin,
that Dragon of the mountain saddlebacks,
though one might not die of it, one's skin would fall off.[7]

Xang Liang plowed the mountains,
plowed all the way to the Earth God's village,
where seventy thousand persons lived.
The ox couldn't go there,
and Xang Liang couldn't enter.
Who could go there?

A: Ant could go.
   Ant could go and plow there.

There was still a stony gorge
that was deep as an urn;
Xang Liang couldn't go there,
and the ox couldn't enter.
Who was able to go into the stony gorge to plow?

B: Crab could go.
   It could go and plow the stony gorge.

The land was nearly all plowed,
and only one field was left on a mountain peak.
Who was called to plow it?

A: Wild Pheasant was called to plow it.
   If Jang Vang were plowing,
   he would plow to the edges of the paddy,
   and meeting the corners, turn around.
   But that's how it would be with Jang Vang.

But looking back on Xang Liang,
to where did he plow?
To where did he harrow?

B: He plowed to Huangping
   and harrowed to Yuqing.
   Huangping is a level plain;[8]
   Yuqing is a stretch of flat land.
   From the river's source he plowed East;
   from the place of sunrise, he plowed West,
   plowed until his plowshare was dull,
   plowed until the harrow bands broke.

He still wanted to go on West,
but he had no harrow with which to rake:
The mountain valleys seemed bottomless;
the mountain peaks reached the clouds.

The land was plowed;
the hills were all harrowed:
Everything was flat as a woven bamboo mat;
level as the foundation of a grain crib.
Now to hurry and plant the Tree Seeds!

"Hold on, not so fast!"
The tools had to be sent away before the planting could begin.
The plow was taken to a mountain peak,
where the share turned into Ba Hlio,[9]
changed into Gha Xiu,
who came for Ancestor sacrifices.[10]

There was also an ox hoof;
when thrown beside the garden,
it turned into a *wushao* snake.
There was still the harrow harness;
when cast at the base of a cliff,
it turned into a red-striped snake.
There was still the ox yoke;
when put at the East side of the vegetable garden
it turned into a *gebang* snake;[11]
its head and tail were both the same size.
There was still the curved plow beam;
the plow beam turned into a *didi* bird,
that cried: "didi-didi!"
There was also the rope in the ox's nose
that looped down to the ground,
and that turned into a mud-dwelling eel.
There was also a whip;
it was placed at the foot of a paddy dike,
and after a few years turned into a straw sandal bug.
The harrow was sent to Lu Men's home,[12]
where it turned into a little dog harrow
and was buried crosswise in the road.

If it were today,
after the paddies were all plowed,
the ox would be put in its pen,
and wine would be brought to toast it.
When Xang Liang finished plowing,
where was the ox sent?
What was brought to toast it?

A: The ox was sent to the mountain forests,
and rain water was brought to toast it.
After a year went by,
the ox turned into Vi Vang O Rock,[13]
and the rock wanted to eat Paper and Books.

Sowing the Seeds

A: The tools were all sent away.
"Now quickly—plant the Seeds!"
Whose hands were so fragrant
that he was called to sow the Seeds?

B: Xang Liang's hands were the most fragrant,
so he was called to plant the Seeds.
Were the nine kinds of Seeds sown in one handful,
or were there nine separate ways of sowing them?
Did the nine kinds of Seeds sprout into nine sorts of Shoots,
or did only one kind of Tree grow from them?

A: The nine kinds of Seeds were separately sown,
and from the nine kinds of Seeds grew nine sorts of Trees.

Where were two handfuls sown
that didn't sprout?

B: One handful was sown in the water;
one handful was sown on stone.
Those two handfuls never grew.

There was also one more place,
and why didn't the Seeds grow when sown there?

A: That place was in the mountain saddlebacks;
 people kept coming and going along the pathways,
 and that the place was left for people to rest on,
 so no seeds were sown there.

 Though the nine kinds of Seeds had been sown nine times,
 and the Shoots had sprouted thick and strong,
 Xang Liang still hadn't seen them.
 But who went to look for them?

B: Wild Rat went to look;
 returning, he told Xang Liang:
 "Your Tree Shoots are growing well;
 they are strong and in good order."

 Though Xang Liang had sown the Sweet Gum Seeds,
 he still hadn't gone to look at them.
 Who went to see?

A: Paddy Rat went to see them;
 returning, he told Xang Liang:
 "Your Gum Shoots are really lovely,
 each of them is thick and strong!"
 Who climbed up a tree?

B: Magpie climbed up a tree,
 stood in the top of a shagbark tree,
 and "zha-zha-zha-zha" called to Xang Liang:
 "You sowed the Seeds on the hillsides,
 and then just stayed at home.
 The Tree Sprouts are growing like flowers in blossom,
 just like the duckweed in the fields;
 come quickly and take a look!"

 The Sweet Gum Shoots
 looked just like little kapok shoots;
 the Fir Shoots
 looked just like rice shoots;
 the Pine Shoots
 looked just like chestnut shoots.

 Bird Catching Day, on the Tenth Earthly Branch,[1]
 is good for bird hunting;

the Third and Fourth Earthly Branches are good
for settling lawsuits.[2]
Which day was chosen as best for planting the Trees?

A: On a cloudy day the Seedlings were taken to plant,
taken on a cloudy day so that the Trees could survive.

When the Tree Sprouts were pulled out,
they went along the mountain peaks
until coming to Green Water Pool.
Xang Liang's pool was really beautiful!
It had four sides and eight corners.
Who built the first side?

B: The first side was built by Wang Wu.
Who laid the second side?

A: The second side was laid by Ghe Lu.
Who built the third side?

B: The third side was built by Bang Xang Ye.
Who laid the fourth side?

A: The fourth side was laid by Wang Nang.
Those persons constructed Green Water Pool,
and that pool of Xang Liang's was really beautiful!
Who came to sink the well to divert the water to flood the pool?

B: There was Bo Jen Hsa;
he sank the well to flood the pool.
The pond had eight corners,
and the water was a beautiful clear green.

There was also Bo Jen Hsang;
he diverted the water to flood the pool.
The pond had four sides,
and the water was a beautiful dark blue.
Bo Jen Hsa and Bo Jen Hsang
were born by which mother?

A: Green moss in the pond made blue algae;
blue algae in the pond grew green moss,

green moss and blue algae gave birth to them.
Where were the Trees planted?

B: Since the Sweet Gums were trees used in the Ancestor sacrifices,
they were planted by the roadsides.³
The tall, pointed Firs were beautiful,
so they were planted in the mountain valleys
where their wide-spreading branches touched the Sky.
The Pines were tall and their needles beautiful,
so they were planted on the hillsides,
their branches spreading out straight;
when planted on the ridges,
Pines could grow as high as the summits.
Camphor Trees were planted beside the mountain roads,
so passersby could enjoy the shade.

There were also Nong Ji Trees.
They were planted in the mountain saddlebacks;
their rustling leaves made moving tunes,
bringing happiness to the young.⁴

Horse-chestnut and *Wubei* trees
were planted from the peaks to the feet of the mountains.
The Thorn Trees were strong and powerful,
so they were planted beside the hills.
Anyone daring to touch them would have their clothing torn.

The trees all had clothing to wear.
What did the Sweet Gum's clothing look like?

A: The Sweet Gums dressed in old-fashioned tunics;
the Firs were dressed like eels;
the Pines were dressed like pangolins.
Where were the Sweet Gums planted?

B: They were planted in the pool,
but the Gum Trees didn't like that place.
In one morning they shrank to one-tenth their size;
when they shriveled up, they were thrown away.
When planted on the pool banks,
the Sweet Gums were unhappy;
in one morning they shrank to one-tenth their size,

and when they shriveled up, they were thrown out.
Where was a suitable place to plant them?

A: They were planted beside the pond's source.
Early each morning they got plenty of water;
late each evening they got plenty of water.
The Sweet Gums were really happy;
in one morning they grew ninefold,
and after growing ninefold, they were cut.

If Jang Vang were planting trees,
what would he plant to accompany them?

B: He would plant cogon grass and winter grass as company.[5]
What did Xang Liang plant as company for the Sweet Gums?

A: He planted bamboo as company;
bamboo to accompany the Gum Trees as they grew;
it was so green at the Gum Trees' feet!
The Sweet Gums wanted bamboo as company:
The bamboos grew as high as the Sky,
so it was deep green at the Gum Trees' feet.

The Trees were all planted.
The Sweet Gums grew taller every day,
their branch tips reached straight to the clouds,
parting them to reveal the Sun.

Thus the myriad of mountain ranges could enjoy the shade,
and the myriad of valleys could relax in the coolness.

From where did the young man come?
And a girl from what family played with him?

B: A young man of Gha Liang's family came,
and a girl of Xang Liang's family played with him.
They courted beneath the Sweet Gum Tree.
Who else courted in the tree?

A: Eagles and magpies
screeched and cackled as they courted.

Cutting Down the Ancient Sweet Gum

A: Xang Liang planted the Trees beside the pool,
   then in the pool raised fish.
   One morning he put in nine pairs,
   but by evening he had lost nine fish.
   Where did the fish go?

B: Xang Liang's wife
   came every day to scold;
   every night she raised a ruckus,
   but never said for sure whom she was cursing.
   A boy of Niu Liang's family came,[1]
   and a girl of Ni Liang's family merrily played with him.[2]
   They courted beneath the Sweet Gum Tree,
   making the ground bare with their dancing.

   Xang Liang said to them:
   "I'm so good to you,
   letting you court beneath the Tree.
   Have a good time,
   but don't get any evil ideas!
   Don't sneak into my pond
   and make off with my fish fry!
   In the morning I put in nine pairs,
   and in the evening I lost nine fish;
   but I don't know where the fish went!"

   "We are a boy of the Niu Liang family,
   and a girl of the the Ni Liang family.
   Our courting has been proper.
   We haven't entered your pond;
   we haven't touched your fish;
   we don't know where your fish have gone!"

   Old Man Xang Liang looked the tree over carefully,
   and saw that the Sweet Gum's leaves
   were covered with fish scales.
   Xang Liang blew up,
   roaring like thunder:
   "I'm good to you;
   the fish need water to live,

and because of me you were planted.
How can you have such a bad heart as
to sneak into my fish pool
and steal off with my fish fry?"

"It is those Egrets and Wild Geese
whose wings are wide as bamboo mats,
whose legs are big as posts,
whose bills are thick as shinbones.
They came from the East,
flying here at night
and returning at dawn.
It is they who went into the fishpond
and stole off with your fish fry."

"If you bring those Egrets and Geese to me,
I'll let you go!"

"The Egrets and Geese can fly past nine villages in one night,
can visit sixteen places in all.
But where can I go to find them?
Though my leaves are covered with fish scales,
I have no mouth to eat fish fry.
If you excuse me, I live;
if you want to kill me, I die.
What else is there to say?"
After the Tree had pleaded its case,
who was asked from above?
What person was asked from below?

A: Jen Hsong Ghang was invited to come;[3]
   Wang Lu La was the cleverest.[4]
   Wang Lu La rode up on a male tiger
   and wanted to slaughter a cow when he came
   and kill a water buffalo to put in his house.
   After eating and drinking he had a great sleep
   and didn't go to plead the Tree's case.
   Who was invited from upstream?
   Who was invited from downstream?

B: Wang Lu La was invited,
   but Jen Hsong Ghang was more capable;
   he came riding a great stallion,

and after arriving butchered a fat hog,
and butchered a water buffalo to put in the village.
He said he would state the case after eating;
but who would have known that after eating
he would fall asleep?
So he didn't state the Tree's case.
Who was invited from above?
Who was invited from below?

A: Grandpa Xiu Niu was invited.
   He neither ate nor drank,
   he just pleaded the Tree's case.
   He brought five judgment sticks;[5]
   five sticks made of bamboo.
   "Whap-whap" he slapped the Sweet Gum's roots
   till the Sweet Gum was quaking.
   He declared:
   "You are the accomplice of thieves;
   because you are here, the thieves come.
   If you were not here, the thieves would leave.
   Anything else to say for yourself?"

The case was pleaded for several days;
though the Sweet Gum had an excuse,
it couldn't express itself clearly.
The Sweet Gum was to be cut,
so the Sweet Gum's voice trembled.

When the Sweet Gum was cut down,
it turned into a myriad of things.
The sawdust chips turned into fish;
the woodchips turned into honeybees;
the heartwood bore butterflies;
the buds turned into flying moths;
the knots turned into owls,
who at midnight call "hoo-hoo";
the leaves turned into swallows,
and turned into high-flying hawks and vultures;
there were also two forked branches
that wavered in the wind;
they turned into a Ji Wi Bird[6]
that came to sit on Butterfly's eggs.

Part IV
Song of Butterfly Mother

Introduction

In the last song, as the giant sweet gum transformed into myriad beings, a pair of its forked branches become the Ji Wi (Jix Wib) bird. This mythic bird eventually hatches the eggs laid by the matriarchal butterfly, Mai Bang (Mais Bangx), as reported in the *Song of Butterfly Mother*. This series of songs was performed in a different social context than the other ones in this book, and was sung only by ritual specialists during ceremonies in the cyclic buffalo sacrifices. The songs mention several aspects of these *bu mai* (*but mais*) sacrifices.

As we have seen in earlier songs, these aspects usually involve images of material objects that suggest certain social processes—in this case, ritual activities. These items include the *mo liang* (*mos liangx*), or hat, worn by the leader of the ceremonies (who must engage in numerous expensive and time-consuming activities and lives under the constraints of many taboos). Other prominent items are the black-and-white striped bamboo poles, one of which is erected in front of each family's home. At a predetermined time, the poles are brought to the ceremonial grounds, along with soot. The pole-bearers form two lines, letting the poles drop simultaneously at a signal. Then the pole-bearers cover themselves with soot so as to provide entertainment for the mythical ancestors. Such ceremonies are rarely held and constitute the least common and least familiar of the performance contexts in which the epics are performed.

In this series of songs, Mai Bang, or Mother Butterfly, who is also called Bang Lie (Bangx Lief) or Mai Lie (Mais Lief), emerges from the heartwood of the sweet gum. She makes love with the wave foam on the river and eventually gives birth to twelve eggs, hatched with the help of the Ji Wi bird and a few swipes of a god's knife. Jang Vang's egg is broken first, the breaking of his shell being regarded as the origin of mankind. The pieces of the eggshell become the role names of the organizers of the *bu mai* sacrifices.

Other beings born from Butterfly Mother's eggs are the Thunder God, a water dragon, a tiger, a snake, and an elephant. Each of the creatures has its umbilical cord cut. Jang Vang's cord is cut with a piece of bamboo, as is common in some cultures of south China and Southeast Asia. Raw copper is used to cut the dragon's cord, which is why dragons fear copper. In the end, a torch is used to cut the Thunder God's cord. The umbilical cords turn into various things: the dragon's into a soft-shelled turtle, Thunder God's into earth, and Jang Vang's into rice and mountain ferns. There is also mention of the origin of spirits (ghosts) and of the *gu* poison, derived from a lazy snake that crawled up a girl's carrying pole when she was fetching water. Finally, the leftover eggshells turn into dark clouds, while the membranes turn into clear skies. A last shard of shell turns into the sacrificial bowls, kept in the special shed used to house the drums between ceremonies.

Song of Butterfly Mother

The Birth of Butterfly Mother

A: We've come to sing "The Birth of Butterfly Mother,"
tell the ancient story of Mai Bang.[1]
As the Sweet Gum was transforming into myriad beings,
Butterfly was forming within the heartwood.
Who opened the door to let Butterfly out?

B: The King of the Moth-Borers opened the door
to let Butterfly out.
As the door opened,
Butterfly lightly turned her body, then raised her head.
Who flew from the East?

A: Woodpecker flew from the East.
His bill was thick as a leg;
he pecked at the wood, then ate the Moth-borers.

"Peck all you want on the roots and trunk,
but don't peck in the center.
Don't hurt the Butterfly's hands and feet!"
After another day, Butterfly was strong enough to come out.
When Mai Lie was born, her face was mottled;[2]
her tangled locks were like balls of hemp.
What did she use to wash her face?
What did she use to comb her hair?

B: Her fingernails grew long and sharp;
she used them to comb her hair;
rainwater washed the spots from her face.
Who was her elder aunt?
Who was her younger aunt?

A: Tree Root was her elder aunt;
   Tree Branch was her younger aunt.
   They brought milk to nurse her,
   and Butterfly grew strong.

   Three mornings after her birth,
   Butterfly was carried to Grandfather Xang Ghe's home.
   He named her Bang Xang.[3]

   When Butterfly was born, she wanted to eat fish.
   Where were the fish?

B: The fish were in the Ji Wi Pond,
   in ancient Ji Wi Pool,
   where there were fish galore!

   Ladybug was as big as a straw hat;
   Mud Eel was as thick as a grain crib post;
   Carp was the size of a crossbeam.
   These fish were given to her to eat,
   so Butterfly was happy.
   What was used to make paper umbrellas?[4]

A: The high mountains were the umbrella,
   covering the pots and stove.
   Beneath the umbrella the fish were boiled;
   Butterfly ate them happily,
   her heart sweet as honey.

   As Butterfly grew she wanted clothing.
   What kind of clothing did Butterfly wear?

B: Xang Ghe was born diligent;
   every day he was busy collecting manure,
   storing the manure by the stock pens.
   He split bamboo with a "crack"
   to weave into manure baskets.
   When he cut the bamboo, he got pulp for paper
   and took it to make clothing.
   When Butterfly put on her new clothing,
   she was so very happy!

As Butterfly matured she wanted to dress up.
Who made the bracelets and neck rings
to give Butterfly for courting?

A: Icicle made the neck rings
as well as bracelets to give Butterfly.
When Butterfly wore them courting,
she was really happy.

B: When Butterfly grew up she wanted a mate.
When the Ji Wi Bird came flickering about,
Butterfly went quickly to a treetop.
When the Ji Wi Bird flickered away,
Butterfly went up a mountain to find him.
But the Ji Wi Bird wouldn't play with her.

Some people are born at favorable times
and can easily find a mate;
but Butterfly was born at an unlucky time
so it was hard for her to find one.
With whom could she court?

A: She courted with Wave Foam;
they played beside a clear water pool;
in a muddy pool, fish and shrimp frolicked.

Butterfly and Wave Foam courted[5]
and later became a couple.
For how many years was Butterfly married?

B: She was married for twelve years
and laid the Twelve Eggs.

THE TWELVE EGGS

A: Now for the Twelve Eggs,
those ancient round coins.
Moth gave birth to caterpillar eggs
but afterward didn't care for them.
Who came to care for them?

B: Moth laid caterpillar eggs
   on a piece of rough paper,[1]
   then gave them to the Stove to care for.
   Each egg grew into a lovely caterpillar.
   Were they so lovely because the Stove
   had helped to care for them?

A: They had all eaten ashes,
   so in that way the Stove had helped them.

   Mantis' eggs were like wave foam.
   Since Mantis didn't hatch the eggs after birthing them,
   who came to help?

B: Cogon Grass came to help hatch them.
   The eggs were all well acquainted with the yellow earth,
   so Cogon Grass came to help them.

   Duck eggs were white with a greenish tint;
   when Duck laid the eggs, she didn't hatch them;
   instead, the eggs were given to Hen.
   In those ancient times,
   Hen had no way to cross the Nanhe River;[2]
   Duck carried her across on her back,
   so later Hen came to hatch Duck's eggs.

   Soft-shelled Turtle's eggs were like round-washed stones;
   after laying the eggs, Turtle didn't hatch them.
   The river sands helped warm the eggs,
   and the muddy waters helped to hatch them.
   When the water was high
   and floods washed away the sands,
   Turtle helped to hold the sands in place,[3]
   so the sand helped to hatch the eggs.

   Butterfly laid Vang La's Egg—laid it[4]
   but didn't hatch it!

   She let the Ji Wi Bird come to hatch it.
   Since she and the Bird were born by the same mother,
   the Ji Wi came to help her hatch the Egg.

The Ji Wi made a ball of its tail feathers,
then sat on Butterfly's Eggs
to hatch those ancient Ova.
Gha Vang made a nest and waited;[5]
Fu Fang brought grass to line it.
Rocky cliffs bordered the West side;
rocky cliffs bordered the East side,
so the Ji Wi was completely surrounded;
thus the Ji Wi could care for Butterfly's Eggs
and hatch those ancient Ova.

As for Vang La's nest,
if it were a *ge* bird's nest,
or a mountain sparrow's nest,
it would be shaped like a rice bowl,
the rim like that of a grain measure—
but that would be a sparrow's nest.
As for Vang La's nest,
what did that nest of the Ancient One look like?

A: The nest bottom was the wide Earth,
and the rim was the Sky.

If a hen were caring for her eggs,
that kindhearted mother
would bring stalks of rice straw
to shore up the nest,
putting it in the corners of the room to hatch her eggs.
As for the Ji Wi Bird,
where did it hatch the Eggs?

B: It hatched them at Nang Te's house,
hatched them in a place called Guduyin,[6]
for that place was really wide and open.

The Ji Wi's feathers were very full—
it had huge, wide wings—
so it dared come hatch Butterfly's Eggs,
hatch those ancient Ova.

The Ji Wi sat on the Eggs for three and a half years.
Three cold winters passed,

but even after three years the Bird could not hatch the Eggs.
Its feathers molted, so it dared sit no longer.
But after only a day, its feathers began to regrow,
and when the Ji Wi's feathers grew back completely,
it came again to hatch the Eggs.

The Ji Wi curled up its tail feathers,
and with its wings again full-fledged,
it dared to cover Butterfly's Eggs
to hatch those ancient Ova.
The Ji Wi sat on the nest for three years;
three years passed and the Ova still hadn't hatched.
The Bird's head became bald, without a feather.
After its feathers regrew,
the Ji Wi came again to hatch the Eggs.

The Ji Wi sat on the Eggs for three and a half years,
but none of them hatched.
The Ji Wi stamped its feet angrily;
finally, the Bird flew off.
It flew to a mountain valley
to find some grubs to eat.
It declared:
"All work's the same—why should I waste my time
doing that?"
What was it given so that it would hatch the Eggs?

A: It was given a hillside
where it could go to look for insects.

The Ji Wi sat on the eggs for three more years;
when the third spring came around,
the eggs still hadn't hatched.
The Ji Wi rose angrily
and, flapping its great wings, flew up nearly to the clouds.
It declared:
"Such hard work; I'm not doing that any longer!"
What was it given so it would return to hatch the Eggs?

B: It was given a great mountain forest.
The Ji Wi was so happy
that it returned to sit on the Eggs,
to hatch the Butterfly's Eggs.

After three and a half years the Eggs
still hadn't hatched,
and the Ji Wi wanted to fly away.
Who was it who wrote the words,
then stuffed them into Vang La's mouth?

A: Hsen Yen wrote the words,
then stuffed them into Vang La's mouth.
Vang La gurgled out some words,
then from inside the Egg called to the Ji Wi:
"Don't be in such a hurry to leave,
don't be in such a hurry!
Don't just run off and abandon me!
Don't be so lazy!
In one more night I'll hatch;
but if you neglect me, everything will be ruined;
everything will be ruined,
and not just for me—
there's also Dragon Brother,
and Uncle Thunder—
why, the whole family will be ruined!"

If it were chicks being hatched,
clever Mother would carry the eggs to the threshold,
then hold them up to the light at the crack in the door;
but that's how chicks are examined before they hatch.
As for Butterfly's Eggs,
who came to look at them?

B: Clever Hsen Yen
took the Eggs to the side of a mountain range,
then held them up for the Sun to watch.
From inside the Eggs a slight pecking could be heard,
as if the Eggs were going to hatch.
The next day they would certainly hatch,
then that good fellow Jang Vang would be born.

Vang La's eggshell was too thick—
only a god's knife could break it open.
With one swipe of the blade, the shell
was broken into several pieces:
One piece changed into Gha Hsang;

two pieces changed into Din Wang;
three pieces turned into Gha Liong;
there were still two small pieces,
and they turned into Gha Dang Hniang.[7]

When they were all born,
they slept together in the nest.
The white one was Gha Hva;[8]
the black one was Jang Vang;
the bright one was the Thunder God;
the yellow one was the Water Dragon;
the striped one was Tiger;
and the long one was Snake.
At the First Heavenly Branch Gha Hva was born;
at the Second Heavenly Branch Jang Vang was born;
at the Third Heavenly Branch Tiger was born;
at the fourth Heavenly Branch the Thunder God was born;
at the Fifth Heavenly Branch Water Dragon was born;
at the Sixth Heavenly Branch Snake was born.

Raw copper was used to cut Dragon's belly cord;[9]
a torch was used to cut the Thunder God's belly cord;[10]
when Cogon Grass was born, it cut itself.
Jang Vang's belly cord was cut with a piece of bamboo;[11]
Snake's belly cord was cut with a stone;
there was still that fierce old Tiger
who wouldn't let anyone do it,
so Wild Grass and Brush came to cut its cord.

Dragon's belly cord turned into a soft-shelled turtle,
which went to live deep in the waters;
the Thunder God's belly cord turned into earth,
then the Earth God went to live in the West side of the village.
Jang Vang's belly cord turned into rice,
and turned into mountain ferns.

There was also Tiger's belly cord—
it turned into wild cats, brush wolves, and foxes.
There was also Elephant's belly cord,[12]
which turned into Dliang Ge Ghosts,[13]
who in the middle of the night eat people's chickens.

When they were all born,
they lived in the nest;
one by one they took each other's hands;
one by one they helped each other up,
till everyone was standing.
*Who was the one who lay at the bottom of the pond,
so spoiled he was unwilling to get up?*

A: That old Snake was lying on the bottom of the pond,
so spoiled he wasn't willing to get up.
When a girl went to fetch water,
she used her carrying pole to poke him;
Snake crawled up the pole,
then went with the girl back home.
Thus, Father got the Dliang Ge Ghosts,
and Mother got the Gu Poison—[14]
that's how the Ghosts got here;
that's how the Gu Poison got here.

That old fellow Gu Vang[15]
huffed up to the edge of the nest,
then standing at the side laughed out:
"I'm all by myself, and it's great—
too bad you're all in there together!"
*When everybody came down from the nest,
what did the eggshells become?*

B: The eggshells became dark clouds;
the egg membranes became clear skies.
There was still a bad egg—
after another year,
it became a Demon,
a Demon that eats up sows.[16]
*They had all been born,
but what did the nest become later?*

A: It became Ve Khang.[17]
There was still a half of a bit of eggshell left.
What did it become later?

B: It was put into the Drum Shed,
then later became a Sacrificial Bowl.[18]

THE BROTHERS DIVIDE[1]

A: A family with no children is an unhappy family,
   but if the children are too many, it's chaos.
   If seven sisters share only one spinning wheel,
   the younger ones will be upset when the elder ones spin;
   the elder ones will grab it when the younger ones spin.
   When crocks and pots and urns are dropped,
   everything inside spills out.

   If seven brothers share only one knife,
   the younger ones will protest when the elder ones use it;
   the elder ones will want it when the younger ones use it.
   They will struggle till the ridgepole snaps,
   till the walls are ready to collapse,
   till the door planks topple and the eldest brothers are hurt.

   Jang Vang was really clever.
   He went out and cried to everyone:
   "What's the big fuss inside?
   Hurry out and find some food,
   find some meat and we'll eat!"

   When no one listened to him,
   Jang Vang started a fire.
   Front and back, the house was encircled by flames,
   and dense black clouds of smoke rose up.
   Everyone was running about for their lives,
   and all the brothers and sisters ran off in every direction—
   you couldn't have found them if you had wanted to.

   Clever Jang Vang
   cried out to them all:
   "Don't worry, don't worry;
   sit down and listen to me—
   let's go to Nantu;
   Du Yen's house is really huge."

   They went to Nantu,
   where Water Dragon found a good house,
   and the Thunder God found a very spacious house.

But Jang Vang's house was a shack.
Every day he climbed the mountains to cut soft cotton bamboo,
which he took to weave walls to keep out the wet.
Jang Vang went to the mountains to cut bamboo.
But what was he really doing?
Who was told to go and find out?

B: Housefly was told to go and see.
Housefly returned
and, waving his hands and feet, said:
"Jang Vang was doing this and doing that;
he's busy gathering moxa;
I'm afraid he wants to burn down some houses again."

Each and every one of the brothers wanted to be head:
Water Dragon said, "I'm the longest."
The Thunder God said, "I'm the heaviest."
Tiger said, "I'm the fiercest."
Jang Vang said, "I'm the cleverest."

Each and every one wanted to be head.
How was it decided to whom everyone would listen?

A: Everyone agreed to cross a bridge,
cross the Gold Bridge to test their weights,
and that bridge was built up in the Sky.
Whoever was the heaviest would become the head.

Water Dragon was first to cross.
When he went across, the bridge didn't move.

The Thunder God was told to cross.
When he crossed, the bridge swayed lightly.
Tiger was told to cross.
When he went across, the bridge didn't even creak.
They had all crossed, when Jang Vang said:
"I'm going to cross;
all of you watch carefully!"

Clever Jang Vang
went down the path to the bridge,
carrying a *ge* bird in the corner of his shirt.

He'd take a step, then pinch the bird—
the bird would cry out;
he'd take two steps, then pinch the bird—
the bird would cry out.
Everyone heard the squawks and said:
"When we went across, the bridge didn't move;
but when Jang Vang crossed, the bridge nearly broke—
since the Sky Bridge was creaking so much,
let's call Jang Vang Elder Brother"!

When sparrows are too many, they overflow the nest;
when people are too many, they crowd the land—
there is no place for fire pits,
no place for grain-husking treadles.
Everyone spread out;
one in each direction.

The living places had to be divided,
and that required a scale.
What was used as a measure?

B: A torch was tied to Tiger's tail;
pine sap was lighted on Green Snake's head;
getting fire to the five hills and six stream banks—
those were the places that were divided.
The flatlands were divided into paddies;
the hills were dug up into soil.
Afterward, the paddies were plowed to raise crops
to support the parents.

Water Dragon was given a deep pool,
a pool nine thousand feet deep,
and Water Dragon lived there in its depths.
What did he use to repair the pool?

A: He used his horns to repair it;
after repairing the pool, he lived there.
When Water Dragon left for the deep pool,
the way was so dark he could hardly walk.
Who came to light his way?

B: Glow Worms came to light some pine oil,

so on both hillsides the lamps glowed,
so brightly that the Dragon could easily go.

When the Dragon went, he forgot to take something.
What did he forget?

A: He forgot some precious things,
those valuables handed down from the Ancestors.
Who went out to look for them?

B: Glow Worms helped to carry them;
when the Dragon got them, he put them in his mouth.

Tiger was given a mountain forest,
then entered that forest.
Snake was given a rocky lair,
then slithered inside.

Centipede was given the legs of grain cribs,
then went into the legs.
What place was Jang Vang given?

A: He was given the Ancestors' fields,
and lived in the ancient house foundations of the first gods.
The fields and orchards weren't cultivated—
only wild grasses grew;
the houses were vacant and full of brambles.
What did Jang Vang use to repair them?

B: He used a sharp knife to repair them.
The Sun King lighted his lamp,
lit the pine oil so it glowed brightly,
lighting his way back home.
When Jang Vang went, he forgot something.
What did he forget?

A: He forgot to bring his hoe to open the wilds.
Who took it to him?

B: Niang Ni took it to him.
The Thunder God was given the Western Sky,
given that region of high clouds.
What did he use to repair it?

A: He used a gong and a drum to repair it,
and after repairing it, he lived there.

When the Thunder God went to the Sky,
Grandpa Earth lighted a lamp,
took bright pine torches to light the way.
When Thunder God went, he forgot something.
What did he forget?

B: He forgot his silk chair.
Who took it to him?

A: Grandpa Earth took it to him;
he carried the chair,
running along behind the Thunder God.[2]

Jang Vang was the eldest brother,
and the Thunder God was a younger brother.
When the Thunder God wanted to go to the Sky,
he called over and over again to Jang Vang:
"Elder Brother, what road do I take to the Sky?"

In Winter, snow falls;
in the seventh month, it hails;
the floodwaters surge from the West,
surge forth full of driftwood and tangled grass.
Jang Vang took such fuel to burn,
and dark swirls of smoke curled up to the clouds;
Jang Vang called in a high voice:
"You may follow the smoke!"

Jang Vang was the eldest brother,
and Water Dragon was a younger brother.
Water Dragon wanted to go deep into the pool,
that pool was nine thousand feet deep.
He called over and over to Jang Vang:
"The waters flow from West to East—
follow the flowing waters!"

When the Thunder God left, he said to Jang Vang:
"When I go you should work hard.
Open the fields to support Mother—

you can't let Mother starve to death!
If Mother starves to death, I'll disown you."

Jang Vang replied to the Thunder God:
"When you get to the sky don't be lazy—
let down rain while I am plowing;
that way Mother won't starve to death."

When the Thunder God went to the Sky,
he didn't let down the rain;
Jang Vang wanted the god to return to find out the reason.
The Thunder God lowered his head from the Sky,
saying to Jang Vang:
"The water is dammed up in the West;
you go and release it if you want to use it—
you can't just sit around waiting for rain."

When the Thunder God went to the Sky,
he had advised the Water Dragon:
"If you follow the rivers,
don't cross any mountains
and trespass on other people's land;
for if I find out, it will be bad for you!"

When the Thunder God got to the Sky he had nothing to do,
so he sat around taking charge of affairs on Earth.
What did he take as a model for his booming voice?

B: In the early years when the Pillars of the Sky were erected,
    a big hammer was left over.
    The Thunder God took it to rule over Earth,
    scaring everyone witless.
    There was also the shimmering lightning.
    What was it modeled after?

A: In the early years, when the Sky Pillars were being made,
    the bellows blew "whew-whew"
    and the golden sparks crackled;
    lightning was made that way.

    There was also the Thunder God's hat.
    What was it made of?

B: In the ancient times, when Bang Xang Ye died,
every part of him changed into something—
all except his nose,
which changed into the Thunder God's hat;
and the Thunder God wore it when looking into things.

The Thunder God wore richly embroidered clothing.[3]
What clever person helped to sew it?

A: Ni Wo Niang was the clever one
who helped embroider the clothing
that the Thunder God wore when taking charge of things.

Other families have only one set of scales,
but the Thunder God had three steelyards
that he used when looking into people's affairs.
The first he used to settle legal disputes;
the second he put on the West side of the Sky
to use when checking people's fields
to make sure things on Earth didn't get out of order;
the third he put on the grain measure—
Persons with their hearts in the wrong place—
those who weigh things in their favor,
will have their heads struck
by the Thunder God.[4]

Killing the Centipede

A: *What place was Jang Vang given?*

B: He received the Ancestors' ancient fields
and lived in the old-time house foundations.
The fields grew trees instead of crops,
and the houses were empty, filled only with brambles.
Jang Vang was given Zhanxi,[1]
so he returned there.

Some people are too lazy
and won't do what they should.
Jang Vang worked very hard;
every day he worked to open the fields.

He opened paddies on the high mountain peaks,
and dug dirt on the steep mountain slopes;
he opened much wild land,
and opened land all the way to distant Zhanxi.

Jang Vang opened the mountains:
After opening the East, he went to open the West;
as he dug to the corners of the paddies,
he met Centipede.

Centipede said to Jang Vang:
"When you open land, you may do so only in the East;
don't clear my lands here in the West.
The West is my cow pen;
the West is my water buffalo pen.
There is also my father's grave—
my father is buried over there."

Jang Vang was busily working
and paid no attention to anyone's words;
he opened the fields Westward,
and dug up Centipede's graves—
that was the root of the trouble.

Each night Centipede sharpened his teeth;
each day Jang Vang sharpened his knife.
They agreed to meet in the forest to fight.

Centipede went early and waited,
but Jang Vang didn't come;
so things were left unsettled.

The second time, they arranged to meet on the plains.
Centipede came,
but Jang Vang didn't come;
so things were left unsettled.
Later on, where did they agree to meet?

A: They agreed to meet on the treacherous cliff tops.
  Centipede really went,
  but Jang Vang didn't come;
  so things were left unsettled.

In Winter the skies are snowy;
in the seventh month hail falls—
the floodwaters surge from the west,
surging full of driftwood and tangled grass.
Jang Vang went to the riverside
and collected driftwood for firewood.
Centipede crouched on some wood
and flowed along with the current.
Jang Vang mistook Centipede for a piece of driftwood
and used his hand to pick it up;
he used his feet to carry it.
Centipede bit him three times.
Jang Vang's whole body became blistered,
and he flopped down on the riverbank.

Old Man Yu Dang was kindhearted;
he hurried home from the riverbank
and told his wife:
"Centipede has bitten Jang Vang's foot;
hurry and carry him home."
What sort of medicine is put on centipede bites?
What sort of water is used as a rinse?

B: "Catch a louse to come suck;
use lice-water as a rinse."[2]
Rinsed away with lice-water,
Centipede's poison was gone,
and Jang Vang's foot got better.

Jang Vang's little sister was kindhearted;
when she heard her brother was sick,
she carried a ham hock
and brought a bundle of fresh fish.
She brought chicken and duck as well,
when she went to see Jang Vang.
Jang Vang was just recovering from his illness,
but seeing all the food, he became too greedy.
He stuffed himself so full
that his wounds swelled up again,[3]
swelled till they were the size of crocks—
they were horrible to see.

Centipede was too poisonous.
He harmed people too often;
he had to be captured,
otherwise, he would hurt people again.
Who went to capture him?

A: Ghe Bo and Ghe Hxu
went East on the river and set a fish trap.
Centipede flowed down river, right into the trap.

Some people are just too lazy—
they won't do what they should.
Jang Vang worked very hard,
digging the dirt on the steep hillsides;
on the flatlands he made fields.
He used his sleeve as a scoop,
his fingers as rake tines,
and an ox horn as a spike.

When Jang Vang went to open the hillsides,
he left for home at dusk.
He placed his scoop on the field dike,
and placed his spike beside the spillway.

Jang Vang went to open the mountains.
When the East was cleared, he went West;
as he dug to the corners of the paddies,
he uncovered a great piece of rock.
The rock was so big,
Jang Vang couldn't dig it out;
so he just left it there in the paddy,
where later it was a good place to set lunch baskets.

Jang Vang opened the paddies;
inside, rice seedlings were planted.
On the banks, hemp was planted—
hemp three armspans tall.
When making sacrifices to the Ancestors,
the hemp is used to make the sacrificial hats,[4]
worn for Butterfly to see.
When Butterfly sees them, she is very happy:
"My Grandsons are so hardworking!"

Jang Vang opened the paddies,
planting the rice seedlings inside.
On the banks he planted bamboo;
the bamboo shoots were three armspans long.
Why was the bamboo grown?

B: It was kept to make sacrificial poles:[5]
When decorated they are so lovely,
that when Butterfly sees them, she is very happy,
saying, "My Grandsons are really capable!"

As the paddies were opened, roads had to be left;
roads for people to race horses,
roads for people to carry sedan chairs.
As the paddies were opened, brooks had to be left;
brooks for water to flow in,
water that can be channeled into the paddies,
where it is good for raising fish.

There was still a mountain slope.
Why was it left?

A: It was left to dry grain upon.
When other people open land and come upon a spring,
they mark it with a piece of grass
so that the field can be laid out properly;
then they will dig wells to divert the water for irrigation.
What did Jang Vang use as a marker
when he opened the fields and came upon a spring?

B: He scattered a bunch of duckweed.
The duckweed became greener and greener
and filled up the spring,
awaiting the building of the paddies,
awaiting the wells dug to feed the paddies.

Jang Vang cleared the hillsides.
The paddies were nearly all opened,
and only one little hill was left.
The host brought a duck;
the guest brought a jug of wine.
They worked together to dig up the little hill.
After the little hill was all dug up

and the paddies built,
the duck was killed and the wine drunk in celebration.⁶

Honeybee was hungry,
so he came to eat and drink with Jang Vang;
drinking dry a jug of wine,
eating up a whole duck,
Honeybee was full.
He then taught Jang Vang to dance;
Jang Vang learned to dance from Honeybee.

Jang Vang cleared the mountain slopes
and the paddies were nearly done.
What were the foundations made of?

A: They were made of wood.
   What were the walls made of?

B: They were made of stone.
   When the paddy walls were finished,
   yellow earth was daubed inside.
   The long paddy walls
   surrounding the deep paddy water—
   so lovely to behold.

   Jang Vang cleared the mountain slopes
   by the middle of the second month,
   he carried big baskets home,
   returning home to celebrate New Year's.
   Why did Jang Vang want to celebrate New Year's?

A: Because after New Year's, trees and flowers start to grow.
   Why did Jang Vang want to celebrate the festival?

B: Because after the festival the flowers blossom.
   When flowers see the festival approaching,
   they all blossom.
   When Spring sees the New Year,
   Spring returns.
   Flowers blossom on the tree branches;
   when Spring comes, the rivers gurgle
   to awaken the flowers and grasses.
   When the flowers and grasses awaken,

the mountains are filled with green.
Who got up the earliest?

A: Girls got up the earliest
and opened the door to look:
Clouds were floating all over the Sky—
clouds white as cotton bolls,
white as froth on the waves—
floating in the Sky, high and low,
it would soon be dawn.
The girls returned home
and called Jang Vang to get up
to go cut grass for the livestock.

Jang Vang took a clasp knife
and in two or three steps was on the mountainsides,
where he cut a bundle of grass.
When he returned home
he fed his water buffalo till it was full,
then afterward led it to plow the paddies.
When the water buffalo mounted the paddy dikes,
when the water buffalo mounted the paddy walls,
it looked at the dark green water,
and the water seemed too deep—
so the buffalo was afraid to enter the paddy.
Clever Jang Vang stretched out his arms longer and longer,
rolled up his pant legs higher and higher;
and just like a little frog,
dived into the water.
He said to the water buffalo:
"The water comes up only to my ankles,
it's not even as deep as my knees.
What are you afraid of?
Hurry on down here!"

When the water buffalo saw this,
it jumped into the water,
and huffed along as it drew the plow.

When Jang Vang was plowing the paddies,
Woodpecker flew from the East.
Woodpecker ate moth larvae,

and with a "dong-dong" noise
pecked into the hollow trees.
When the girls heard it,
they ran quickly to call Jang Vang:
"It seems that Mother's festival has arrived,
it sounds like the sound of Mother's drum.
Let's hurry and see!"

Jang Vang quit plowing,
left the buffalo in the middle of the paddy,
then ran up on the banks to dance the drum dance.
As the drum sounded "dong-dong,"
he danced forward three steps.
He could dance, but he didn't know how to turn;
after he learned to turn, he still couldn't circle.

That good swimmer, Waterbug, taught him to turn;
flying Honeybee taught him to circle.
Jang Vang learned the drum dance,
learned it better and better.
He twisted like a waterbug
and moved like a honeybee.
It is said the best drum dances are held
during sacrifices at Nanjiang,[7]
but Jang Vang danced even better than those.

Woodpecker was beating a drum,
"dong-dong, dong-dong."
Jang Vang danced on the paddy walls,
the buffalo danced in the paddy fields,
tail dancing between its legs;
dancing till they forgot they were tired.
The buffalo whip heard the drum sound
and also wanted to come dance,
so it brought the buffalo to the dance ground;
the mosquitoes were hovering around,
surrounding the buffalo's head,
all dancing for joy.
There was also a harrow,
circling all about the paddy field,
dancing so much that waves kicked up.
Everyone was dancing;
everyone was singing.

SEARCHING FOR THE SACRIFICIAL DRUMS

A: Some people are idle by nature.
 Even if they have something to do,
 they are too lazy to do it.
 Jang Vang naturally liked to make paddies,
 and to go to the high mountains to open land;
 he made paddies at Horse Saddle Mountain,
 all the way to Zhanxi district.

 By the time the eighth month was half gone,
 Jang Vang had harvested three big storehouses of grain;
 six grain cribs beside the village were completely filled.[1]

 The oxen's eyes were red and their bodies strong;
 the pigs were fat as door planks;
 the fish in the paddies were big as crossbeams;
 the babies were all plump as could be,
 just like melons.

 Everyone discussed making sacrifices to the Parents,
 making sacrifices to that ancient Gho Do:[2]
 He made us wealthier;
 he let everyone prosper.

 "For an Ancestor sacrifice a wooden drum is needed;
 everyone hurry to look for one!"

 The double drums were taken to invite the relatives;[3]
 brothers-in-law and uncles were invited.
 Li was invited;[4]
 Liong was also asked to come.
 When Li came, he brought something;
 when Liong came, he carried something.
 Li brought a big knife;
 Liong carried a long sword.

 Liong got up early to set up the pot;
 Jang got up early to light the fire
 for hot water to wash their faces.
 After washing, they put on their neck rings;

after donning their neck rings, they put on dove feathers.⁵
This was their attire for seeking the drum.

As the two sat and stirred up the ashes,
and stood to put the horse halters in order,
little children used their mouths as drums,
as cymbals, to rouse the village:
"Is everything ready yet?
If it's all done, let's go quickly!
The drum is in the Jiuli Mountain Forest;
let's quickly go to find it!"

Walking out the gate, to the corner of the house,
they saw a white chicken sacrificing to the Ancestors,
and heard a drum making a good sound.⁶
Liong Hlie tried to beat the drum;
Jang Vang tried to dance.
Liong Hlie beat the drum, but not smoothly;
Jang Vang danced, but was out of step.
The sound was that of the later generation's cymbals,
not the Ancestors' drum.
The first people's drum was in Jiuli Forest:
"Let's hurry to find it!"

Arriving at the corner of the pond,
they saw a fish sacrificing to the Ancestors,
and a drum was making a good sound.⁷
Liong Hlie tried to beat the drum;
Jang Vang tried to dance.
Liong Hlie beat the drum, but not smoothly;
Jang Vang danced, but was out of step.
These were the cymbals of the later generations,
not the Ancestors' drum;
the first people's drum was in the Jiuli Forest:
"Let's hurry and find it!"

Arriving at the paddy banks,
they saw a frog sacrificing to the Ancestors
and a drum making a good sound.⁸
Liong Hlie tried to beat the drum;
Jang Vang tried to dance.
Liong Hlie beat the drum, but not smoothly;

Jang Vang danced, but was out of step.
These were the cymbals of the later generations,
not the Ancestors' drum.
The Ancestors' drum was in Jiuli Forest:
"Let's hurry to find it!"

Arriving at Bamboo Mountain
they saw five bamboo gardens
and six bamboo forests planted long ago.
Why did Jang Vang plant them?

B: The bamboos were split, then plaited into grain-drying ovens,
now used to dry rice.
After twelve years,
they were used to dry rice for grinding into *baba* cakes
for the Ancestors.

Arriving at Qinggang Bluff,
they saw five *qinggang* forests
and six stretches of those hardwoods, planted long ago.
Why did Jang Vang plant them?

A: They were planted to make *baba* moulds,
used to make *baba* cakes for a New Year's Festival,
after twelve years,
made for an Ancestor sacrifice.

Arriving at the Sweet Gum Mountains,
they saw five Sweet Gum forests
and six stretches of Sweet Gums planted long ago.
Why did Jang Vang plant them?

B: They were used to lash on the Ox's horns,
to let the horns accompany Butterfly,[9]
so today we can prosper and grow rich.

Arriving at Horse Chestnut Forest,
they saw five forests of chestnuts
and six stretches of chestnuts planted long ago.
Why did Jang Vang plant them?

A: They were planted for making cattle pens;
used to keep draft oxen.

After twelve years
the pens were used to hold the sacrificial oxen.

Arriving at Tea Mountain,
they saw five tea gardens,
and tea trees and flowering bushes were planted everywhere.
Why did Jang Vang plant the tea trees?

B: When the Ancestors return,
tea is boiled for them to drink.
The Ancestors laugh happily
and give us happy lives,
much wealth, and many descendants.

Walking onward,
they arrived at Jiuli Forest
and found a good tree for making a drum.
What was used as a marker?

A: If knives or axes had been used for marking,
the cuts would later heal, and moss would cover them.
A stone had to be left as a marker.

They arrived at Jiuli Forest.
Each tree grew so nicely:
The trunks were straight and tall,
and the limbs beautiful.
Which one did Jang Vang choose?

B: Jang Vang chose the straightest one:
The branches stretched out widely and the leaves were full;
the crown was round as a paper umbrella,
just like the wings of a goose.
Each tree grew so nicely.
But which one did Jang Vang choose?

A: Jang Vang chose that tree,
the one with the branches growing into the clouds.
Its branches were like a bamboo hat,
and the top seemed the same as a duck wing.
That was the tree chosen to make the drum;
to make the drum for sacrificing to the Parents.

Jang Vang was called to make the first cut;
so Jang Vang cut first.
Liong Hlie was called to take a cut,
and Liong Hlie did so.
If the tree were allowed to fall toward the bluffs,
it might have crushed other people's grain;
if it were allowed to fall toward the mountain streams,
it might have hurt the paddy crops.
"Let it fall to the East;
falling to the East is best!"[10]

The tree was cut down,
then taken to the flatlands.
It was used to make a drum
so everyone could dance.
When everyone danced forward,
the wild pig danced backward
and stepped on Jang Vang's gown;
Jang Vang was very angry,
and cut the pig with his knife.

SEARCHING FOR THE SACRIFICIAL OX

A: The wooden drum was found,
   but it was still necessary to find an ox.
   Only after finding an ox
   could an Ancestor sacrifice be held.
   Let's look at the search for the Ox.
   Where did they go to look for it?

B: The Ox ran to the East,
   so it had to be followed and found in the East.

   Boys were told to tend the geese;
   girls were told to pasture the oxen.
   Who came from the East?

A: Liong Hlie came from the East,
   wanting to court with the girls.
   In one hand he carried a *lusheng* to play;
   in the other hand he carried a tree leaf to blow;

the songs of the *lusheng* and the tunes of the leaves
were soft and soothing;
the girls cared only for courting,
forgetting to look after their oxen.
So the oxen followed the flowing water,
wanting to go to the home of the waters and the Sun,
to that rich, ancient home of the waters.

Horse left the second month.
What did he say when he left?

B: Horse said to all the saddle-packs:
"You wait for me here;
I'm going East.
I'm going to pack cotton bales;
I'm going to transport silks and satins,
bring them to the West
to make an offering to our Butterfly,
so everyone will prosper."

When the Ox went,
Hemp was just beginning to sprout.
What did the Ox say to it?

A: "When I go East, you should all grow quickly;
grow thick and strong.
I'm going East to have the hair whorls painted
on my shoulders;
I'm going East to have my horns fastened on.[1]
Wait till I come back to the West,
I'll twist you into ropes,
then we'll make an offering to Butterfly Mother together,
and everyone will prosper."

There was also a big fat Pig.[2]
He went East to have his hair whorls painted on.
When he left,
the Bamboo Shoots had just started to grow.
What did he say to them?

B: He said to the Shoots:
"While I'm gone, grow up quickly;

I'm going East to be decorated,
to be painted with hair whorls, then return to the West.
I'll use you as offering poles,
and together we'll make offerings to the Parents,
and everyone will be prosperous."

When the Yellow Cow went East,
Spring tilling had just begun to get busy.
What did he say?

A: He said to the *Gha Gang* tree:
"I'm going East to be decorated,
to have my horns fastened on and
be painted with whorls.
When I return to the East,
I'll use you as a plow-shaft
as we two till the fields;
we'll bring in nine big cribs of rice
to use in an Ancestor Sacrifice to the Parents;
after sacrificing to Butterfly Mother, we'll prosper."

The Ox went to the East.
What family's things did he eat in the bamboo garden?

B: He ate the leaves of the Cotton Bamboo,
and the Bamboo was very angry.
The Ox said to it:
"Don't be angry; don't be upset!
Together we'll make a sacrifice to the Ancestors.
We'll split you into strips
and use you to fasten the ox horns to the center post;
to accompany Butterfly Mother is a great honor."

The Ox followed the river water,
wanting to go to the hometown of the waters and the Sun,
that prosperous, ancient, watery hometown.[3]
He passed the foot of another village,
and that place had a crock of indigo.
The Ox trampled over it,
and a girl of those people became angry.
She went to the cliff tops,
then stood there and shouted:

"This isn't your place.
Why do you want to come East?"

"Don't be angry; don't be upset!
When it's time to make a sacrifice to the Ancestors,
that wooden bucket won't be left out!"
Later, when making an Ancestor Sacrifice,
only one bucket was needed;
a bucket with nine bands on it,
used to carry water to raise the sacrificial fish.[4]

The Ox wanted to go East,
wanted to go to the hometown of the waters and the Sun,
that prosperous, ancient, watery hometown.
He went below the long paddies
and ate White Gum's things;
White Gum was very angry.

"Don't be angry; don't be upset.
You won't be left out of the Ancestor Sacrifice!"
Later, when making sacrifices to Butterfly Mother,
White Gum was used to make the yoke
to lead the sacrificial bull to the flatlands.

The Ox wanted to go East,
wanted to go to the hometown of the waters and the Sun,
that prosperous, ancient, watery hometown.
Arriving at the foot of a cliff,
Kind-hearted Banana was building a house at the foot of the cliff,
building a house for the Ox to live in—
where the Ox spent the night, then left.

Walking onward, onward,
arriving at a river pool,
the Ox trampled on Fish's house,
and Fish was angry.

"Don't be angry; don't be upset.
We'll make an Ancestor Sacrifice together!"

Later, when making an Ancestor Sacrifice,
three fish were needed.

The Ox wanted to go East,
wanted to go to the hometown of the waters and the Sun,
that prosperous, ancient, watery hometown.
Arriving at the edge of a mountain forest,
he trampled on Squirrel's home,
and Squirrel was angry.

"Don't be angry; don't be upset.
You won't be left out of the Ancestor Sacrifice!"
Later, when making Ancestor Sacrifices,
a squirrel was needed.[5]

The Ox wanted to go East,
wanted to go to the hometown of the waters and the Sun,
that prosperous, ancient, watery hometown.
Arriving at Cogon Grass Bluff,
he trampled on Pheasant's home,
and Pheasant was angry.

"Don't be angry; don't be upset.
The Ancestor Sacrifice will include you!"
Later, when making Ancestor Sacrifices,
some pheasant plumes had to be
put in the crowns of the sacrificial hats.
The hats had to be well decorated,
so Butterfly Mother would be happy when seeing them.

The Ox followed the flowing water.
He wanted to go to the hometown of the waters and Sun,
that prosperous, ancient, watery hometown.
Onward, walking onward,
on to Butterfly Mother's home.
Who came to paint the hair whorls upon him?
Who came to fasten on his horns?

A: Uncle Bang Xang Ye's family had a good pond.
   The Ox went to bathe,
   rolling back and forth,
   so that the pond water sent out whorl upon whorl.
   Thus the whorls were printed on the Ox's body;
   his four legs had a whorl on each shoulder.
   That's how the Ox got his hair whorls.

Butterfly Mother fastened on his horns;
fastened the two horns above the Ox's eyes.
The Ox got his horns and whorls,
then happily returned to the West.
He returned to make a sacrifice to Butterfly Mother,
a sacrifice to the Ancestors for prosperity.

Returning home, he still didn't have cloven hooves;
returning home, he still didn't have a wide mouth.
On the rocky mountains,
on the red-pebbled bluffs,
the sharp stones cut his feet,
and his feet became cloven;
the sharp cogon grass sliced across his mouth,
and his mouth became wide.

Without his horns he couldn't return;
only after getting his horns did he return.
When the Ox left he had no clothing,
and his back was bare as could be.
Crossing the piney mountains,
pine needles dropped on his back
and became clothing for the Ox to wear;
then he happily returned to the West.

Walking Westward—
at Nanmendang and Nanga E,[6]
whose house did he trample on?

B: He trampled on Crab's home.
Crab was angry:
"Wait a few years,
then I'll get even with you!"

Coming Westward,
the ox arrived at Jang Vang's home.

Today, when oxen are put on the flatlands,
and see each other, they fight.
Why is this?

A: Once, two oxen competed
to grab a single stalk of cogon grass;

because of that,
when they meet, they fight.

SEARCHING FOR THE SACRIFICIAL VESTMENTS

A: The Ox returned to his home,
but he still had no sacrificial vest,[1]
and still had no sacrificial hat.[2]
How could he make an offering to the Ancestors?

"Hurry and find the Vestments;
hurry and find the Hats!"
Where did the Vestments live?
Where did the Hats live?

B: The Vestments lived in the Han people's homes;
the Hats lived in the Han people's homes.

"Go to the Guests' home to find the Vestments!"

Other people's homes had only one girl;
but Jang Vang's home had nine girls.
All the nine girls were married.
The eldest was called A Niang,
and she married Yu Liong.
This Yu Liong,
where did he live?

A: His family lived at Wenglao.[3]
What gifts did he owe Jang Vang?

B: At the Six Month's Festival,[4]
A Niang visited her parents' home
to get Mother's bamboo pole to dry clothes on;
but she took an offering pole by mistake.
At Ancestor Sacrifices she has to bring the offering poles,
bring them back to her parents' home.

The second sister was called A Ni,
and she married Yu Li;

Yu Li took her in marriage.
This Yu Li,
where was he from?

A: He was from Wenglao.
What gifts did he owe Jang Vang?

B: In the sixth month they feasted;
A Ni visited her parents' home
to get Mother's indigo crock.
That indigo crock was at the foot of the village,
but she mistakenly took the brine vat;
at Ancestor Sacrifices,
she must come to look after the brine.

The third sister was called A Mai,
and she married Yu Hniang.
This Yu Hniang,
where was he from?

A: He was from Wenglao.
What was his mistake?

B: When A Mai visited her parents' home,
she took two bowls;
she took away two plates for her guests,
but she took the sacrificial bowls by mistake.
At Ancestor offerings
she must come to look after the sacrificial bowls.

The fourth sister was called A Lie,
and she married Yu Ve.
This Yu Ve,
what village was he from?

A: His family lived at Ong Lo Vang Niu;[5]
his family lived at Dli Dong Bi Di.
What was his mistake?

B: When A Lie visited her parents' home,
she borrowed a shuttle from her mother
because she wanted to work her loom,

but she took a *lusheng* by mistake.
At Ancestor Sacrifices
she must come to look after the *lusheng*s.

The fifth sister was called A Yu,
and she married Yu Ju.
This Yu Ju,
where did he come from?

A: He came from Ong Lo Vang Niu;
he came from Dli Dang Bi Di.
What did he owe Jang Vang?

B: When others return home, it takes a whole season,
but when A Yu returned home it took three years.
The road was too long,
and she birthed a child at her parents' home.
She carried a ham hock and a duck
for a sacrifice to the Ancestors;
and thus everyone prospered.[6]

The sixth sister was called A Gi,
and she was born fair and beautiful,
but she was unwilling to marry suitable relatives[7]
nor friends.
Instead, she married Liong Tong,
then climbed the high cliffs to live happily.
This Liong Tong made what mistake?

A: His family lived in Je Hsang Vang,
and every night he came to dally with A Gi
and cheated her away.
At times for making sacrifices to the Ancestors,
he comes as the crier
walking through the villages
and spreading the word around.[8]

The seventh sister was called A Diu.[9]
She didn't know how to sing,
and she didn't know how to embroider.[10]
Thinking that no one would want to marry such a girl,
her mother grew very sad.

Later, the girl was sent to a Han family
who used her as a maidservant;
then she became the son's wife.

The eighth sister, A Ge,
was promised to a man who did not satisfy her;
she would rather have died than go to his family.
She filed a complaint and made a stir,
forcing her parents to sell several paddies
to cover court costs.
Later she became a Han's wife
and finally calmed down.

The ninth sister was called A Ju;
her husband-to-be was no good, and she wouldn't marry him;
she didn't care if she was driven to death.
She went to the officials and made a row,
forcing her parents to sell a large section of paddy to cover costs.
Later, she married into a Han Family,
and finally calmed down.

They had to go out,
go and find the Vestments,
go and find the Hats.
Liong Hlie got up earliest,
set a pot of water to boil,
washed his face, then went to search.
Where was his food bundle?

B: It was hung on his scabbard;
that's how he carried his food on the search.

*He wanted to find the Vestments and Hats,
but what would serve as hunting dogs?*

A: Grass sandals served as the hunting dogs.
He wore grass sandals to go search,
search for the Vestments and Hats,
only after finding them could a sacrifice be made to Gho Do.

B: *How did Liong go?*
How did Jang Vang travel?

A: They followed crooked passes through the mountains,
   and built bridges across the streams;
   thus they went faster, and drew nearer.

   Onward, going onward.
   They arrived at the edge of a village.
   Seeing a child tending the horses,
   Jang Vang asked him:
   "Where does my sister's family live?"
   Jang Vang gave him a little piece of silver,
   and the child took it and said:
   "Your aunt's family lives here!"

   Arriving at a fork in the road,
   they came upon a little herd boy
   and gave him a string of *yimi* seeds.[11]
   Jang Vang asked him:
   "Where does my sister's family live?"
   "Your aunt's family lives here!"

   By the door of a Han family's home,
   a big tree was planted,
   and in the tree was a magpie's nest,
   and at the foot of the tree crouched a dog;
   the dog was really friendly,
   and came quickly to ask the guests:
   "Where are you from?"

   At the Han family's home,
   the lintel was hung with a black lacquer plaque,
   and there were couplets on each side of the inner doorway;
   the main hall was wide as could be.

   Arriving at the Han family's home,
   Liong was received by the Guests as an in-law,
   brothers-in-law count as brothers,
   so Liong Hlie sat on a wooden chair.[12]
   Jang Vang was a distant uncle,
   so he sat on a chair made of lead.

   The Guests were very hospitable,
   and they slaughtered a spotted hog to entertain their guests.
   For three days and nights the Han people sewed silk downstairs,

while upstairs they made the Hats.
They were making the Hats and sewing the Vestments
to be carried to the West to honor our Parents,
so that everyone would prosper.
What were the Vestments like?

B: A horse leg was taken as a pattern
for sewing the Vestments.
*As for the Hats,
what were they patterned after?*

A: Chestnut burrs were the pattern,
that is how the Hats were made.

Without the Vestments, the two would not have returned;
without the Hats, the two would not have returned.
Only after getting the Vestments did they return;
only after getting the Hats did they return.
Jang Vang's foolish sister, A Diu,
sent him a string of *yimi* seeds.
Jang Vang's sister, A Ghe,
sent him a Hat.
Jang Vang's sister, A Ju,
gave him a set of Sacrificial Vestments.

Coming, coming westward.
They arrived at Cogon Grass Bluff,
where they spent New Year's Day with Golden Pheasant;
after New Year's they continued on.
Arriving at Je Hsang Vang,
they spent the holidays with Liong Tong;
after the holidays they went on.

Without the Vestments, they would not return;
without the Hats, they would not return.
Only after getting the Vestments did they return;
only after getting the Hats did they return.
*When Jang Vang returned home,
where were the Vestments put?*

B: They were put on a long table.
Din Hsai had quick, clever hands:

The clothing was well sewn
and suited Liong Hlie perfectly;
Jang Vang's clothing was just right, too.

THE ANCESTOR SACRIFICE HUNT

A: The Vestments were brought home;
the Hats were brought home.
After preparing the beams, a house would be built;
then the wild beasts would be hunted
to sacrifice to the Ancestors.
After each Ancestor Sacrifice,
the Drum is sent back to the mountains.[1]

If it is the New Year's Send-off festival,
the Han people do the dragon dance to send off the auspicious year.
Our parents round up chickens and ducks,
and make *baba* cakes for the send-off,
which is part of the New Year's festival.
But what is brought to send off the Drum?

B: A fat hog is brought to the send-off,
and the Drum is escorted to the Silver Cliffs;
the Lead Mountain Hollows are so lovely
that the longer one stays, the more one likes them.

The Drum lived in the Lead Mountain Hollows;
the Drum lived on the Silver Cliffs:
Stones were its pillow;
pebbles were its mat;
lion grass was a roof,
which also served as a mosquito net.

The longer Butterfly lived there, the more she liked it.

The Drum should live there for eleven years,
and on the twelfth year return.
*Why did the searchers go only six years,
and after only five years return?*[2]

A: Adults remember the customs;
but children can't remember them.

The rattling of the carrying poles resounded through
the Silver Mountain Hollows.
When Butterfly Mother heard it, she arose
and quickly left for home.

People can remember customs,
but Pheasant didn't understand the "Principles."
It was collecting chestnuts in the mountains
when an avalanche of rocks and stones rolled down.
The big stones struck against the small ones,
and struck against the drum-head with a "dong."
The Sacrificial Drum quickly replied, "Let's go!"
The Sacrificial Drum couldn't say, "Stay put."[3]

*When the Drum returned home,
who went to welcome it?*

B: Watered wine welcomed it;
white rice escorted it home.
When the Drum comes, an Ancestor Sacrifice must be held:
"Quickly, go and hunt!"
Where was the wild beast?

A: It was in the Jiuli Mountain Forest:
"Go there quickly to catch it;
use its skin to cover the Drum!"
In the early times,
Mountain Goat and Dog
were sisters born of the same mother.
Their legs worked together grinding grain
and pounding rice.

In those early years,
Dog and Mountain Goat were sisters.
Their feet worked together grinding grain
and pounding rice.
When Mountain Goat took Dog's horns,
Dog was very angry
and fiercely chased Mountain Goat into the hills.
Which road did Mountain Goat take?

B: If it fled through the main gate,
it might have been bitten,

for many dogs were on guard there outside;
so Mountain Goat fled through the back door,
then leaped into the vegetable patch.

The vegetables were plentiful and sweet,
but the leaves cried out when touched.
Hearing the noise, the goat was frightened.
What way did it take when it fled?

A: It escaped along the waste-water trench.
Mountain Goat fled,
fled to the forest on Jiuli Mountain.
The mountain forest
was on nine bluffs linked into one great one.
"Let's hurry on the chase
to get its skin for the drum-head!"

If Mountain Goat was to be chased,
it was necessary to have a hunting dog.
Today, there are dogs in the market;
if you need one, you can buy it.
In those ancient times,
where were hunting dogs to be had?

B: In Liong Tong's family.
Liong Tong's family had many dogs.
Nine of them were the fiercest.
Jang Vang spent seventeen silver ingots;
with seventeen silver ingots he bought the dogs.

He bought quail dogs,
then chased Mountain Goat to Je Wang.[4]
Jang Vang spent seventeen silver ingots,
bought the dogs with seventeen ounces of silver,
dogs for chasing Mountain Goat,
and they chased the beast to Jiuli Mountain.
Did Jang Vang spend the seventeen ounces of silver?

A: Jang Vang did not spend silver.
So what did he spend?

B: Other families had only one girl,
but Jang Vang's family had nine girls.

The nine sisters all married,
and one of them married Liong Tong.
Liong Tong and Jang Vang were brothers-in-law,
so Liong Tong gave a dog to Jang Vang for free,
which he used to pursue the wild beast.

Without getting the dog, Jang Vang wouldn't have returned,
but after getting the dog, he returned.
When they came home,
where did the dog sleep?

A: It slept at the foot of the grain crib.
When judging a person, you look at his face;
but when it's a dog, where do you look?

B: To judge a dog, you look at the hair whorls on its head.
If there is a hair whorl on the left side,
then the dog is a fierce one;
if it chased Mountain Goat, the prey would be lucky
to get over one mountain.
When looking over a dog, you look at the whorls.
If a whorl is on the left side,
then that dog is savage;
if it chased after beasts,
they would be lucky to cross one mountain range.

"The hunting dog was found,
hurry and catch the beast!"

Din Hsai was an old hand at things.[5]
He ran from the bottom to the top of the village;
in a high voice he urged everyone:
"Everyone stop grinding grains;
the beast will be frightened by the noise,
Mountain Goat will be scared away."

Din Wang was extremely clever;
he ran from the foot of the mountain to the peak,
then cried on and on to them all:
"Everyone stop grinding grain;
Mountain Goat will be frightened by the noise,
the beast in the mountains will flee!"

Mountain Goat fled to Je Wang.
"Now, in this mountain forest,
nine bluffs are linked into one.
Everyone go quickly for the chase!"
The wild beast ran to Jiuli.
"Now, in this great forest,
nine mountains are linked into one.
Let's hurry and make chase!"

Arriving at the mountain forest,
Jang Vang crawled over the craggy cliffs.
As he crouched at Crib Door Saddleback,[6]
Mountain Goat came up the mountain.
With what did Liong Tong point?
With what did Jang Vang kill it?

A: Liong Tong pointed with his finger;
    Jang Vang used a knife for the kill.

    If an arrow had been used, it might have broken a leg;
    if a knife had been used, it might have damaged the skin.
    They still wanted the skin to cover the Drum,
    so what was to be done?

B: When Liong Tong pointed his finger,
    Jang Vang struck with his fist;
    Mountain Goat dropped dead to the ground.
    Where was Mountain Goat captured?

A: It was captured in the fish grass.[7]
    What sort of carrying pole was used to carry it?

B: A *wubei* wood carrying pole
    and a dry birch timber were used to carry it.

    They were back, they were back;
    back at Jang Vang's home.
    Who came to admire Mountain Goat?

A: Jang Vang's elder sister praised it:
    "This Mountain Goat is really beautiful!"

PART V
THE GREAT FLOOD

Introduction

This song concerns the conflict between the clever ancestor of humankind, Jang Vang, and the vengeful Thunder God. Though both born of the same nest, one lives on earth and the other in the sky. The two engage in a dispute that begins over the division of the house foundations of the ancients. The Thunder God feels short-changed by his share and returns to the sky, where he vents his wrath by flooding the earth. Jang Vang delays inevitable destruction by employing various tricks, meanwhile growing a huge calabash in which he and his sister just escape the rising floodwaters, which destroy the earth. The Thunder God sends out a variety of bird and animal scouts to see if Jang Vang is alive. After a fearful chicken lies to him that it did not see the floating calabash, the god finally lowers the water.

Surviving the flood, Jang Vang eventually finds himself in need of a wife. His sister is the only female available. Some practical bamboos suggest that he marry her. In a rage over their suggestion, Jang Vang slices the bamboos into nine pieces with his ox-sacrificing knife, promising, when they ask, to put them back together again if he does indeed marry his sister. Eventually, need gets the best of him, and he attempts to trick his sister into marriage by making nine iron baskets and placing a thrush in each of them. When the girl puts her hands into the baskets, she cannot pull them out. Jang Vang replies to her screams for help by saying that, if she marries him, he will free her. She decides that if he can roll two millstones down a mountain and have them land on top of each other, she will submit. He tries and fails. He then chases her around a mountain on horseback and again fails to gain her agreement. Finally, he sets a snare, catching his sister by the foot when she comes to grind rice. When she cries out for her "elder brother" to come save her, he ignores her in silent anger. At last, when she cries out, "my husband," Jang Vang gleefully marries her.

After a year his sister gives birth to a lump of flesh. Why? Because "Jang Vang had not done things correctly. / He didn't find a wife elsewhere. . . ."

The lesson was: "When looking for a wife, he hadn't searched far enough." Gho Do (Ghot Dol), the resulting flesh ball, is shaped like a fire-bundle (an irregularly shaped packet of vegetation, used for transporting live coals on journeys) or like the grass used to wrap up fish when carrying them. In his rage Jang Vang slices the flesh ball to bits with a sickle, then fills up nine manure buckets with the pieces. After he scatters the pieces over the mountains they turn into the ancestors of the present ethnic groups in Southeast Guizhou province. The Han Chinese (the "guests") were transformed from the meat; the bone became the Miao; and so on. Exactly what portions of the flesh ball (intestines, sweat, hair, etc.) turned into the other ethnic groups was not included in the text by the original editors. In a note they explain that they did not wish to hurt the self-esteem of the respective groups (especially those who were transformed from the lower bowels).

In any case, none of the peoples transformed from the meat could speak. Jang Vang asks the Earth God to go to the sky as an intermediary to the Thunder God. Jang Vang thus learns that if he burns the bamboos, the people will learn to talk. He takes up a fire bundle and burns off several mountain ranges. The crackling of the bamboo is the catalyst that causes the people to speak:

> The Miao said, *"Mong mong!"* (Mongl, mongl!)
> The Guests said, *"Qu, qu!"*
> The Dong said, *"Bai bai!"*

All the words mean "go" in their respective languages. Afterwards, the people spread out into the blackened hills. But, as time progresses, the population in the east grows, and

> Seven of the grandfathers used one ox-sacrificing knife;
> seven grandmothers used one spinning wheel.
> There were many, many people
> all using one crock of salt.

So the people quarrel, forcing the families to divide up and go their separate ways to find a better life.

THE GREAT FLOOD

A: There are twelve Ancient Songs,
   so you needn't sing *The Great Flood*.
   It will be rough walking back home in the dark
   if you choose that one to sing!
   But, if the song of the flood is to be sung,
   then place a butchered duck on the ground;
   kill a duck before beginning.[1]

   Let's sing *The Great Flood*,
   sing about the murky depths of the past.
   What was done wrong in the daytime?
   What offense was committed at night
   that caused hail and rainstorms to fall
   and floodwaters to rise to the foot of the Sky?

B: In the vastness of the past,
   those two brothers, the Thunder God and Jang Vang,
   contended over the Ancestors' house foundations,
   but finally came to an agreement.
   But there was also a grain-drying yard
   that was a stretch of that ancient Grain-Drying Bluff.
   It was given to Jang Vang,
   but the Thunder God couldn't accept that fact.
   Thus he angrily raced up to the Sky
   to release the hail and rainstorms
   to appease his rage by drowning Jang Vang.

   Jang Vang was terribly worried—
   a great flood would drown everything on Earth!
   What was done wrong in the daytime?
   What offense was committed at night
   that caused hail and rainstorms to fall
   and floodwaters to rise to the Sky?

A: Jang Vang wanted to till the paddies and fields,
   but he had no ox.[2]
   Since Jang Vang and the Thunder God were brothers,
   he borrowed an ox from him.
   After Jang Vang finished plowing the paddies and fields,
   he killed the ox and ate it.
   After sticking the ox's tail in a waterway,
   he said to the Thunder God:
   "I was plowing in a very muddy paddy,
   when the ox sank right to the bottom;
   his tail is still sticking out.
   Let's go quickly and pull him out!"

   Together, Jang Vang and the Thunder God pulled.
   As the Thunder God tugged upward,
   Jang Vang yanked downward.[3]
   They pulled and pulled, until the Sun was hanging in the West.
   Jang Vang was tired out;
   the Thunder God was exhausted.
   Jang Vang said:
   "Let's go home;
   tomorrow we'll put on new silk gowns;
   tomorrow we'll put on long shirts;
   tomorrow we'll come again."

   The Thunder God put on a new silk gown;
   the Thunder God put on a long new shirt,
   then came to pull with Jang Vang.
   They pulled and pulled,
   till the Sun touched the Western horizon.
   The Thunder God was tired out.
   Jang Vang was tired out,
   but he took a deep breath and went:
   "Huh, huh, huh!
   Huh, huh, huh!"

   Then he said:
   "Listen, that's the cow calling!
   Let's give one more big tug!"

   When the Thunder God pulled with all his might,
   Jang Vang let go.

The Thunder God fell "ker-plop" into the paddy,
and was all covered with mud.
At last, the furious Thunder God
went up to the Sky in a rage, crying:
"When I get to the Sky,
I shall immediately release a great rain,
and let the great floodwaters of the Sky drown you!"

Jang Vang answered the Thunder God:
"If you raise the waters right now, I'm sure to run off;
but if you wait three sunrises,
by the third night
I'll have completely forgotten about it;
when the rain comes, it will be hard to escape!"

In a great hurry, Jang Vang planted a Calabash.
And what did he say to the Calabash?

B: "Calabash, Calabash sprout quickly;
Calabash, Calabash quickly flower;
in three days, grow as big as a water crock."

In the morning the Calabash sent out vines;
in the evening the Calabash blossomed.
When exactly three days and nights had passed,
the Calabash had grown as big as a water crock.

As soon as the three days and nights passed,
hail and rainstorms fell from the Sky.
The Thunder God said to himself:
"Jang Vang, you'll have a hard time surviving this!
Jang Vang, this time you will surely die!"

The great rain came down for three days and nights;
the hail fell nine mornings and evenings.
Because of the surging floodwaters, no one could be seen,
and the Calabash floated to the edge of the Sky.
The floodwaters rose to the Thunder God's doorstep.
Who did he send to see how high the floodwaters had risen?

A: He sent a goose to see.
The goose returned and said to the Thunder God:

"Honk-honk-honk-honk,
it seems there is still a mountain peak
floating along in the East."

Hearing that, the Thunder God was angry:
"The great waters have risen to my doorstep;
how could there be such a high mountain?"
He slapped the goose on the bill,
and thereafter it had a big bump on its bill.
Who did the Thunder God send for a look?

B: He sent a duck to go look.
The duck returned and said:
"Quack-quack-quack-quack,
it seems there is still a mountaintop
rocking about in the East."

When the Thunder God heard that he was enraged:
"The floodwaters are up to my doorstep;
how could there still be a mountaintop?"

He tramped on the duck's bill,
so thereafter the duck's bill was flat.
Who else did the Thunder God call to go look?

A: He also called a sheep to go look.
The sheep came back and said:
"Bah-bah-bah,
it seems there's a mountain peak
floating over by the side of the Sky."

Hearing that the Thunder God was angry:
"The floodwaters are at my doorstep;
how could there still be such a high mountain?"

He grabbed the sheep's horns in his hands
and twisted them into curves.
Who else did the Thunder God call to go look?

B: He also called a chicken to go look.
The chicken returned, but didn't dare tell the truth:
"Bruk-bruk-bruk,
below the Sky is a vast, calm sea!"

When the Thunder God heard that, he was very happy:
"I'll give you a nice pointed beak,
so you can peck grain from the ground."

After the great flood had risen a long time,
it slowly receded.

The mountain peaks were all exposed
and the earth could be seen!
Jang Vang was so happy!

As the floodwaters receded
the waters lowered day by day;
the river bottoms appeared
as one stretch of white, glimmering sand.
Upon seeing it, Jang Vang was so glad!
Now to return to the land
and confidently get to work.

The days slip by
and people grow older.
Without a companion
Jang Vang grew restless.

We are born in such fortunate times,
yet even now a companion is hard to find!
Jang Vang was not born in such fortunate times,
for there was only his sister on earth.
It was like a lone silver ingot,
it was like a single reed-pipe;
even if he wanted leave, it was impossible.

Jang Vang looked to the East,
and then gazed to the West.
In the West he saw no fields,
in the East he saw no one to love.
So Jang Vang was really nervous.
*Who was it
who taught Jang Vang to find a wife?*

A: The *nan* and cotton bamboos
   helped Jang Vang to find a wife:

"If you want to find your true love,
you needn't go far;
just there beside your home's rock pile,
find your sister and talk of love,
and brother and sister will become a pair."

When Jang Vang heard this he was very angry!
He picked up the ox-sacrificing knife[4]
and sliced the bamboo to pieces;
in nine slices the bamboo fell to the ground.
The bamboos were still not dead,
and the bamboos opened their mouths, saying:
"If in the future you get your sister,
how will you treat us?"

"Later, if I can marry my sister,
I'll put you bamboo pieces back together,
fuse you back together like a trunk;
you'll certainly live as one piece."

As the days pass by,
wrinkles grow on the forehead,
but still he could find no mate,
and Jang Vang was really sad.
Jang Vang looked to the East
but in the East he could see no fields;
he also looked to the West,
but in the West he could find no lover.
Jang Vang was getting desperate.

If he were to marry his sister,
his sister would not agree.[5]
Clever Jang Vang
came to the west of the little bridge
and wove nine iron cages
and captured nine thrushes
and put them in the cages;
then he called his sister to let them out.
His sister put her hand inside,
but the iron cage would not release her;
she was so upset she began to cry:

"Brother, quickly come and save me!
Brother, quickly come save me!"

Jang Vang answered, saying:
"If I want to take you as a wife,
will you agree?
If you agree, then I'll free you."

"Go find a pair of millstones
and put them up on the mountainside
then let them roll down.
If the two halves
roll down and land in place together,
then I will marry brother."

Most families have only one pair of millstones,
but Jang Vang's home had two pairs of millstones.
Clever Jang Vang
put one pair up on the mountainside
and placed the other down below.
When the stones rolled down the slope,
his sister went to look
and saw the two halves were indeed together.
But sister would still not marry brother,
and Jang Vang was really angry.

Jang Vang rode a red horse,
his sister rode a speedy horse.
The two agreed:
Jang Vang would chase his sister,
one escaping to the West,
one chasing to the East;
chasing and catching up in the East,
chasing and catching up in the West.
The two were eye to eye,
their two horses head to head;
their horses' tails tangled together
and the brother took the sister in marriage,
and the sister agreed to be the brother's wife.
How did the sister escape this?
How did Jang Vang chase after her?

B: When the sister escaped to the West,
   Jang Vang chased after her to the East.
   Jang Vang had a good plan:
   He circled round and round a mountain,
   and the two of them came face to face,
   and the two horses were head to head.
   Jang Vang urged his horse to circle back,
   and the horses' tails tangled together,
   but sister wouldn't relent,
   and still called Jang Vang brother,
   so Jang Vang was very angry.

   But Jang Vang had many tricks.
   He went and set up a snare,
   with the trigger by a rock pile.
   When sister went to pound rice,
   the snare caught her by the foot.
   His sister called to Jang Vang:
   "Brother, come and save me!"
   Jang Vang didn't make a sound,
   for Jang Vang was really angry.
   The sister called to Jang Vang:
   "My mate, my man,
   please come and save me!"
   Jang Vang laughed merrily:
   "Will you agree or not?
   Let's hurry and decide to marry!"

   The brother and sister married.
   After a few years
   they gave birth to a child,
   but it was a ball of flesh.
   What was this?

A: Jang Vang had not done things correctly.
   He didn't find a wife elsewhere;
   he took Niang Ni into his home,[6]
   taking his sister as a wife.
   The tree sapling had grown twisted.
   The child born was as round as could be:
   It had feet but no arms;
   it had no face, but had eyes.

It reminded one of a fire-bundle,[7]
like a fish wrapped in paddy grass;[8]
just as ugly.

Jang Vang was extremely angry,
and he took up a crooked sickle
and found a fir tree stump,
then chopped "it" up by the granary.
Filling up nine manure buckets,
he went out and spread it over the nine hills.
The pieces turned into many, many peoples,
turned into myriads of persons.
They had feet to do the drum dance,
they had mouths to suckle milk,
but they had no words to speak.
Who did Jang Vang ask for advice,
to go up to the Sky and ask the Thunder God?

B: The feet and hands of the Earth God were very light,
and the Earth God's ears were keen;
Jang Vang asked him to go to the Heavenly Palace.

When the Earth God was beside him
the Thunder God said nothing;
but when the Earth God left,
the Thunder God softly spoke:
"This happened in Jang Vang's home—
if it had happened to me,
I would find some bamboo and burn it.
When the bamboo cracks with a 'pop-pop,'
the people will be able to talk."

One spoke softly,
one listened on the sly.
The Earth God went to the side of the horse pen
and heard the Thunder God's words,
then went back to tell Jang Vang.

With a torch in his hand,
Jang Vang went to set the fires,
burning five or six mountain peaks,
scorching a whole bamboo forest.

As the bamboo cracked, "pop-pop,"
the people followed along and spoke:
The Miao people said, "*Meng-meng,*"
the Han people said, "*Qu-qu,*"
the Dong people said, "*Bai-bai.*"⁹

Everyone was all spread out,
there on the blackened slopes.
Seven of the grandfathers used one ox sacrificing knife;
seven grandmothers used one spinning wheel.
There were many, many people
all using one crock of salt.
So many people couldn't keep from chatting,
but there was no way out, they had to divide;
each going off to find their own way of life.

PART VI
WESTWARDS, UPRIVER

Introduction

The last song in this volume has been assigned the title *Westwards, Upriver*. The narrative has a flavor of legendary memories more than myth, in that it concerns the wholly human "grandparents" of the present Miao ethnic group in Southeast Guizhou as they encounter and overcome a series of obstacles when migrating into the region. Though this song is not understood as a direct continuation of the events related in *The Great Flood*, it is often sung in conjunction with that epic. The present song provides the names of various towns and geographical features. Some are still recognizable and can be found on maps of the region today, others are lost in now obscure recesses of collective epic memory. According to the content of the song, the Miao ancestors left their original home because of population pressures, traveling by foot and by boat towards the West where the "rice stalks shimmer like gold."

On their way to the promised land, the migrants meet a host of difficulties, including a river-churning dragon (quelled by throwing copper into the water), an evil toad, and a great eagle, which is shot from the sky and put on trial for its transgressions. Though at times they think of turning back, the ancestors continue on to "find a better life," which they ultimately do, killing an ox for the mythical ancestors when they arrive. The theme of migration is prominent in the folklore of the Miao ethnic group and other ethnic minority groups in southwest China. It is also a major theme in the stories of Hmong in Southeast Asia and in their diaspora communities worldwide.

Westwards, Upriver

A: Come see the five pairs of Parents,[1]
sing of the six pairs of Westwards-moving Parents.
Who gave birth to them?

B: It was old Jang Vang.
He raised the five pairs of Parents,
gave birth to the six Westwards-moving Parents.
Where did the Parents originally live?

A: They lived in this sort of place:
The earth and waters were as one,
the shining waves billowed up to the blue sky;
everything was as flat as a bamboo mat,
like the river flats where grain is dried.
*When the parents lived in the East,
what clothes did they wear?
What food did they eat?*

B: They ate "clear and bright" greens[2]
and wore sheaths off bamboo shoots;
jong hfi lu root was their food,
cliff vine leaves were their clothes.
Each day they wore out nine suits;
after searching nine nights,
it was hard to find replacements.

If they wanted to eat, they grew bitter buckwheat;
if they wanted clothes, they used banana leaves;
in one night they would wear out nine suits;
after searching nine evenings
they could not find anymore.
Like this they were often hungry;
like this their clothes wore out quickly.
"Hurry and come together to talk
about going West for a better life."

When the Parents lived in the East,
the earth and waters were as one,
the shining waves billowed up to the blue sky;
the earth was as flat as a bamboo mat,
just like the floor of a grain crib.
The widest places were as narrow as horse pens,
the flattest places were as steep as kettle rims.
One nest can only hold so many nestlings;
only so many people could live in one place.
Hearths next to hearths when cooking,
feet tramping feet when working rice treadles;
houses were built like beehives;
pots and urns cracked when crammed together.
"Hurry and come discuss the move West,
the move to find a better life."
How did the sons urge on their fathers?

A: The sons urged on their fathers, saying:
"Gather your steel-edged tools!"
How did the aunts urge their nieces?

B: The aunts urged their nieces, saying:
"Gather up your spindles!"

"Hurry and come discuss the move West,
the move to find a better life."

When everyone had discussed it,
they decided to move West.
*Those Ancestors who moved West,
what were their names?*

A: They were Grandpa Yen and Grandpa Mo,
Grandpa Xen and Grandpa Sai,
Grandpa Li and Grandpa No,
Grandpa Jang and Grandpa Wen.
These five pairs of Grandparents,
these five pairs of the first to go West.

Six grandfathers said to hurry and leave,
go West to live a better life.
Six grandmothers were unwilling to leave,
six grandmothers shed tears.

"The best place is still home,
less food and clothes—that's alright,
but we shouldn't abandon our Parents' place!"
Who was it?
Who came from the East?

B: Bee Person came from the East,[3]
blowing a trumpet plant stem,[4]
"woo-woo-woo!"
The sound shook the sky
and it traveled to Grandma's vegetable patch.
Bee Person came to trick Grandma, saying:
"The village dragon has already left,[5]
hail and rain are ready to fall,
the pillars of the sky are tumbling down,
you and I will certainly be crushed to death!
What are we still doing here?"

Grandma was so frightened,
she couldn't but leave.

The steel tools of the Ancestors,
Father put in place.
And where did he put them?

A: He put them on the yellow sand banks,
where they later turned into "sweet talkers,"[6]
and at that place the wisemen passed judgment.[7]

The weaving tools of the forebears,
Auntie put in place.
And where did she put them?
To whom did she give the spinning wheels?

B: They were stored in the yellow sandbars,
and the spinning wheels were given to the weaving maidens.
When the fifth month came around again,
the weaving maidens came and made
the spinning wheels clatter.

Elder brother forgot to take something.
What did he forget to take?

A: He forgot to take the *lusheng* pipes.
   Who would want his lusheng tunes?

B: The *gang lia* cicada took them;[8]
   when the fifth month came around,
   the *gang lia* cicada blew them with a "lia li" sound.

   Mother forgot something.
   What did Mother forget?

A: She forgot her walking stick;
   later it changed into a stumbling stone.
   When brother tripped over it,
   when sister tripped over it,
   "ker-plop" they fell down
   and cried out "Mother!"[9]

   "Get married, then go."
   Who would the maiden marry?

B: The maiden married the mountain flowers;
   among them the cherry blossom is best known.
   "Marry off Mother's sister, then go."
   Who did Mother's sister marry?

A: She was wed to the blooming flowers,
   married that most beautiful one, the cherry blossom.[10]

   "Come see the five pairs of Parents,
   sing of the six pairs of Parents going Westwards."
   Who had such great strength
   that he was called to measure the road?

B: The Eagle's strength was great,
   so he went to measure the earth.
   Measuring East and West,
   going just as far East as West;
   thus the Parents went Westwards,
   going West for food and shelter.
   Which child was the kindest one?

A: Magpie was the kindest.
   He flew over nine mountains

flying up to the seventh level of the sky.
He saw green tea plants on the Western mountains;
he saw yellowing rice along the Western rivers;
he returned home to report to the Parents:
"The Western mountains produce tea leaves,
the Western fields overflow with grain,
the rice fields are glimmering yellow,
the cotton stems are as thick as hammer handles,
the cotton bolls are as big as horse hearts;
one boll can make a suit of clothes,
one hundred bolls can clothe a family."
Hearing this Mother was happy—
To seek a rich life, they must go West.

Who was the most capable?

B: Magpie was the most capable.
He circled over nine mountains
flying high up to the seventh level of the sky.
He spied green fruit trees on the Western mountains;
he spied ripening grain along the Western rivers;
he returned home to report to the elders:
"The Western mountains produce fruit,
the Western paddies overflow with grain,
the ripening grains shimmer like gold,
the cotton stems are as thick as hoe heads,
the cotton bolls are as big as cow hearts;
one boll can make a set of clothes,
one hundred bolls can fit a family.
The rice grains are like sticky-rice cakes;
throw nine grains into nine waterfalls
and when flowing down seven cataracts,
they won't melt apart."
Mother jumped for joy
and wanted to go West to seek a comfortable life.
The Parents lived in Jang Xi Go,[11]
and it was from Jang Xi Go that they set out.
They followed the sandbars Westwards;
their steaming breaths came so hard,
they were dizzy, with eyes unclear,
walking until they seemed like roving night ghosts.

The family of the Ant King is huge;
when moving they all go in file,
longer and longer, an unbroken chain.
The ants came to teach the Parents to go,
in long files, to the West.

Coming, coming, really coming,
coming to a pomegranate forest.
The pomegranates there could be husked like grain.
Who was it who came to husk the grain for the Parents?

A: Grandpa Xong Tin,
he came to husk the grain for the Parents.
In one morning he would husk one heap;
in nine mornings, he husked nine baskets.
The Parents ate their fill,
and their legs were strong for climbing over the hills.

Coming, coming, really coming,
coming to the fallen mountain rocks;
the fallen rocks were sharp as saw teeth,
sharper than the sickles of the Guests;
Mother's tunic was in shreds,
and the soles of her feet were cut;
fresh blood flowed endlessly.
What was to be done?

B: Mother made grass sandals to wear,
wore woven grass sandals to cross the rocky mountains.
What were these sandals like?

A: If it was today,
the soles would be woven from the stalks of sticky-rice,
and threaded together with straw grass.[12]

That's how to get grass sandals to wear,
when cutting grass and firewood in the mountains.
*But when the Parents were crossing the rocky mountains,
what were their grass sandals like?*

B: Green vine was used for soles,
and cogon grass for the thread;
thus the Parents crossed the rocky mountains.

Coming, coming, really coming.
They came to Dang Vi Mong.[13]
It's said that at this place,
thousands of years ago,
the waters left good soil on the banks,
the fields were flat and treeless;
it would be a good place for a family to live.
But who would have known?—
the tangled grasses went as far as the eye could see;
cogon grass, bamboo, reeds, and undergrowth grew all about.

When Mother saw it, she was really sad.

The frog was a good fellow.
He went to invite the rooting pig;[14]
night and day he called:
"Rooting pig, rooting pig."
Echoing through the cliffs and valleys,
"Rooting pig, rooting pig!"

The rooting pig's father said, "Go!"
The rooting pig's mother said,
"Over my dead body you'll go!"
She was just that narrow-minded;
as if she had only one ingot of silver;
it would be ruined if it were cut in half.
She had only the one son,
and she was afraid to lose him
if something happened.
What was brought to invite the rooting pig?

A: Bring a swath of bamboo forest as reward,
give him a bare riverbank
on which to build a house.
The presents should include a pair of drums,
so that the pig will come to cut the bamboo,
cut it so nice and smoothly.

The rooting pig could only cut things apart,
it was unable to sweep them away.
"Give the Sun a summons,
call the Wind to take a look."

The Sun shone and the Wind blew
the reeds and bamboo dry.
Fire brother then came to sweep things away,
and thus the cogon grass, bamboos, reeds,
and undergrowth were swept clean.
When Mother saw it, she was happy as could be.

When the cogon grass, bamboos, reeds,
and undergrowth were gone,
it was time to build a new house.
The house was built in Gang Ye Meng,
and the parents lived there.

Old Spider
wove a silver thread for an ink line.
"Pa-da" it was strummed on the moxa pillar,
the sound traveling to the home of the Sun.
The Sun hurried out its door,
and the Sun saw the web and praised it.
By the time the Sun shone past
the peak of the grain crib,
the roof of the house was already in place.

The houses at that time
used rafters made of moxa stems,
banana leaves were used as roof tiles.
When the house was built at Dang Vi Mong,
when it was all finished,
there was a sacrifice to the Ancestors,
a sacrifice to the first person, Gho Do.

A leech was the ox,
and empty-heart vegetable stalks were the drums;
locust wings were used to cover the drums,
locust legs were used as drum sticks,
"dong-dong" the beat arose,
sounding through the whole village.

There were over six circles of drum dancers,
and there were seven circles of onlookers.
People crowded on the drum grounds.
Nothing could be more lively,

there was no room to stand.
It's never been so lively!
There was not a dull moment!

Before it was time, it was hard to get up,
but once they arose, they just kept going.
Arriving at Zang Pa Bi Mountain
the trees and brush were thick
and it was hard to get through;
the trunks were twisted and tangled,
and the leaves were thick and clustered.
Even though the Sun shone in the sky,
it was as dark as before a thunderstorm.
Mother was so worried!
"If we had known this before,
what would be the use of going West?
Living in our Eastern home,
though hard to eat and drink, life was still sweet."
Who was it?

B: It was Old Man Yu Yang Dai,[15]
who broke through the brambles to build a road,
to give Mother and Father a way to go.
Mother was so light-hearted!
Going West to seek a rich life.

Going, going, moving along.
Arriving at Nang Lu, where
the Nang Yu River water washes into Nang Ngo,
the Nang Hxi River waters lap Nang La;[16]
five rivers join into one,
nine great flows become one great one.
Moving from East to West,
a thick rolling mist rose above the water,
the river water was black as charcoal,
blacker than tung oil used to coat bamboo hats.

The clever Han people
put their writing in their topknots,
and crossed the river with their heads above water.
So today, they have writing to keep accounts,

relying on their pens to remember things.
But those silly Miao people!
They chewed up the writing with their teeth,
and swallowed it into their stomachs,
so today they memorize accounts by heart
and fret over remembering things.

Coming, coming, really coming,
arriving at muddy Nang Hsei Le;[17]
but the road was slippery and hard going,
falling every step,
falling twice every two steps.
Mother didn't have an easy path to follow,
so Mother again cried bitterly:
"If we had known this before,
why would we have come?
Living in our Eastern home,
even if harder, it would be easier to take."
Who was it?

A: It was Grandpa Sun,
who came to give Mother and Father a way to go.
Mother got a path to walk,
and happily went on Westwards,
going West to seek a better life.

Coming, coming, really coming,
arriving at Zang Ghai Plain.[18]
Which one was it?

B: It was Old Man Xong Ghai,[19]
who gathered the Parents from nine routes.
Uncles and aunts lived in how many cities?[20]
Uncles and aunts lived in how many towns?

A: Maternal aunts lived in sixteen cities;
paternal aunts lived in sixteen towns.

The Parents came together at Zang Ghai Plain,
got together for an Ancestor Sacrifice,
a sacrifice to the Ancestor, Gho Do;
only sacrifices yield benefits,
otherwise, it's only hardship.

If it were today,
the sacrifice would require a drum,
a drum made of yellow sandalwood,
with a white chicken to go through it,
going in and going out;
only then could an ox be slaughtered;
yellow cow skin for the drumhead,
and cudrania wood for the drumsticks;
beating the drum "dong-dong,"
the sounds going in every direction,
like the cry of a dragon.

Looking back on those early times,
what was the drum like?

B: Bugle Grass was the body,
and a wood-borer would go through it,
going in and going out;
a water scorpion would be the ox,
a locust would be killed for the sacrifice;
a toad skin would cover the drum,
and a locust would be the drumstick;
the drum sound spreading in all directions,
sounding like a dragon's roar.

After sacrificing to Gho Do,
they decided to go on Westwards,
going to find a better life.

Coming, coming, really coming.
arriving at a long, deep pool.
The pool water was a dark green.
How were they to cross?

A: They quickly called everyone together
and discussed it all night.
They had to make some boats.
The boats had to be made in the hundreds,
to get the Parents across,
to send thousands of people Westwards.

Wild fires had scorched the slopes many times,
floods had often fallen from the skies;

the fires had burned the hills bare,
   and the floods had drowned all the wild vines.
   Where could they go to find trees?

B: There was still a white parasol tree
   that grew beside the Thunder God's vegetable patch.
   The Thunder God covered it with his hat,
   and used a hemp rope to tie it fast,
   so the floodwaters couldn't wash it away,
   and the fires couldn't burn it down.

   Go cut down the white parasol tree!
   Go chisel out a big boat!
   What was that thing,
   that raised its children in the tree?

A: That old Rock Eagle
   raised its children in the tree.
   He stammered, saying:
   "If you are going to cut down this tree,
   destroying my home
   and killing my children,
   I am going to eat your Parents."

   Today's rock eagles
   are only the size of a foundation post
   and eat only chickens and ducks.
   The Rock Eagle then
   had a beak like a blacksmith's tongs,
   claws as thick as harrow spikes,
   and wings as wide as grain-drying mats;
   opening its great mouth,
   it could swallow a fat cow,
   and it was going to eat the Parents!
   What was to be done?

B: They quickly called everyone together,
   and discussed it all night long.
   The Rock Eagle in the tree had to be killed,
   if the Parents were to be safe
   and escape to the West.

A bow and arrow was needed to kill the Eagle.
What wood was used for the bow?
What wood was used for the arrow shaft?
What vine was used for the bowstring?

A: *Nong hniang* wood was used for the bow,[21]
   nang ong vine was used for the bowstring,[22]
   nong hniu was used for the arrow shaft,[23]
   to make the bow and arrow to kill the Rock Eagle.

   Aiming at the Eagle's head,
   striking it in the neck.
   The Eagle fell to the ground,
   its legs quivering,
   the great wings folding.
   Who was it?

B: It was Big Brother Hornet King
   who climbed into the Eagle's wound to listen.
   "The head and body are separated,
   but it is not dead;
   the neck is separated,
   yet it's alive!"

   The arrow-shot Eagle had fallen dead to the ground.

   Who came to accuse it,
   enumerating its crimes,
   then dividing it up to eat?

A: Call the Mynah Bird to come accuse him;[24]
   the Mynah's body was black;
   the Mynah Bird didn't dare accuse it,
   didn't dare enumerate its crimes.

   Call Oriole to come accuse it;
   Oriole's body was yellow;
   Oriole didn't dare accuse it,
   didn't dare enumerate its crimes.

   Call Swallow to come accuse it,
   let him eat the innards.
   He said he only wanted the Eagle's chin,

because of this, its beautiful name was handed down,
carried to the nine drum clans,
six generations of people
have praised him down until today.
When making the accusations, what sort of hat did he wear?

B: He had to wear a silver hat,
he wore a silver crown on his head
when making the accusations,
so awe-inspiring in appearance.

"You live in your place,
we were making our boats.
If you had minded your own business,
no evil would have been committed today.
But you wanted to eat your Parents,
so the arrow was shot into your body."

The Eagle's meat had to be boiled to eat.
What would be used as a pot?

A: If today, the vegetable pot would be made
by those skilled Han people in the East,
who make excellent iron pots.
The fathers make them
and the sons take them out to sell.
The Han people carry them Westwards
and grow rich by selling them for silver,
returning home with their fortunes.
But looking back at that time,
what sort of pot was used to cook the Eagle?

B: Moxa stalks were used to make the pot.
Who came to eat the kidneys?

A: Liong Bi came to eat the kidneys.[25]
He ate the Eagle's innards;
when he finished eating, his tongue was sluggish;
his tongue was so numb he mumbled.
He said *gad*, instead of *niaf*.[26]

Liong Bi came to eat the Eagle's innards,
eat the Eagle's chin;

after eating his fill, his mouth was mushy,
his tongue was so stiff he mumbled.
He again said *niaf,* instead of *gad.*

The great boats were carved out.
Who came to row them?
Who came to steer them?

B: Our Fathers came to row them;
our Mothers came to steer them.

Who poled in the front?
Who steered in the back?

A: Our Grandpa poled in the front,
our Grandma steered in the rear.
With one push, seven pools were passed.
They were soon at Sickle Bar,[27]
but they were moving too slowly.
Who was most capable?

B: Xong Za was most capable.[28]
He was so powerful that
in seven pushes he passed a whole mountain,
the boat seemed to be flying;
in eleven strokes he passed nine shoals,
the boats seemed like arrows from a bow.

Coming, coming, really coming,
arriving at Sickle Bar.
Who was it?

A: It was the Dragon King
who kicked up waves the size of grain cribs,
the wave tops pouring over the horse pens,
the churning waters out of control.

He wanted to eat the Parents.
When Mother saw this she was startled:
"If I had known this before,
living and eating a bit less in the East
would have been alright."

Coming to Sickle Bar,
the Dragon King wanted to eat the Parents.
What was to be done?

B: Hurry and call everyone to discuss it,
discuss it all night long.
Throw raw copper into the river,
and the dragon will retreat to its rocky lair;
the parents could then proceed Westwards.

The dragon, thick as double drums,[29]
wanted to eat our Parents.
What act was committed in the daytime?
What act crime was committed at night?

A: At dawn
they had cut down that white parasol tree,
cut it down to make the boats;
the parasol tree fell down,
and crushed the Dragon's mother.
It was because of that morning's crime,
that he wanted to eat the Parents.

Coming, coming, they were really coming.
Arriving at a big bridge,
the wind blew so cold
that Mother lighted a charcoal firepot.
Who came from the West?

B: A Han man following the rivers
gave a boat of *de niang khai* wood to Mother,
rowing the parasol boat to follow the river's flow.
As the Han man was preparing to go,
what did he say?

A: "I am going East to weave cloth,
I am going East to sew brocade;
at the time of the Ancestor Sacrifice,
I will send cloth and hats to the West,[30]
for sacrificing to Butterfly Mother,
sacrificing to the Ancestors for a bountiful life."

Before starting, it was hard to get up;

but once up, they just kept going.
Arriving at the dark and dangerous cliffs,
they ran into a giant Toad;
its body was six spans thick,[31]
as big as a water buffalo;
its mouth seemed like a great broken basket,
with a roar like a tiger or wolf.
It wanted to eat Mother.
What was to be done?

B: Call everyone to discuss it,
discuss it all night long.
A knife had to be made
to kill the Toad at the foot of the cliff,
so the Parents could go Westwards,
go West for a better life.
What was used to make the knife?

A: The Eagle's leg bone was used as a knife,
and carried to the foot of the dangerous cliff
to kill the giant Toad,
so the Parents could go Westwards.
The Toad with a body six spans wide
seemed the size of a water buffalo
and wanted to eat the Parents.
What crime had been committed during the day?
What evil had been done at night?

B: In the morning
when they came to Zang Ghai Plain,
and sacrificed to Gho Do,
they had killed a Toad
and used its skin for a drumhead.
Because of that,
the Toad wanted to eat the Parents,
wanted to eat the Parents in revenge for the crime.

Coming, coming, really coming.
Arriving at the foot of a broken cliff,
old trees filled the mountain passes,
old vines locked the mountain valleys,
blocking the Parents' path.

Mother was kindhearted:
"If we had known this before,
we needn't have come;
staying in our Eastern home,
eating a bit less would have been alright."
What was to be done?

A: Monkeys in droves
swung on the cliff-top limbs,
playing on vines as they pleased.
Mother unwound her leggings,
Father unwound his turban;
the monkeys came to help,
pulling the Parents up the cliffs.
Mother was so happy!

Coming, coming, really coming.
Arriving at a brambly forest,
the whole slope was thorns,
the Parents couldn't find a way through.
Mother was in low spirits:
"If we had known this before,
we wouldn't have come;
staying in our Eastern home,
eating a bit less would have been alright."
Who was it?

B: It was Old Man Xong Tin
with a sickle in his hand.
He took a right-handed sickle[32]
and cleared a clean path:
"Follow this road to go
straight to the tea-producing hills,
straight to the grain-producing river bottoms,
with rice heads glimmering yellow as gold."
When Mother heard this she was so happy,
following the road Westwards.

Coming, coming, really coming.
Arriving at Khong Xong Wang,
to Je Hsang's Western place.[33]
Westwards, the Parents cleared the wastelands for fields,

and dug the dry earth layer by layer
to make the water courses in the rice fields.
Mother led a good life,
Mother was so happy!

Coming, coming, really coming.
Arriving at Dang Gho Saddleback,
at Dlong Ji they killed an ox,[34]
killed an ox for the Ancestors.
Everyone had sons and grandsons,
sons and grandsons as abundant as minnows,
all of whom had to divide up
and go to other places.

Fang and Fu went where?[35]
Dli and Nie went where?

A: Fang and Fu went to Je Mi,
Yi and Nie went to Fang Jang.

Dai Ne stayed in the old place,
stayed with the Ancestors.
There was still your grandfather and mine
who foot by foot climbed the mountains,
step by step went down the hills,
together arriving at the "river place," Fang Ni.

In the ancient times
you and I were of the same ancestors,
born by one grandmother;
washing in the same basin,
wearing the same indigo cloth;
as one slice of meat sacrificing to the god of drought,
as one string of meat sacrificing to the wild ghosts.[36]
As people increased there were towns and villages,
sons and grandsons increased and spread out.
You and I may not be acquainted,
but we need only to meet
and raise the affairs of the olden days,
and the mouths will sweeten,
and will begin to speak without end.

NOTES

Notes to the Preface

1. During the Cultural Revolution (1966–1976) many aspects of traditional culture associated with "feudalism" were suppressed under the category of the "Four Olds."
2. Jin Dan wrote this Preface in 1986—in anticipation of my completed translation—which has taken somewhat longer than expected to publish due to intervening events over the years. (M. Bender, 2006)

Notes to the Introduction

1. In Chinese the official umbrella term is *Miaozu*, for decades translated as "Miao nationality." In recent years, however, the term "nationality" has also been translated in China as "ethnic group" (a term used in the present text), generating the alternate translation "Miao ethnic group." In reality there are many names that the dozens of Miao subgroups call themselves. Such ethnonyms include those of the four major subgroups : Hmu, Hmong, Hmao, and Gho Xang (Schein, 37–41; Wu and Qian, 64–8; Tapp, *The Hmong of China*, 9). Though in the past a host of different names were in use by individual groups—such as White, Black, Buffalo Horn, Magpie, and Flowery Miao—today local place affiliation often serves to differentiate subgroups in publications and other media or public contexts such as government-sponsored ethnic festivals. Thus, as with subgroups of other minority groups like the Yi (located in Western Guizhou, as well as Sichuan, Yunnan, and Guangxi), various Miao subgroups are associated with specific places such as Wenshan in Yunnan, Rongshui in Northern Guangxi, Taijiang in Southeast Guizhou, and so forth. In the following descriptions, the term Miao (unless otherwise specified) refers to the groups in and around the cities of Kaili and Taijiang in Southeast Guizhou who commonly, though not exclusively, go by the ethnonym Hmu (Hmub). (According to Jin Dan, whose hometown is Gedong, some Miao in the Taijiang area refer to themselves as Hmong [Hmongb]).

It should also be noted that the Mandarin Chinese term "Miao" meaning "sprouts" appears early in Chinese records. By the fourteenth century or so the word was written with the addition of a radical meaning "canine" and applied to people in southwest China whom researchers regard as the Miao ethnic group of today. Since the canine-bearing term held a derogatory meaning, after 1949 the more neutral "sprouts" character was restored on the Chinese mainland. The name "Miao" may have been a way of transcribing words similar to "Hmu" for which the Chinese did not have sounds in their language (the "hm," for instance). Today the term *Miaozu* is normally used by many Miao, especially when speaking in Chinese. As Tapp ("Cultural Accomodations," 97–8) has noted, however, some Miao intellectuals and officials in China (including Southeast Guizhou) are now using the term "Hmong" in public contexts, though they themselves may go by other ethnonyms (such as Hmu) in their respective dialects. I have been told that in English it is spelled "Hmong," though in the medium of Chinese it is *Meng ren*, meaning "Hmong people" and employing the same character for *meng* as that used in part of the Chinese name for "Mongol." This phenomenon seems to be related to contacts with Hmong in diaspora communities in North America and Europe where, in recent years, the term "Hmong" has become a rallying term for related peoples who migrated from Southeast Asia beginning in the late 1970s. Tapp believes that the term Hmong may someday replace the term Miao in China—which, if he is correct, would result in "Hmong ethnic group" being the umbrella term for the various subgroups (assuming that the present subgroups will remain under the same general classification rather than being reclassified into more homogenous, smaller groups).

2. Locally, the name Butterfly Mother is literally "mother butterfly" or Mais Bangx. As explained in the Key to Pronunciation for Eastern Miao Dialect Romanization, I have omitted the tone markers from the words presented in the Eastern Miao Romanization, placing the actual renderings in parentheses only on the first occurrence (unless otherwise warranted) in the Introduction and Notes. Thus, for the general reader the term "Mais Bangx" becomes "Mai Bang," "Hmub" becomes "Hmu," and so on.

3. In contrast to the elaborate ceremonial cycle common in Southeast Guizhou, Graham describes a less elaborate ceremony held before 1949 by the so-called "Chuan Miao" in Sichuan.

4. Certain words, for instance, were thought offensive to the Ancestors and could not be spoken during the sacrifices. For example, the word "salt" sounds the same as "tiger," which is among the animals born with the mythic trickster-hero, Jang Vang (Jangx Vangb). If a tiger or snake entered a village, it could not be harmed, as such creatures were sent by the mythical Ancestors. Moreover, snakes were regarded as baby dragons.

5. Two verbs meaning "to give birth" appear in the epics: *yi* (*yis*), an archaism, and *diang* (*diangl*), which is colloquial. In the translation, the terms are respectively rendered as "birthed" and "bore" when they appear together.

Notes to the *Prelude*

1. The number twelve is an indefinite sum meaning "many." (Other indefinite numbers include five, six, and nine.)

2. Niang E Sei (written as Niangx Eb Seil when the tone markers are added) is the most beautiful girl in the myth epics.

3. "The Birth of Butterfly Mother" (Mai Bang Diang [Mais Bangx Diangl]), as the title indicates, concerns the birth of Butterfly Mother who, after emerging from the ancient sweet gum tree, was impregnated by wave foam and laid twelve eggs, which later hatched into proto-humans, dragons, thunder, tigers, and other entities. In the historic past, this song could only be sung in years during which the sacrifices to the mythical Ancestors were held. It is also called "The Song of the Black Drum Society," for previously, there were exclusive black and white drum societies. The Black Drum Society had many restrictions and duties concerning the sacrificial cycles, which the White Drum Society members did not have.

4. "Bang Xang Ye" (Bangx Xangb Yel) describes how a man eats the *De Le* (*Deb Lel*) fruit in the sky and returns to childhood: According to Jin Dan, oral sources relate that "The teeth that fell out filled seven baskets; / the skin he shed filled seven baskets." He lived for 89,000 years and was later called Bang Xang Ye. After he died his mouth became a cave, his hair turned to grass, his eyebrows changed to indigo, and his teeth to borax, and so on. This story is similar to the myth of Pan Gu, found in the traditional lore of a number of southern minority groups as well as that of the Han Chinese.

5. *Transporting Gold and Silver* (Qa Jen Qa Ni [Qab Jenb Qab Nix]) is set in the ancient past and concerns transporting Gold and Silver to make the Sun, Moon, and Stars.

6. "Niong Ji Bong" (Niongx Jib Bongb) tells of a pheasant that searched for wild chestnuts in the mountains. Its pecking caused rocks to fall down and kill a girl who was fishing. The pheasant is typical of characters that like to place blame on others. As the story goes, the pheasant was later tried. During the interrogation, it described itself as having "a head the size of a wine cup, legs as thick as chopsticks, and a body as big as a small calabash." Thus it claimed it could not have possibly dislodged the rocks with its small beak. It then blamed the deed on a wild pig, claiming that the animal, with its "big feet and long legs that stride a foot at a time," had rooted up the mountain stones. Later, when the case was investigated further, the real culprit was found. According to custom, this and similar songs can only be sung outdoors because the characters are believed to represent humans.

7. "The Five Pairs of Parents" (Za Gang Na [Zab Gangx Nal]) concerns the ancient Ancestors when, according to legend, they still lived in the east along a seashore. Later, because of poverty and overcrowding, the story says they moved west.

8. The pronoun "we two" is used here because pairs of singers perform the songs antiphonally, each pair singing as one voice.

9. The first god.

10. According to an ancient custom, barren mothers construct a small bridge in hope of conception. Every year the bridge is the subject of a ritual known as "Blessing the Bridge," held the second day of the second lunar month.

11. These characters represent places where gold, silver, iron, copper, tin, and other metals were mined.

12. *Ye fang* (*yet fangb*) is a courting activity that includes singing, dancing, flirting, and so on. (Hereafter, I have translated this term as "courting.")
13. Called *caigu* in Chinese, this is a popular dance held on festival occasions in which people dance in large circles to the beat of a drum.
14. Hsen Yan (Hsenb Yenl) is the local Miao dialect pronunciation for the Chinese term "immortal, transcendent" (*xianren*).
15. The mythical figure who plowed and harrowed the land and planted the Tree Seeds.
16. Jang Vang was the first mythical ancestor of humankind and the first being to emerge from Butterfly Mother's eggs. He is also called Vangb or Lax and sometimes Vangb Lax (Vang La). He is often used to represent humankind in the epics.
17. This god is said to be the earth.
18. This god is said to be the waves.
19. This being is said to be a mythical figure that would reason and mediate on important issues.
20. This character is an enormous woman who husks rice and whose hands stretch to the ends of the sky.
21. The mythical man who created fire.
22. According to the myth, the time before Jang Vang was born was the age of the gods. Only after his birth did the present age of humans begin.

Notes to the Introduction to *Song of Gold and Silver*

1. In the Chinese tradition, time was marked by complex cycles of interactions between ten Heavenly Stems and twelve Earthly Branches.

Notes to *Creating the Sky and Earth*

1. The original lines in the local Miao dialect are (the final consonants—the tones—are not pronounced):

> *Waix haib dab dlel dlel,*
> *dab haib waix dlel dlel.*

The verb *haib* means "stuck together" and the adverbial reiteratives *dlel dlel* indicate that they stuck together instantly.

2. Huangping and Yuqing are both in Eastern Guizhou province.
3. An obscure place name.
4. The term *ji* (*jid*) means "son-in-law" in colloquial Miao, but in the songs may mean either "son" or "son-in-law." Since the intended meaning is not clear, in this line it is translated as "son-in-law," while below it is "son."

5. Length of the arms widespread.
6. In some versions these two lines read: "The Sky was like a roof tile; / the Earth was like a bamboo mat."
7. The birch is known as *de gang fu* (*det gangb ful*) in the Eastern Miao dialect, or *huagao* in Standard Chinese. Some versions say they used a plant called *laobao* (*Arafia*) in Chinese. In the past, the roots of *laobao* and *wubei* (*de pa* [*det pab*] in Miao; *Rhus chinensis*) were bunched together and hung on the door to drive away ghosts. This custom may have some relation to the story.
8. Some versions say his four legs had seven joints, and that he had four feet and eight hands.
9. Hongjiang is located in Hunan near the upper reaches of the Yuan River. It is a commercial center and on the only route by land or water from Southwest Hunan into Southeastern Guizhou.
10. Leigong Mountain is called Vu Ghang Ho (Vud Ghangb Hob) and is located in the Southeast Guizhou Miao-Dong Nationalities Autonomous Prefecture.
11. Located along the banks of the Wuyang River in Southeastern Guizhou.
12. Bie'e is east of the Jian River Hot Springs Commune; the area has seven mountain peaks surrounding a small valley. Because of its similarity to a smelting tool, the locals call this place Tripod Mountain for, according to legend, this is where Gold and Silver were melted to make the Suns and Moons. Zhandang Mountain is west of the commune.
13. Gedong is east of the Taijiang district.
14. A large, clear-running river in the autonomous prefecture named for its clear, blue water.
15. A mesa-like mountain near the city of Kaili that looks like an incense burner. The town of Kaili was formerly known as Lushan (Censer Mountain) because of the bluff.
16. A place near Leishan County, the largest Miao village in the autonomous prefecture.
17. A "short melon" is a length of wood (*duangua* in Chinese) used to lengthen support posts in the roof.
18. All are names of mythic characters.
19. A crossbeam (*chuanfang* in Chinese) that connects the main support posts of a house.
20. A legendary medicine.
21. *De Le* (*Deb Lel*) is the name of a mythical fruit. According to the story, Bang Xang Ye ate this fruit in order to be rejuvenated. When a rooster ate the discarded seeds, its face became bright red and its feathers were beautiful. The juice of the fruit is known as "Fruit of Immortality" water.
22. A species of black tubeworm that lives under rocks in water. It can be eaten or used as fishing bait.

23. A hand span is the distance between the stretched thumb and middle finger.

24. Hxu Niu (Hxub Niux) is interpreted by some singers as "unicorn" (*kaili* in Chinese). However, a comparison between Han and Miao pronunciations makes "rhinoceros" (*xiniu* in Chinese) a more likely possibility. The Han have a saying: "The blue sky is high, but I have a ladder to heaven; / the blue waters are deep, but I have a rhino to divide them."

25. Water buffaloes are major offerings in rituals honoring the mythical Ancestors. After a bull was killed, the horns, still connected to the base of the skull, were hung on a house post. If the collection of horns grew too large, the horns were tied to a sweet gum ladder, one pair on each carved step. The ladder was stood on end and used for sacrifices, used in a manner similar to that of Han altars.

Notes to *Transporting Gold and Silver*

1. The Dragon King is a popular figure in the folklore of many ethnic groups in China and in other parts of East Asia. He is said to live in a palace deep in the rivers.

2. It is said that Ye Ju (Yet Jus) Pool was located in Leishan County.

3. Though there is a place in Taijiang County named Fang Liang (Fangb Liangx) River, there is no river in the vicinity. The name is obscure.

4. Gha Nang Liang (Ghab Nangl Liangs) means "birthplace" but can also be understood to mean "the place of the origin of things." There are places in the Miao areas with such names, but it is not known if any refer to the one mentioned in the song.

5. According to the singers, Ghe Lu (Ghed Lul) is another name for the earth or the land.

6. Bo Ji Li (Bod Jit Lil) is a mythic being's name.

7. The drum societies (*jang nie* [*jangd niel*]) were social organizations determined by descent through the father's line. Marriage between society members was prohibited. During sacrifices, all members came under the jurisdiction of the ceremony leader, no matter where they lived. As time went on, these rules were less strictly enforced. Here "nine drum societies" implies that the people were spread out in many places.

8. See Introduction to *Song of Gold and Silver*, note 1.

9. *Xini* is a kind of shrub. Here it may imply a relation between mining and vegetation.

10. According to folk beliefs, there are sheep dragons, water buffalo dragons, and snake dragons. The horns of sheep dragons are like sheep horns, and those of water buffalo dragons are like those of water buffaloes. Snake dragons, however, do not have horns.

11. A kind of wild grass.

12. The term "Emperor" refers to the Emperor of the East, above. There is no clear link to any Chinese emperor.

13. *Ja yu* (*jab yux*) may be a substance used to brighten gold and silver.

14. When a girl married, the groom's family gave money to his wife's uncle. (The money is called *ni diang* [*nix diangb*] in Miao.) The amount was determined by the economic situation of the groom's family. According to Jin Dan, a folk saying describes this calculation as "Entering the water buffalo fold in search of a water buffalo; / entering a cow pen to get a cow." The uncle's family customarily used some of the money to buy wine and meat for a clan celebration. Another part of the money was used to buy salt to send to each clan member. Thus, little girls were sometimes called "salt grains" by the uncle's family. Some of the money was also sent to the new wife as umbrella money (local Miao brides must have a delicate paper umbrella). The rest of the money belonged to the uncle's family. The next year they were supposed to send a gift of ducks in accord with the amount of the "nephew money." Generally, every *liang* (a Chinese measurement equal to about an ounce) would require one duck in return. The ducks were not divided among each clan family. These customs survive in some areas, though have largely disappeared.

15. The references to the marriages of the metals concern substances commonly associated with a particular stage of working a given metal. For example, a pipe bellows is needed for smelting iron, pine resin for soldering tin, borax for polishing silver, and so on. The term *ji nang* (*jib nangl*), like many terms in the epics, is now obscure.

16. This may be some sort of personified metal.

17. This is possibly a personified metal.

18. This is the name of a mythical character.

19. The meanings of the terms *Ni Jen Ghen* (*Nil Jent Ghenb*) and *Bo Ji Ghen* (*Bod Jit Ghenb*) have been lost.

20. This is possibly another personified metal.

21. A tiny ceramic crucible (of a sort still in use today) used for melting gold and silver in a forge.

22. It was customary to let a white chicken walk through the hollow of a newly made drum for the Ancestor Sacrifices before the instrument was covered. Today it is only necessary to toss the chicken over the drum.

23. The names of two species of snake.

24. According to the story, at one time water buffaloes had neither hair whorls on their shoulders nor horns. Later, the bulls went east to have the hair whorls painted on and the horns attached so they could participate in the Ancestor Sacrifices. Much attention is paid to the position of the whorls on a sacrificial bull as well as the distance between its horns and how they are situated on an animal's head.

25. The *gha gang* (*ghab gangd*) is a species of strong hardwood (possibly in the *Palmae* family) traditionally used for plow bows. The local Han people call it

huapilang ("slippery skin fellow") for its bark emits a kind of slippery, oily colloid liquid.

26. The *ge* is a species of migratory bird. The local Han people call it the *gege* sparrow because of its cry. The bird is somewhat smaller than a thrush, flies over in huge flocks in winter, and can be seen flying off mountain roosts *en masse* before dawn. Local people use sticky tung oil daubed on a decoy tree to trick the birds (used for food) into alighting, whereby they are stuck.

27. The bird lime is made of sticky tung oil and is kept in a container made of bamboo or in a calabash.

28. Special bait birds are pestered so that their cries attract passing birds to the lime. (Songbirds are highly territorial and will drive out trespassers.)

29. An old superstition. When someone was ill, a duck egg was used to divine what ghost was causing the problem. This was termed "egg divination." Special words were recited over the egg before it was boiled. After boiling the egg, the yolk was removed and the whites held up to a light. The shadows in the whites revealed the ghost's name.

30. The name of a mythic grandfather.

31. Wild sparrows are similar to those around farm buildings except that their tails are longer. They often nest in banks along roadways.

32. Earth God (called "Earth Buddha" in Southeast Guizhou) altars are simple brick and wood structures. A family may build one, and they are often seen along roads.

33. An obscure name.

34. According to legend, the Earth God comes out at night to stir the roosters so that they crow the dawn.

35. A kind of stone wall, built in rivers, in which a weir is set. This is a common fishing technique.

36. A kind of bird called "the fisherman," a small kingfisher.

37. A wooden dipper used to bail water from a boat.

38. Grandpa Yu (Yux).

39. This is a dragonfly nymph.

40. A huge wooden dipper used to move coals and ash.

41. This is a kind of amphibious spider.

42. The taste of the water may indicate mine tailings.

43. The name of a place.

44. The brackets in which the axle of a grain-husking tilt-hammer is set.

45. The name of a place.

46. According to the story, when the first dragon was born, a copper knife was used to cut its umbilicus. It hurt so much that ever since, dragons run off in the presence of copper.

47. The tree is a *Catalpa ovata*.

48. *Ghan Nang Dang* (*Ghand Nangl Dangt*) means "Creation Site."
49. There is another passage often sung in connection with the end of this song. The original editors decided to place it in the notes, feeling it did not follow with the rest of the text. (The speech tones are included here.)

> A: What did Xang Ghed get?
> What did Lix Ghed get?
>
> B: Xang Ghed got sorceror's songs;
> Lix Ghed got a compass.
> Each one got something.
> Everyday they dragged their feet around the villages,
> going all about telling fortunes, not working at all.

Notes to *Creating the Suns and Moons*

1. The "tunic" is the weight on a small steelyard.
2. This "rich soil" (*dab mux mongl*) may be a mixture of mud and charcoal.
3. The reference is to a shooting star. It is said that a fire will start where a meteor falls.
4. The name of a ghost.
5. The names of mythic characters.
6. An aquatic centipede called the "straw sandal" insect by the local Han people. It lives under river rocks, is dark in color, resembles a land centipede, and is edible.
7. "Greasewood" is another name for resinous pinewood. It is used for kindling fires.
8. If a woman is born on a day and at a time unsuitable in relation to the scissors star, she will be barren; or if a child is thus born, it shall not survive. This is an old superstition.
9. *Bong yu lio* (*bongt yux liod*) means a blast of air that can blow away a cow; that is, a storm.
10. *Bong yu nin* (*bongt yux ninx*) means a blast of air that can blow away a water buffalo; that is, a storm.
11. See Introduction to *Song of Gold and Silver*, note 1.
12. In these passages, "long" means the day is long; "heavy" means the weather is hot; "short" means the day is short. In colloquial Miao, a hot thing may be termed as "heavy."
13. This implies that the vegetation will turn color after a frost.
14. The names of most of the following stars do not correspond with known stars today. This is another example of once meaningful references that are now lost yet still handed down as part of the living epic tradition.
15. This is the name of a mythical character.

16. This is a place name.
17. This is a place name.
18. This is the name of a mythic character.
19. It is said that diseases come after a hailstorm. Thus there is the saying, "If it hails, there is disease."
20. The meaning of the lines is that it snows when the New Year comes; when spring comes, it rains.
21. This is a place name.
22. This is a place name.
23. Refers to a man and a woman, respectively.

Notes to *Shooting Down the Suns and Moons*

1. The following names refer to mythic characters.
2. According to myth, in ancient times the horse-mulberry (*de wi* [*det wik*] in Miao; *masang* in Chinese; *Coriaria sinica*) could understand human language. When it was told to grow taller or shorter it would comply. Later, it let Hsang Sa (Hsangb Sax) stand on its branches to shoot down the excess suns and moons. Later, the remaining sun and moon chanted incantations over the tree, and thus it grew crooked and useless. Horse-mulberry trees are therefore never used in house building.
3. Probably a reference to the mythical Sky Dog associated with plagues in Chinese folklore.
4. A *jin* is a Chinese measurement weighing about one pound.
5. According to the story, three stars in the sky are transformed members of Hsang Sa's family. The star that comes out at dusk is his son, because he shot him at dusk. The star that comes out after dark is his wife, for when she heard of the death of her child, she ran out in the dark to find him. The star that appears at dawn is Hsang Sa himself, for he waited at home until dawn, but went out after his wife failed to appear. Since the stars do not appear at the same time it indicates that the family cannot be reunited.
6. A female god living in the sky.

Notes to *The Seeds' House*

1. "Rusty water" is a kind of orange liquid that seeps from the earth (usually in streambeds) that Miao women dry and make into powder. To make a dye they mix it with the leaves of a plant called *de ja ji* (*det jab jib*) (*huaxiang* in Chinese; *Platycarya strobilicea*). It is said that where there is "rusty water," there must be metal to be mined. According to this song, however, "rusty water" resulted from a China fir being buried in a landslide. Since many mines have chemical tailings, the former explanation is most reasonable.

2. The original for "Ghe Lu's house" is "Nge Ge Lu" (Ngex Ged Lul). *Nge (Ngex)* today means an animal stable, but the old meaning is "house," as it is translated here. The full meaning of the phrase, however, is "the house the Seeds lived in." According to the singers' explanation, Ghe Lu is a personification of earth.

3. This is a place name. In some versions, it is Fengtan Mountain. The names are both obscure.

4. This is an ancient place name.

5. When a new house is about to be built, a thick ink line of string will be stretched the length of the main house beam and plucked during a special ceremony. A clean, symmetrical line of ink was a symbol of good luck. (Soaked in ink, an ink line is stretched taut across a beam and plucked so that it leaves a purple line on the wood for the carpenter's saw to follow.)

6. A measuring pole is a carpenter's tool made of bamboo. It is the length of the longest house post, and the lengths of all shorter posts are marked on it.

7. This is said to be a mountain rock.

8. Vong E (Vongb Et) is Jang Vang's elder brother-in-law. He is sometimes called simply Vong (Vongb).

9. In Miao names, the first name is one's own, the second (similar to English surnames) is one's father's name, the third is one's grandfather's name, and so on up to ten generations. In this passage, the lack of common ancestral names shows there is no blood relationship.

10. A square of blue or red cloth, the size of a large bandana, is fastened to the middle of the center roof beam of a newly built house. Copper coins are nailed on the corners of the cloth and some silver is placed inside. A pair of chopsticks, made of Chinese toon wood, and several pieces of cotton are tied to the center of the cloth with raw hemp cord.

11. Carambala (*Actinidia chinensis*) is also called *nihoutao* in Chinese. It is a kind of fruit-bearing shrub.

12. This is the god who controls the fire in the sky. He wears red clothes and likes to drink blood. Therefore, when dealing with him, ritual specialists wear red clothes and kill a beast for blood in a sacrifice. The reference here is to lightning or meteors.

13. References to ancient "Rites," "Rules," and "Principles" indicate a now-obscure ethical code.

Notes to *Seeking the Tree Seeds*

1. The name of a mythic character.

2. A type of clasp knife with a curved wooden handle. It is held by a ring on the third or fourth finger when cutting stalks of glutinous or other rice.

3. The original is "nine thousand pool" (*ji je hsang* [*jid jex hsangb*]). In the epics, a special structure is used in which numbers are put after nouns as modifiers. The numbers do not refer to any specific sum and are exaggerated.

4. This is a place name.

5. The reference here is understood as referring to common paddy rats. It is said that in years when rats severely damage crops there will be famine. Another explanation is that when the Tree Seeds were in the East, the rat made a contribution by looking for them. Therefore, at the beginning of every cotton or grain harvest, a small amount of the crop was left on the ground with the words, "This is for the rats!" One reason for this is that the people never forgot the mythical rat's help in getting back the Seeds; another is that if today's rats get part of the crop, they will leave the rest alone.

6. The original Miao word for "scales" is *dei* (*deid*). The Miao language has words for five *jin* (a *jin* is a Chinese measurement of about one pound), ten *jin*, and fifty *jin*, which are *fi* (*fit*), *dei* (*deid*), and *du* (*duf*), respectively. In the Guizhou dialects of Han Chinese, ten *jin* is called "one scale," making "three scales" about thirty *jin*.

7. The *didi* bird is small and has a call that sounds like its name. It likes to live with *huangdou* sparrows and has unkempt feathers; thus the saying, "As unkempt as a *didi* bird." Both words are given here in Chinese.

Notes to *Plowing and Harrowing the Earth*

1. This is the name of a ghost who specializes in making mischief. As the saying goes, he was delighted to "Agitate the Miao people to fight, and put the Han in a position of killing in revenge." He is very loquacious. The lines in the song can be understood in two ways. One way is that the mouth cannot keep up with the speed of the words; the second is that one thought cannot be kept in mind for a long time—implying a lover of gossip.

2. A place name in Huangping County.

3. A place name in Huangping County.

4. A local custom. If one passes by a relative or friend's village on the way home from buying a sacrificial bull, the villagers will celebrate by hanging chickens and ducks on the bull's horns. If one doesn't pass through the villages but relatives still hear about it, they will bring chickens and ducks to one's home to celebrate, sprinkling wine on the ground and on the bull's nose.

5. This simply means "many" grandfathers, not an exact number.

6. A kind of small bamboo basket with a small mouth and a large body that is strapped to a person's waist for convenience. It is often used to carry fish and freshwater shrimp.

7. According to an old superstition, anyone who sees a pangolin roll up in a ball and roll down a hill will suffer from terrible sickness. However, if the following song is sung, disaster may be averted:

> I say I'm an unlucky one,
> but who would know I had the luck
> to meet a pangolin.
> I'll live for a hundred years
> and sacrifice to the Ancestors nine times.

8. The Huangping mentioned here is not the present Huangping County. This refers to an ancient kingdom of Huangping located on flat mountain land.

9. This refers to a clever man known for his dependable wisdom and his fondness for speaking and singing.

10. The special singer who sings praise songs in the Ancestor Sacrifices.

11. The name of a snake. It is said that the head and tail are as symmetrical as a single tree on the plow lines. Every part of the snake is treasured for medicine.

12. A different name for the ghost mentioned earlier (see note 1). When dealing with this ghost, a small bamboo plow is made. After the ceremony, the plow is buried in the road with the leftover bones from the sacrifice.

13. The name of a rock. According to legend, when paper was first made, *goupi* (in Chinese) hemp (*Broussonetia papyrifera*) and other materials were beaten on the rock. Later, to revenge being struck, the rock came to eat the paper and books.

Notes to *Sowing the Seeds*

1. The Miao word for "surround" or "capture" is *wai* (*waix*), which is used when describing the capture of birds or animals. On another level, the word is pronounced the same as that of an auspicious day related to the twelve stars of the ancient Chinese calendar (Wei, Jian, Qu, Man, Ping, Ding, Zhi, Puo, Cheng, Shou, Kai, and Bi).

2. Wisemen (*lu* [*lul*]) who acted as mediators in legal disputes (which were sung), regarded the Third and Fourth Earthly Branches as times of fire, with the implication of a fast burning that produces a powerful heat. It was said that these Earthly Branches were good times for deciding court cases.

3. When sacrificing a bull, a sweet gum (*de mang* [*det mangx*] in Miao; *fengshu* in Chinese; *Liquidambar formosana*) branch was used in conjunction with a wooden nose plug to raise the beast's head. When its snout pointed to the sky, the edge of a large knife was whacked against its throat. Sweet gum was also used to fasten the horns to the main house post where the ancestral memorial tablets (for human ancestors) were set. This was because the sweet gum tree gave birth to Butterfly Mother.

4. The leaves of this tree are of moderate size and produce a nice sound when blown like an instrument.

5. In the past, when rice seedlings were transplanted, a stick of *wubei* wood as tall as a man was stuck in the middle of the paddy and a clump of cogon grass was tied to it. The mention of the grasses here parallels that custom.

Notes to *Cutting Down the Ancient Sweet Gum*

1. This is the name of a mythical character.
2. This is the name of a mythical character.
3. This is a person's name, possibly a famous wiseman of the past. Some versions say he was born in Maha (today called Majiang).
4. He is also a wiseman.
5. When a wiseman decided a case he used sticks made of bamboo that he would rap on the table after hearing an argument.
6. A mythical giant bird.

Notes to *The Birth of Butterfly Mother*

1. Mai Bang (Mais Bangx): *Mais* means "mother"; *bangx* means "butterfly"; thus the name literally means "mother butterfly." It has been translated in this text as "Butterfly Mother."
2. Bang Lie (Bangx Lief) simply means "butterfly." Sometimes Mais Bangx is called simply "Bangx" or "Lief," or "Mais Lief."
3. In accord with custom, a baby is given its own name when three days old, as well as taking its father's first name as its last.
4. The third day after a baby is born a table filled with fish, wine, and rice—covered by a paper umbrella—is set outside the door. A specially invited middle-aged man or woman known to be healthy and fortunate will carry the baby to see the sun rise. At that time, the child is symbolically given something to eat and drink and is named. Fish are used because fish scales stand for dragons, indicating wealth and the promise of a great son. Also, fish are aquatic animals that never get fevers, an ailment common among babies. It is hoped that the baby will always keep a normal temperature and have good health.
5. According to legend, butterflies prefer to lay their eggs along rivers. The season after laying, a river will rise to the height the eggs were deposited. So it is said that Butterfly Mother and Wave Foam made love.

Notes to *The Twelve Eggs*

1. A heavy sort of construction paper is made from *goupi* hemp. It is coated with tung oil to make a waterproof material that is used for wrapping. When silkworm eggs are laid on it, the paper is rolled and placed in a warm spot until spring.
2. The name of an ancient river.
3. Other versions say, "Floods covered both turtles and sand, / that's why they knew each other."
4. Another name for Jang Vang (see *Prelude*, note 16) is Vang La (Vangb Lax). Since Jang Vang was the progenitor of the human race, the hatching of his egg is regarded as the genesis of humankind.

5. Gha Vang (Ghab Vangx) may mean "mountain ridge," as the pronunciations of the words are similar.

6. An ancient place name.

7. The above transformed objects are the names of positions of the organizers of the Ancestor sacrifices.

8. The name of a protector god. A white chicken is sacrificed to it. Because the god is very poor and wears shabby clothing, it is too ashamed to be seen in daylight, so sacrifices must be held before dawn.

9. See *Transporting Gold and Silver*, note 46.

10. The use of "torch" here is unclear, but seems related to a word in the local Miao dialect.

11. In many cultures in East and Southeast Asia, a bamboo knife was used to cut the umbilical cord of infants.

12. Elephants were found in south China well into historical times, though they are found only in parts of Yunnan province today.

13. According to legend, this sort of ghost attaches itself to living persons and not only can be passed on to one's descendants but also can rub off on friends. The ghost is very terrible and does its best to harm people, its victims dying in a short time. Those unfortunates who were thought to be victims of this ghost became social outcasts. However, not all of these ghosts were harmful. Only those associated with rich and powerful families went about killing or eating people. The richer the families, the more terrible were their ghosts. Thus the folk saying, "*Diangs wat bongx gangb mangl, / dlas wat bongx dliangl gel.*" ("Too fat, so you have pimples, / too rich, so you have *dliang* ghosts.")

14. This is a kind of poison known as *gu* (*ku* in the Wade-Giles Romanization) in Chinese. According to legend, it is controlled only by women. It is made of snakes, scorpions, toads, leeches, hornets, and so on. If a person eats food doctored with the poison, the creatures will grow in his stomach and may pour out of his body orifices. It was believed that the poison lost its power when in contact with heat, so if a person heard that someone was afflicted by the poison, they would boil foods, such as fruits, that they would normally eat raw. If someone was poisoned, medicine was taken or physical therapy performed, but gods or ghosts were not invoked. It is said that the bewitching poison was handed down from mother to daughter and never to sons or daughters-in-law. So there is a song like this:

> Mother got the *gu* poison
> and died with the secret;
> so when father got a *dliang* ghost,
> he couldn't be cured in a million years.

The Miao are not the only people with legends about the *gu* (*guk*) poison. Other minorities in southwest China also have beliefs about it. A doctor of the Shui ethnic group who graduated from medical school in the 1950s made an investigation in his region. After visiting an old woman who had been bewitched by *gu* made of poisonous snakes, the doctor concluded that she was actually suffering from a parasitic disease. Investigations in some Miao areas in recent years also confirm that what some people believed were symptoms of *gu* poisoning were actually diseases such as angina, tonsillitis, and various sores and boils. These beliefs in *gu* differ slightly from modern disease and medical theory. (See Diamond for more on the *gu* poison and Miao/Han relations.)

15. According to an old superstition, the Gu Vang (Guk Vangx) is a demon sent by persons trying to harm others in revenge. A ritual specialist is asked to make a curse by chanting special lyrics while tying a red silk thread around a crab or centipede. The creature is then placed in the intended victim's home, and the demon thus enters and destroys the family. If such a creature is seen inside a home, it will immediately be thrown in the manure pit.

16. According to an old superstition, certain ghosts like to eat sow meat. If a sow is not sacrificed to them, illness will spread and sows will eat their offspring.

17. During a major sacrifice, the walls of the house of the ceremonial head (in the past this was translated as "drum society head") must be completely torn down. On a certain night everyone (except babies and their mothers) in the village comes to that place. They sleep randomly on straw and eat chicken and rice porridge. The place they stay is called *ve khang* (*vel khangt*) and the porridge is called *ga khang* (*gad khangt*). (Also, the day a child is born, the women and children of the clan get together to eat chicken porridge, in hopes of prosperous descendants.) The entire ceremony just described is called Ve Ve Khang (Ved Vel Khangt) and means "keeping watch over the houses left by the Ancestors."

18. Two sacrificial bowls made of pottery are filled with vegetable oil and burned for the Ancestors during the sacrifices.

Notes to *The Brothers Divide*

1. Some singers take the first part of this episode as an epic unto itself, rather than as a subdivision. If so, it is called "Nang Diang Hmong Hsong" ("Nangx Diangs Hmongt Hsongl" or "Passing the Sky Bridge Trial") and ends after Jang Vang crosses the Sky Bridge.

2. The story goes that the Earth God made a contribution by giving a chair. Therefore, when sacrificing to the Thunder God, some of the wine and meat on the table is put underneath for the Earth God. (Before any meal, a small amount of wine is poured on the floor for the Ancestors.)

3. This indicates rosy clouds.

4. In the ancient times, the Thunder God was very strict. Whenever he caught someone making a mistake, he thundered. Once a girl washed some scallions and threw the white skins in a pond. From so far away the bright skins looked like rice to the Thunder God. Becoming angry, he struck the girl dead for wasting food. Her bereaved mother wailed and called for redress each day. Finally, the Thunder God heard her and came down to investigate. Discovering

his mistake, he declared a new law: Only after a person has made a mistake nine times would he punish them.

Notes to *Killing the Centipede*

1. This is a place name. Today it is called Ronggangjiang in Chinese.
2. There are several ways of dealing with bites from centipedes or poisonous snakes; all of them require the use of lice. For example, a clay needle is inserted in the top of a victim's head. After a small hole is made, it is filled with powdered lice and roundworms.
3. According to traditional Miao medicine, when a person is ill or has just recovered from a serious disease, he must avoid certain foods, such as roosters, duck and goose meat, mutton, dog meat, sow meat, and so on. As for fish, crucian carp and eels are especially to be avoided.
4. A special ceremonial hat, called a *mo liang* (*mos liangx*), is worn by the ceremonial head. The brim is only a few inches wide, and the pointed crown is about a hand's-length tall. A bunch of hemp is tied around the point of the hat.
5. The sacrificial poles are made of entire bamboos, including the roots. The middle of a pole is dyed in black and white bands, and several pieces of cotton are tied to the top. Their use is described in the Introduction to the *Song of Butterfly Mother*.
6. In the past, the ceremonies were held for field clearings. A small mound of earth was left in the middle of the field (called the "earth heart," *lai dlui li / laib dluid lix*) and friends or relatives were invited to dig it up at the start of the ceremony. Guests brought a duck, a bottle of wine, and a small basket of glutinous rice.
7. This is a place name.

Notes to *Searching for the Sacrificial Drums*

1. A grain rack was used for glutinous rice and millet. It had several tiers, and a roof was above it to shield the grain from the weather. In the past people planted crops primarily in high, cold areas, and grain was difficult to polish. When the rice was ripe, it was harvested with a clasp knife in sheaves and hung on the grain racks. During the slack winter months the grain could be polished at leisure.
2. Gho Do (Ghot Dol) (or *dai gho do* [*daib ghot dol*]; literally "Child Gho Do") was the ball of flesh birthed by Jang Vang and his sister after the mythical flood.
3. The original is *nie bong* (*niel bongl*), or "double drums"; "a pair of drums." This refers to the two long drums always stored inside the drum keeper's house. The drums are kept on racks as tall as a man, and under them are kept two bowls of oil that are lighted when necessary. On every holiday, the drum keeper must light the oil, burn paper, pour out wine, and hang meat under the racks to

feed the Ancestors. Then the drums are beaten. After hearing the sound of the drums, the villagers may begin their dances.

4. These are persons' names. Li (Lil) is Jang Vang's second brother-in-law.

5. On the occasions of mass bull sacrifices, the head and second head of the ceremonies should wear turtledove feathers in their hats and heavy neck rings of twisted silver.

6. A noise made by a chicken represented here as being made by a drum.

7. A noise made by a fish represented here as being made by a drum.

8. A noise made by a frog represented here as being made by a drum.

9. See *Creating the Sky and Earth*, note 25.

10. Since the East is respected, when a tree is felled for an important reason, it must fall eastward. Another custom is called, "The elder lives in the East, and the younger lives in the West." When brothers live apart, the elder must live to the East, because according to legend, the people originally lived in the East. It is a way of remembering the ancestors and the place of origins.

Notes to *Searching for the Sacrificial Ox*

1. See *Transporting Gold and Silver*, note 24.

2. Water buffalo bulls are sacrificed at one point in the Ancestor Sacrifice cycle; in some places, a pig will be sacrificed the year after the bulls and the drum is sent back to the mountains. Pigs also have hair whorls on their bodies.

3. The original editors, Ma and Jin, suggested these two lines are of value in considering the origins of the Miao people in Guizhou (in terms of how they may have migrated from the East). The original words (final consonants not pronounced) are "*Niak hlongt eb hnaib diangl, / eb dlas xongt hnaib niongl.*"

4. During the sacrifices, two women (an aunt and a niece) were required to carry water for the sacrificial fish. The niece would hold the bucket while the aunt poured water into it.

5. The squirrels must be black.

6. These are place names.

Notes to *Searching for the Sacrificial Vestments*

1. A *xi* (*xib*) is a special kind of ceremonial vest said to be made of sheepskin.

2. These are the ceremonial hats. (See *Killing the Centipede*, note 4.)

3. A place name, now in Rongjiang County.

4. The first day of the sixth lunar month.

5. These and the following names are places in Rongjiang County.

6. Women were not allowed to give birth in their mothers' homes. If such were the case, gifts had to be prepared to appease the gods and Ancestors afterward.

7. Marriage with certain close cousins was once common in some areas.

8. Liong Tong (Liongx Tongb) was a sort of crier, in charge of communications during the Ancestor sacrifices.

9. A Diu (Ah Diub) means "foolish sister."

10. The inability of a young woman to sing or to embroider her courting attire would virtually rule out normal social activities with the opposite sex before marriage, and thus make finding a mate nearly impossible if she had such a reputation.

11. *Yimi* (a Chinese name) are the seeds of a plant known in English as Job's Tears (*Coix lacryma-jobi*), related to maize. The seeds are used as natural beads.

12. Brothers-in-law are regarded as actual brothers, though there is no blood relation.

Notes to *The Ancestor Sacrifice Hunt*

1. The "Drum Mountain" is a section of forest that is specially planted with trees; no felling is allowed. The sacrificial drum is kept inside a cave or under a cliff to protect it from bad weather. The Silver Mountain Cliffs and Lead Mountain Cliffs mentioned below indicate such places. The drum is only brought to the village during sacrifices and is sent back afterward. (New single drums are ritually made for each ceremony.)

2. Times of sacrifices are calculated in various ways. (See the Introduction.)

3. It is forbidden to beat drums after the ceremonial drum is sent back to the mountain. Even children may not imitate drum sounds verbally, or beat on bamboo or wood. An old superstition requires that whenever a drum sound is heard, a sacrifice must be made, for the Ancestors have returned home. The lines explain why there are different dates for sacrifices.

4. This is a place name in Taijiang County.

5. This is the name of a man among the sacrificial leaders.

6. This is a place in Taijiang County.

7. Locals like to raise fish in their paddies (which they describe as a unique custom, though it occurs in other areas in China and Asia). During winter they put branches, straw, thorns, and so on, in the center of the paddies to allow the fish a place to congregate for warmth and protection from predatory animals. This shelter is called *hse nai* (*hseb nail*). Also, when using the technique of surrounding animals during winter hunts, they often drive the animals into the paddies where they are easy to corner.

Notes to *The Great Flood*

1. This song cannot be casually performed. It must be sung outside, and a duck or a chicken must be killed in commemoration of the Ancestors in their confrontation of danger. This song also deals with brother-sister marriage, a

topic later generations refrain from discussing. In order not to insult the Ancestors, it is not sung in the home.

2. According to the story, when Jang Vang and the Thunder God divided up the wealth of their home, the Thunder God took the water buffalo and left his brother Jang Vang only a dog, which was useless for plowing. Thus Jang Vang went to the sky to ask the Thunder God for the water buffalo.

3. Other versions say that Jang Vang stepped on it firmly with his foot.

4. The knife for sacrificing water buffaloes has a square point and is several feet long. It is very sharp and is used to cut the bull's throat during the sacrifices.

5. In this instance, the original wording says, "Mother wasn't willing," but for the sake of consistency, here "mother" has been changed to "sister."

6. The name of Jang Vang's sister.

7. Fire bundles were made of folded and tied cogon grass or straw and were used to carry live coals across the mountains before the Miao had flint and steel or matches.

8. If one catches a fish and has nothing to carry it in, it may be wrapped in a bundle of straw.

9. The spoken words all mean "to go."

The lines that follow this stanza are:

> The bones turned into Miao people,
> the meat turned into Han people,
> the intestines turned into . . .

To prevent "misunderstandings" among people of different ethnic groups, the original editors, Ma and Jin, placed these lines in the footnotes; several lines have been deleted. This is the major acknowledged deletion in the text. Some persons of other ethnic groups wondered why they were identified as descending from intestines (or worse), while Han and Miao were meat and bones. In fact, this motif of the local ethnic groups transforming from parts of the flesh ball is shared by some other peoples, in the southwest, though the divisions are different.

Notes to *Westwards, Upriver*

1. The Miao title is *Nang E Ji Bi* (*Nangx Eb Jit Bil*), or *Going Upstream along the River*. The original for "five pairs of Parents" is *za gang na* (*zab gangx nal*), which is also another name for the song. *Gang* (*Gangx*) means "two," a collective numerative that is equal to a "pair" or a "couple" in Chinese and English. The term is not in the vernacular speech of the region in which the song is popular, but in Kaili its vernacular usage indicates a husband and wife. For example, *i gang wi ya* (*ib gangx wid yas*) literally means "one pair, a husband and wife." Moreover, the term *na* (*nal*) is not in the vernacular. When used in the songs it may mean

"mother," "father," "parents," or sometimes "ancestors." It is similar to the English word "parents."

2. A type of edible biennial plant. It blooms yellow flowers before or just after the spring Grave Sweeping Holiday (*Qingming*), a festival of Han Chinese origin. In the following lines, *jong hfi lu* (*jongx hfib lul*) means "old kudzu root," or the root of the kudzu vine.

3. This is possibly a personified bee, named Liong Wa (Liongx Wab).

4. The trumpet plant blooms every few years and is poisonous enough to kill insects. The root and flower are both yellow and can be used as dye. The stalk is hollow, and in winter it dries and is used by children to make a kind of pipe that they like to blow, thus the name. This is a different plant from the bugle plant mentioned elsewhere in this epic.

5. According to legend, every village has a guardian dragon, and a pond is always dug for it to live in. If misfortune comes (such as a fire), the dragon is believed to have left. A special ceremony must be held to call it back.

6. The original is *gha lo va* (*ghat lot vas*), which literally means "clever mouth."

7. The original wording, *gha niu hlio qe je* (*ghab niux hliod qet jes*), literally means "the clever mouth manages the place." In fact, this indicates a village wiseman (*lu* [*lul*]) who has a capable tongue and mediates in social affairs.

8. A large cicada with a diaphanous abdomen that makes a loud, clear sound. In the vernacular the cicada is called *gang lia li* (*gangb liax lil*), though in the context of the song, it is simply *gang lia.*

9. This is why a person who falls down always cries out, "Mother!" By doing so, it shows one hasn't forgotten the Ancestors' struggles.

10. This is why girls like to wear flowers.

11. The complete term is *jang xi go* (*jangb xib gox*), which means *jangb xib* fruit. Most legends say the people moved from Jang Xi (Jangb Xib), but it is not clear whether this means today's Jiangxi province or another locale. A number of groups of non-Han people in southwest China claim their origins are in Jiangxi province, including some groups of Yi in Yunnan province. Historically, many Han immigrants came from that region in the lower Yangzi River corridor.

12. A perennial root plant. The leaves are long and thin, but pliable and strong. It is used in making rope and paper, and in constructing straw and palm rain gear.

13. This is an obscure place name meaning "rocky plain" (Dangx Vib Mongl).

14. This is a species of wild animal (unidentified) that frequents brakes of bamboo and cogon grass.

15. Yux Yangb Dail is a personified wild animal.

16. The rivers mentioned here are obscure. With tones, Nang Lu is Nangl Luk, while the rivers are Nangl Yux, Nangl Ngok, Nangl Xib, and Nangl Lak.

17. This is a place name (Nangl Hseit Lek).

18. This is a place name associated with a plain (Zangx Ghaib).

19. This is a person's name (Xongx Ghaib).

20. The term *yen* (*yenx*) in Miao, which refers to any settlement with a wall around it, may come from the Han word *ying*, which means "camp."

21. A deciduous hardwood shrub (*nongx hniangb*) called *nongying* in Chinese, used for carrying poles. Its leaves can be used to feed silkworms.

22. A strong, pliable species of cane (*nangx ongb*) that likes marshy gullies. It is called *nanweng* in Chinese.

23. A type of bamboo called "heart bamboo" (*nongx hniub*) because it is not hollow. In Chinese it is called *nongliu*.

24. Mynah birds are black and can be taught simple words. According to custom, when a fierce beast was captured, it had to be "tried" by the village elders before it could be killed and eaten.

25. This is a person's name, possibly derived from the expression *nang nai* (*nangx naif*), which means "to eat."

26. *Ga* (*gad*) and *nai* (*naif*) both mean "food" and are often interchanged in the epics. In Miao vernacular, however, they indicate regional dialects. Hence it is interesting that people's attitudes toward the local dialects are specifically mentioned in the song.

27. This is a place name. Though such a place exists in Jian County, on the Clearwater River, the reference is probably to another place.

28. This is a person's name (Xongt Zax).

29. For a reference to "double drums," see note 3 in *Searching for the Sacrificial Drum*.

30. See *Searching for the Sacrificial Vestments*, note 1, and *Killing the Centipede*, note 4.

31. In the past, people measured things by marking a rope stretched around what they wanted measured. One length is about five inches long.

32. A kind of sickle that is stroked upward with the point to the right when cutting a sheaf of grain. A sickle that cuts downward and to the left is called a "left-arcing sickle." With tone marks, the wielder of the sickle is Xongx Tinb.

33. Literally, "seventy-thousand skies," and "nine thousand places." They are names in Jian County along a mountain chain that runs through Rongjiang, Jianjiang, Taijiang, and Leishan counties. Legend says that Miao living on both banks of the Clearwater River crossed into the region here. When a person dies, his soul is instructed to follow this route back to the ancestral home. If people refer to someone who has "gone to Khong Wang (Khongd Wangs) and Fang Je Hsang (Fangb Jex Hsangb)," it means that the person in question has died.

34. Dangx Ghod and Dlongs jit are both located in Taijiang County.

35. Fang (Fangs), Fu (Ful), Dli (Dlib), Nie (Niel), and Dai Ne (Dail Nes) may be the names of ancient persons that later became names of different branches of the Miao. Villages will call themselves by names of the majority of members. Jiaomi is located in Taijiang County. Fangxiang is in Leishan County. Fangb Nix (literally "river place") is present-day Taijiang.

36. According to an old superstition, persons attending various ceremonies for certain gods are invited by the ceremonial head in accord with blood affinity, from the nearest kin to the farthest. If a close relative is invited before a more distant relative, a quarrel will result. So there is the saying, "Lacking a piece of sacred meat, / kin drift apart forever." Here the "meat" refers to a family member.

Selected Bibliography

Bender, Mark. "Hunting Nets and Butterflies: Ethnic Minority Songs from Southwest China." In *The Poem Behind the Poem: Translating Asian Poetry*, edited by Frank Stewart, 39–54. Port Townsend, Wa.: Copper Canyon Press, 2004.

———. "Three Oral Poetries from Southern China." *Harvard Asia Quarterly* 7, no. 3 (2003): 24–30.

———. "In the (Oral) Territory of the *Mangie*." *Estudos de Literatura Oral* 7–8 (2001): 279–92.

———. "Antiphonal Epics of the Miao (Hmong) of Guizhou, China." In *Traditional Storytelling Today: An International Sourcebook*, edited by Margaret Read MacDonald, 88–90. Chicago: Fitzroy Dearborn Publishers, 1999.

———. "'Felling the Ancient Sweetgum': Antiphonal Epics of the Miao of Southeast Guizhou." *Chinoperl Papers* 15 (1990): 27–44.

———. "*Hxak Hmub:* An Antiphonal Epic of the Miao of Southeast Guizhou, China." *Contributions to Southeast Asian Ethnology* 7 (1988): 95–128.

Bauman, Richard. *Verbal Art as Performance.* Prospect Heights, Ill.: Waveland Press, 1977.

Beauclair, Inez de. *Tribal Cultures of Southwest China.* Taibei, Taiwan: Orient Cultural Service, 1970.

Birrell, Anne. *Chinese Mythology: An Introduction.* Baltimore, Md.: John Hopkins University Press, 1993.

Catlin, Amy. *Music of the Hmong: Singing Voices and Talking Reeds.* Center for Hmong Lore. Providence, R.I.: College Office Publishers, 1983.

Chao, Yuen Ren. *A Grammar of Spoken Chinese.* Berkeley: University of California Press, 1968.

Diamond, Norma. "The Miao and Poison: Interactions on China's Southwest Frontier." *Ethnology* 27, no. 1 (1988): 1–25.

Eberhard, Wolfram. *China's Minorities: Yesterday and Today.* Belmont, Cal.: Wadsworth, 1982.

Fei Hsiao Tung. *Towards a People's Anthropology.* Beijing: New World Press, 1982.

Foley, John Miles. *How to Read an Oral Poem.* Urbana, Ill.: University of Illinois Press, 2002.

Geddes, William Robert. *Migrants of the Mountains: The Cultural Ecology of the Blue Miao (Hmong Njua) of Thailand.* Oxford: Oxford University Press, 1976.

Graham, David Crockett. *Songs and Stories of the Ch'uan Miao*. Smithsonian Miscellaneous Collections, vol. 123, no. 1. Washington: Smithsonian Institution, 1954.

Harrell, Steve, ed. *Perspectives on the Yi of Southwest China*. Berkeley: University of California Press, 2001.

Heberer, Thomas. *China and its National Minorities: Autonomy or Assimilation?* New York and London: M.E. Sharpe, 1989.

Honko, Lauri. "Text as Process and Practice: The Textualization of Oral Epics." In *Textualisation of Oral Epics*, 3–54. Berlin and New York: Mouton de Gruyter, 2000.

Jin Dan. *Bangx Hxab: Miaozu guge gehua* [Song Flowers of the Miao Ancient Songs]. Guiyang, China: Guizhou minzu chubanshe, 1998.

Li Zixian. "Xilun nanfang shaoshu minzu yuanshi xing shi shi chansheng he fazhande lishi genyuan" [On the origin and production of primitive myths of the southern nationalities]. *Xinan minzu lishi jikan* [Journal of the history of the southwest nationalities] 4 (1983): 170–78.

Ma Xueliang. Tan shaoshu minzu minjian wenxuede fanyi wenti [On questions of the translation of folk literature of China's minority nationalities]. In *Suyuanji: minzu minjian wenxue lunji* [From simple garden: A collection of papers on ethnic folk literature], 141–48. Beijing: Zhongguo minjian wenyi chubanshe, 1989.

Ma Xueliang and Jin Dan. *Hxak Hmub: Miaozu shishi* [Hxak Hmub: Miao Epic Poems]. Beijing: Zhongguo minjian wenyi chubanshe, 1983.

Mackerras, Colin. *China's Minority Cultures: Identities and Integration Since 1912.* New York: St. Martin's Press, 1995.

Pan Dingzhi, Yang Peide, Zhang Zaimei, eds. *Miaozu guge* [Miao Ancient Songs]. Guiyang, China: Guizhou renmin chubanshe, 1997.

Parsons, R. Keith. "Traditional Songs and Stories of the Miao of Southwest China." At http://www.hmongnet.org, 2001.

Rossi, Gail. "Enduring Dress of the Miao, Guizhou Province, People's Republic of China." *Ornament* 11, no. 3 (1988): 26–31.

Ruey Yih-fu, ed. *Eighty-two Aboriginal Peoples of Kweichow Province in Pictures.* Taipei, China: Academia Sinica, 1973.

Schein, Louisa. *Minority Rules: The Miao and the Feminine in China's Cultural Politics.* Durham, N.C.: Duke University Press, 2000.

Snyder, Gary. "The Politics of Ethnopoetics." In *The Old Ways*. San Francisco: City Lights, 1977.

Tapp, Nicholas. "Cultural Accommodations in Southwestern China: The 'Han Miao' and Problems in the Ethnography of the Hmong." *Asian Folklore Studies* LXI, no. 1 (2002): 77–104.

———. *The Hmong of China: Context, Agency, and the Imaginary.* Leiden, Netherlands: Brill, 2001.

Tapp, Nicholas, et al., eds. *Hmong/Miao in Asia*. Chiang Mai, Thailand: Silkworm Books, 2004.

Tian Bing, ed. *Miaozu guge* [Miao Ancient Songs]. Guiyang, China: Guizhou renmin chubanshe, 1979.

Tian Bing, et al., eds. *Miaozu wenxue shi* [History of Miao Literature]. Guiyang, China: Guizhou renmin chubanshe, 1981.

Wu Yiwen and Qian Dongping. *Miaozu guge yu Miaozu lishi wenhua* [Ancient Songs of the Miao Nationality and Miao Nationality History and Culture]. Guiyang, China: Guizhou minzu chubanshe, 2000.

Yang Tongru. "Jiefang qian Miaozude zongjiao" [Folk religion of the Miao before Liberation]. In *Zhongguo shaoshu minzu zongjiao* [Religions of China's Minorities], edited by Song Enchang, 367–79. Kunming, China: Yunnan renmin chubanshe, 1985.

Young, Gordon. *The Hill Tribes of Northern Thailand*. Bangkok: Siam Society, 1962.

Zhongguo shehui kexueyuan minzu yanjiusuo [Chinese Academy of Social Sciences Ethnic Studies Research Center], ed. *Taijiangxian Miaozu juan* [Taijiang County Miao Nationality Volume]. Beijing: Minzu chubanshe, 1999.

Zhu Yichu and Li Zixian, eds. *Shaoshu minzu minjian wenxue gailun* [Introduction to Ethnic Folk Literature]. Kunming, China: Yunnan renmin chubanshe, 1983.